No Boy SUMMER

A NOVEL

AMY SPALDING

No Boy
SUMMER

AMULET BOOKS • NEW YORK

Cataloging-in-Publication Data has been applied for and may be obtained from the Library of Congress.

ISBN 978-1-4197-5752-5

Text © 2023 Amy Spalding
Book design by Deena Micah Fleming

Printed and bound in U.S.A.
10 9 8 7 6 5 4 3 2 1

Amulet Books are available at special discounts when purchased in quantity for premiums and promotions as well as fundraising or educational use. Special editions can also be created to specification. For details, contact specialsales@abramsbooks.com or the address below.

Amulet Books® is a registered trademark of Harry N. Abrams, Inc.

ABRAMS The Art of Books
195 Broadway, New York, NY 10007
abramsbooks.com

To my friends Kayla and Jasmine

Chapter One

The whole thing was Penny's idea.

"Lydia," she'd said, in her most serious tone. Penny is thirteen months younger than me, but she's hit almost every milestone earlier. Walking, talking, reading, writing. After she got her period before I did, it was like I was officially demoted to younger sister and there was no coming back. "We need a reset."

I don't remember exactly how I'd responded, but my best recollection is that I made a confused noise while crunching a mouthful of Cheddar Chex Mix.

"You were almost kicked off the crew," she'd said.

"No one calls it *the crew*—"

She'd waved her hand dismissively. "I nearly got a D on an organic chemistry test. Ms. Balsavias made me go talk to Mr. Hockseye, who we would *all agree* is barely competent enough to be a guidance counselor, because I *seemed so distracted.* Mom and Dad nearly got called in."

Then it had been me waving my hand dismissively. Penny is such a good student, and it was only a C– on *a single test*, and if school administration had called Mom and Dad in over anything, it would have been the near-death I'd almost caused in the theater department, not a dip in performance in organic chemistry.

"We can't have another year like this, Lydia." Even though she was maybe blowing things out of proportion, Penny wasn't wrong. Unfortunately, Penny was hardly ever wrong.

It's so annoying.

"What do you suggest?" I'd asked. "Get theeselves to a nunnery?"

"Sort of," she'd said with a raised eyebrow, which, to me at least, had signaled trouble. That eyebrow doesn't come up for general fun. That eyebrow height occurs only when schemes are hatched.

Because Penny is the way she is, I didn't manage to get another single detail from her that night. "It'll be better if it's all from me," she'd said, which was an excuse but also probably accurate, because Mom and Dad know which one of their daughters is more responsible. I'd left it all in her overachieving hands.

∿

We are not on our way to a nunnery, or anything even close to a nunnery. We're in the back seat of Mom's Prius sitting in traffic on the 5 freeway on our way down to Los Angeles. Has anyone, in the history of the world, used Los Angeles as some kind of metaphor for sacrifice, restraint, celibacy? Doubtful.

I was sure right about that eyebrow scheme.

"I can't believe you talked me into this," I mutter to Penny.

"You're lucky that I did," she says. "This is exactly what we need." Ugh, her accuracy is so irritating. Of *course* it's true. I'd be a huge disaster without her.

"What are all these people doing out?" Dad asks. "It's a Saturday morning. Where could they all be going?"

"Exactly," I say. "LA is stupid."

"*We're* here, too," Penny says. "So who are we to judge?"

"That's a great point, Pen." Mom shoots Dad a look. He probably knows that if he doesn't go with the flow his summer could be ruined, so I'm not surprised that he shuts up. I'm not sure how I feel about my dad's dream vacation having absolutely nothing to do with my sister and me, but Penny pointed out that the cost of the cruise and European tour is already high for two people. For four it would be impossible.

"Grace says that the thing about LA is you just need to pick your neighborhood and plan your life around it and everything's fine," Mom says. "I don't get it, but she seems happy enough with that kind of situation."

"That sounds terrible," I say. LA, an hour south of us, has never been appealing to me, with its noise and bad air and lack of greenery, but even so, I don't understand the point of choosing to live somewhere and then sectioning yourself off into only a tiny part of it. Isn't the whole point of living in a big city that you have all of it at your fingertips? But also, I can feel how I don't *want* to understand, because literally none of this was my idea.

I glance down at my phone, but the lock screen is blank. Who would be texting me anyway? Not since Tate. Not since, as my theater advisor Mr. Landiss calls it, *the incident*.

And even before all of that, I can't help but remind myself, my phone was hardly buzzing nonstop. For some stupid reason, I can't stop thinking about the screenshot Darren Nygard posted to his Insta Stories a couple months ago, with his texts showing *sixty-nine* unread messages. *tfw you sleep an hour later than everyone else on the react group text. Nice.*

Sixty-nine messages in one hour, and none of them including me, the copresident of the Rancho El Aderezo Theater Tech Club (REATTC, which we call REACT, because, close enough). The messages weren't about paint or lighting or coupons we found for Home Depot that made our small budgets feel less small, I assumed. They were about crushes and parties and who hooked up with who and who's hanging out after rehearsal, and I wasn't required for any of that.

"Why don't you look excited?" Penny throws a Cheeto at me without warning, and it bounces off my nose. I laugh, despite my mood, and despite everything else.

"You know I'm not excited," I say, even though that wasn't completely true. It was hard not to be at least a little thrilled about a whole plan with my sister, a person I never feel on equal footing with. But of course I couldn't let Penny know all of that. "This is your thing. This isn't a nunnery."

"I'm still confused at how you wanted our summer to be *more* like a nunnery," she says. "Less is more, remember?"

I dismiss her with a hand wave, and she does the same right back to me. I have no idea why this has caught on between us. Sometimes sisterhood is inexplicable.

Grace is waiting in front of her house when we pull up, but unlike up in the far-flung suburbs where we live, there's no driveway and so we have to keep driving. Mom's phone rings with a call from Grace as Mom is slowly circling the Prius around the block.

"Answer it, Craig!" she shrieks, so Dad taps the button on the dash.

"Hello?" Mom and Dad answer at the same time. Penny and I exchange a look. It's not that they aren't always weird, it's just somehow impossible to fully get used to it, ever. It always feels like something new and awkward and unusually loud.

"Hope, you can just double-park right in front so the girls can bring in their bags," Grace says in her cool-as-hell tone. Mom and Grace make Penny and me seem like identical twins. "It'll take forever to find a spot."

I still don't understand living somewhere you can't even park a compact car, but Grace's voice makes me hate it a little less, and by the time Mom swings the car back around, I'm ready to bound out to greet my summer life.

"Lydia, close the door," Mom says. "We have to put the hazards on first."

"I've never used the hazards in this car," Dad says. "Where are they again?"

"You know, that's funny, I haven't, either," Mom says. "Maybe not in the last Prius, either. I still miss driving that one sometimes, that cute little hatchback."

"The hazards are right there," Penny says.

"Time goes by so quickly," Mom says with a sigh. "Remember how little the girls were when we got that car?"

"They're literally right in the middle of the dash," Penny says.

"That giant triangle button," I add.

"Remember when Lydia was born," Dad says with a sigh. "I realized I could put her whole hand in my mouth."

I shriek. "Dad!"

"Dad, why would you *say* that?"

"Oh, *there* are the hazards," Mom says, and presses the button.

"Dad, that sounds like something a goddamn *cannibal* would say."

Mom sighs loudly. "Lydia, don't curse, please."

"It's not as weird as it sounds," Dad says. "I was holding you and eating applesauce—"

"I have literally never seen you eat applesauce," Penny says.

"I used to love applesauce," Dad says. "Then one day, I just didn't. Isn't life funny like that?"

There's a knock on the window and we all scream, though of course it's just Grace.

"What does applesauce have to do with your cannibalism?" I ask.

"Do you understand what cannibalism is?" Penny asks.

"Or are you secretly made out of apples?" I ask, only to make Penny laugh, but it works.

Mom rolls down the window. "Is this OK? Where I parked? If these cars need to get out—"

"So I spilled applesauce on your hand," Dad says. "And I'd dropped my napkin, so I thought I'd just—"

"*Ew*," Penny and I say together.

"You licked applesauce off of my baby hand?"

"Hey, guys, welcome," Grace says. Her red hair is longer than last time I saw her, and she's wearing a faded T-shirt that hangs in that perfect vintage way. I guess there's something in Grace's face that echoes Mom's, but their styles are so different it can be hard for me to see. Mom's hair is always right at chin length, low-maintenance and style-less.

"Come on in," Grace says. "I'm so excited you're here."

"You'll understand when you're a parent," Dad says in a misty-sounding voice. Oh god, I can't handle Dad Nostalgia Tears today. I throw open my door and jump out.

"Lydia! You look amazing." Grace wraps me in her arms and gives me a super tight hug. It's so good to see her that I don't point out that unless *amazing* has a new meaning that equals something along the lines of sweaty-plus-annoyed, she's being way too nice. But I guess that's Grace for you.

I get my bags out of the trunk, though Grace's boyfriend, Oscar, appears and attempts to take them from me. "You can get Penny's. You know she's way more delicate." I say things like this all the time when all that's really true is that Penny is thin and I'm not. It doesn't actually make me better at carrying heavy stuff.

He laughs. "Good to see you, Lydia."

"Come on inside." Grace ushers me toward the walkway, and it turns out that even though Oscar isn't tall or particularly built, he grabs Penny's bags in addition to mine and casually walks them inside. I follow him in as Mom and Dad loudly debate if they can leave the car for a moment or if this will get them "arrested or something like it."

"Everyone on the boat is going to want to murder them," I say, and Grace laughs.

"Only a little," she says. "And only if they talk to anyone else."

Fair point. Mom and Dad don't really have friends; they have each other and they have their jobs, and that seems enough for them. I've been reminding myself of this a lot lately, since Darren's Insta Story and Valentina's party that I found out about from Instagram and not an invitation. High school's a thing to get through and then it doesn't matter if you rank high enough for party invites or group texts. Fall in love and the whole thing is solved. You have your person, you build a life together, and that's that.

"Your mom's watching the car," Dad says, even though we haven't even made it inside yet and the car is about twelve feet away. "Be good for Grace and have fun, Lydia."

I hug him and it hits me I've never been away from my parents for so long before. There's a dangerous chance I might actually *cry*, so I just make a joke about him falling overboard that isn't very funny and end up hiding behind Grace while he says goodbye to Penny.

"We're going to have so much fun." Grace tightens an arm around my waist. "You're excited, right?"

Suddenly I feel anything but, so I just nod very slightly while pasting an extremely fake smile on my face. Mom rushes in, and I cling to her probably for one to two seconds longer than I should. And before I know it, she's saying goodbye to Penny and the Prius is slowly rolling away down the block as I can faintly hear "Craig, how do we turn the hazards *off?*"

"They'll figure it out," Grace says with a smile. "Come on in, guys."

We've of course been to Grace's before, as she's our only aunt (Dad's an only child) and lives only about forty miles away. But usually Mom convinces Grace and Oscar to drive up to us, because we have a guest bedroom and, in general, a lot more space. I guess also so that Grace and Oscar can sit in traffic on the freeway, and not us.

Grace and Oscar's house isn't a tiny home or anything, but it's little. The living room is about half the size of ours, and the kitchen and dining room are the same way. There are only two bedrooms, total, which means for the first time in our lives, Penny and I will be sharing.

"That's better for our plan anyway," Penny had said when Grace brought up this fact earlier in Penny's planning. "We can keep an eye on each other."

She was probably right, but seventeen years is a long time to develop plenty of alone-in-my-room-no-one-can-witness-this habits. Two and a half months will be a test.

"If it's not set up how you guys want it, just move stuff however you want." Oscar walks ahead of us down the hallway with, again, somehow, all of our luggage in his arms. He's shorter than Dad, and thinner, too. Mom says when Grace met Oscar, she gushed to her that he had the good looks of an NPR host. I knew Mom expected us to laugh along with her, but when I think of the boys I've crushed on, kissed, dated, been brokenhearted by…it's not like they fit one particular mold. I'm sure there's room for a wiry public radio type in there, though not now, because now is specifically not the time to worry about boys of any build.

That's why we're in Grace's house to begin with.

If Penny and I keep screwing our lives up because of boys, boys are the problem. Boys *must* be the problem. OK, to be fair, boys themselves probably aren't the actual problem. It's us with boys, us around boys, us thinking of boys when we should be thinking of anything else.

So we're here, in a little bedroom in a little house in a little part of Los Angeles, away from Tate and Miguel and Drew, away from the boys we know and the boys we don't. This summer we're going to hit reset, and that means no boys.

Chapter Two

I'm dreaming of sailing in a gently rocking boat, under a moonlit sky, all bliss and beautiful views, when suddenly the boat shakes rapidly and even though I'm semi-aware it's a dream, my heart pounds and I clasp the edge of—

"Hey, Lydia," Grace sort of whispers, though at least she stops shaking me. "I think you slept through your alarm. We need to head out soon to get to the shop on time."

"I thought I was going to drown," I say, and—at Grace's raised eyebrows—add, "in a dream!"

I'm not sure it helps.

"Meet me in the living room in twenty," Grace says. "Feel free to use anything in the bathroom."

I take a very brief shower even though I feel fuzzy from the early morning and the fact that it's barely even light out yet. I felt *lucky* when Penny worked out this whole plan and told me I'd get to help Grace at her coffee shop while Penny would be interning at Oscar's office. There was no question who could handle business casual and who could focus on latte art. But Penny won't have to be at Oscar's office until nine, and while I'm not exactly sure when the sun comes up, it hasn't made its full grand appearance yet.

"You'll get used to it," Grace says when I zombie into the living room exactly twenty minutes later. There's no uniform, luckily, so I'm just wearing jeans, my usual boots, and my REACT T-shirt from last year's production of *Into the Woods*. Sometimes even a free T-shirt has a perfect fit.

Also, I don't really care about clothes.

"That seems impossible," I choke out through a yawn. My eyes feel too dry, and I'd take off my glasses if I thought that would help or if I'd still be able to see. And I'm worried about what my hair actually looks like, because I pulled it into a messy braid while walking from the bathroom to the bedroom and I have a suspicion that it looks less like a cute hairstyle and more like a hacked-up fraying rope. Suddenly I'm envious of my mom's no-maintenance haircut; mine doesn't have any style, either, but at least hers always looks *done*.

"I used to be a night person, too." Grace leads me out the door and down the sidewalk. "I always had the night shift at The Roast Of, but when I opened Grounds Control, at first I couldn't afford to pay too many other employees and the morning became mine. But now I kind of love it."

"I doubt that's my journey," I say. "Ugh, how far away do you have to park? How do people live without driveways and garages?"

"Oh god, Lydia, you sound *exactly* like your mom," Grace says, and I want to die, at least a little. Maybe more than a little. "And I *have* a driveway *and* a garage. They're both behind the house. But Grounds Control is only about a half a mile away, so unless I have a lot to bring with me, I walk."

A coffee shop job where I'd get to make real money *and* learn how to make latte art sounded like there would be no possible downsides, so of course it's practically in the middle of the night and I have to walk. I thought no one walked in LA? I'd ask Grace but she really got me with that *you sound exactly like your mom* comment. If she says that again while I'm this tired, I might cry.

"I love the city this time of day," Grace says. "Like it's just mine."

"You can have it," I mutter without thinking, and Grace shoots me a look, and I do hear in my voice how I might as well be Mom. So far everything about today is a huge disappointment, and normally during summer break I wouldn't even be up for at least five hours.

"I'm going to win you over." Grace loops her arm through mine. "Mornings, walking, Los Angeles."

"I'm hard to win," I say, which makes her laugh. It hits me how lucky I am to be walking with my supercool aunt, to have this one-on-one time where I'm actually *making her laugh*, being part of her world. Mornings or walking or this city will never be for me, but they're all worth *this*. When we were little, there was no more exciting day for Penny and me than a visit from Grace, and honestly that's still true. When Penny revealed her whole grand plan, despite all my concerns, it felt too good to be real. Grace time has been so relatively fleeting, and now it's all I have for the next two and a half months.

"Hey, Ben!" Grace waves as we walk up to Grounds Control, and—oh, damn. A tall guy waves back with one hand while balancing a huge white box in his other. His hair is nearly black and falls into his face, the kind of hair I think about pushing back so I can gaze into his eyes. His eyes, by the way: extremely good, too. You can tell a lot from someone's eyes, and so I love that his are wide, an extension of his smile. And somehow his bronze skin looks radiant at five-thirty in the morning, even though I'm pretty sure I just look pale and sweaty.

"This is my niece Lydia," she introduces. "Lydia, this is Benjamín."

He shakes my hand and grins at me from under that heartthrob hair and I legit have no idea how I'm supposed to adhere to my pact with Penny if I'm not even twenty-four hours in and forced to interact with the hottest guy I've met in months. Damn.

"Ben delivers our pastries every morning," Grace continues, and I feel relief creep in. So I might have to look through That Hair at Those Eyes on This Face every morning, but all those parts won't be side by side with me as I learn about lattes and muffins and milk alternatives.

"Not every morning," Ben says with a wink. Why can hot guys get away with winking? It should be so gross. "Five days a week is enough this summer. And it's nice to meet you, Niece Lydia."

"It's nice to meet you, too," I say, "Five Days a Week Pastries Benjamín."

Grace unlocks the front door, and once Ben walks off, I follow her inside and watch as she disables the alarm. "Don't get any ideas."

"About breaking in?"

"Oh, you're cute," she says. "Maybe your jokes work on Hope and Craig, but I am here to tell you that I see everything, and there's not going to be any Benjamín in your summer outside of pastry delivery."

"Pastry delivery," I repeat back, like it's an innuendo.

"He's about to start his senior year."

"So am I!"

"*Of college.* Anyway, don't you and Penny have some... nun thing going on?"

"Unfortunately, yes." I follow her as she deposits the pastry box on the counter. "We're chaste for the summer. Aren't you going to tell me the alarm code?"

"For now you'll only be opening the shop with me, so you won't need it." Grace opens a drawer near the register and takes out a binder.

"Here's everything you need to know about how we open the shop, if you want to follow along or study later, but you can also just watch me work. I know everyone learns differently."

I open the binder to the first laminated page, and even though someone—Grace, I assume—went through the effort of choosing a cute font and adorable space-themed clip art, I keep an eye on Grace. She starts giant coffee makers—a dark roast, a light roast, and a decaf—first, so that if people are here at six sharp there will already be coffee ready for them. Then she lines up the pastries in the pastry case and sets up little signs telling people what they are and how much they cost. She counts the cash in the cash register and, briefly, explains to me how to ring people up. Considering it's on an iPad, I assume I can handle it.

Grace brings out four pitchers from the back room. "Fill these with half-and-half, nonfat, soy, and oat. The milk's all under the espresso machine."

I do as I'm told—it's easy because of course the pitchers have been personalized with Grounds Control's logo and what they hold in the same font—and carry them out to the self-service counter. Grace shows me where I can restock all the different-colored packets of sweeteners, though the night crew shut down correctly and refilled everything already, and then somehow it's already six and someone's waiting outside to be let in.

"Grace, is this OK?" I ask, and I know the timing's bad because she's nearly made it to the door to unlock it. "Me being here?"

"Of course it is. Lydia, I love you guys, but if Jenn hadn't just put in her notice, I wouldn't have had an open spot for you. And, sure, you don't have much experience—"

"*Any* experience," I remind her.

"But you'll learn, and I'll get to hang out with you. So, yes. It's OK."

"But, like, don't girls who work in Insta-worthy coffee shops need to be...hot? Am I harshing your whole aesthetic?"

Even though I'm aware of how suburban I am, I am also aware of the vibe of coffee shops. Loads of minimalism, somehow. White walls and tiny decorations. Here the décor is all space-themed, but like that old-timey 1950s idea of space. Grace, in her faded T-shirt and perfectly worn-in vintage jeans, looks perfect here. I, the least-styled person ever, am another story, and maybe I should have thought about this before it was one second until opening.

Grace spins around and stares at me. "First of all, you *are* hot. Not that girls need to be hot to be worthy. I myself am emphatically *not* hot and I've done great for myself. But, c'mon, Lydia. And second, you *know* you're hot. I saw you with Ben. I see how your mind works."

"That's different," I say. "It's just boys. I can win over boys. I'm good at boys."

"I have to let this customer in," she tells me. "He's got a bad commute and is always in a rush and reminds me at least once a week it would be easier for him if I opened at five-thirty like Starbucks does."

"Can't he just go to Starbucks?"

"The eternal question," Grace says, and swings open the door. "Hey, Jeff, how's your morning?"

"Waze says the 10 looks bad," the man mutters. Grace knows his order already, and I hang back and watch her make a double cappuccino before ringing him up and sending him on his way.

"Is everyone that annoying?" I ask, and she laughs.

"I wouldn't be here if they were. Anyway, Lydia, I don't want to guess around at what you mean, but of course you're welcome here. More than welcome! We're going to have a lot of fun."

I smile. "The most fun six A.M. is capable of."

"Beyond!"

More customers begin filing in, though never more than a couple in line at a time. Whenever they want regular coffee, I jump in, filling cups all the way to the top or stopping before if they want room for some dairy or nondairy product. I feel like I'm awkwardly in Grace's way more than I'm contributing anything. And this is like the biggest fat girl fear, anyway, that I'm taking up too much space and keeping people from where they need to be. It's my big fear, at least. I don't believe any of the dumb stuff, like that fat girls can't be cute or healthy, but the stuff that might be true hits differently.

"You'll get the hang of it." An Asian girl around my age walks in and steps behind the counter as I bump into Grace, splashing just enough coffee to sting my wrist. *Ow.* "You're the new girl, I presume? If you're not, I guess you won't get the hang of it, because why the heck are you back here anyway?"

"I'm the new girl," I say.

"I'm Margaret," she says as she ties on her apron. Unlike me, she fits the Grounds Control aesthetic completely. Her thick black hair is braided into one of those flawless crowns, and she has perfect brows and this smudge of gloss that would look sloppy on me but extremely intentional on her lips. And she's not tiny, but she's thinner than I am. I hate that I'm always noticing things like that, but I am. We're technically wearing the same outfit, T-shirt and jeans, but her stuff looks all effortless and—well, mine does too, but in that way where it's obvious that I literally got dressed in the dark and my T-shirt was given to me for free by a school administrator.

"Lydia. Grace's niece, though you probably already know that."

"Grace must be the coolest aunt!" Margaret pretends to swoon. "My aunt is a thousand years old and is always telling me I should wear more makeup."

I want to tell her how perfect her face is without it, but that might be creepy. I'm not good with girl interactions, even though I'm a girl myself. It's not like all girls are the same, and there's something about who I am that makes me worry I'll never figure the rest of them out.

"Grace is a very cool aunt," I say.

"Grace, do you want to get the counter? I can show Lydia how to work the machine," Margaret says. Grace agrees and switches spots with us.

"I knew she'd get coffee to people faster doing it herself," I say.

"Don't worry about it. I was super awkward at first; I spilled an entire decaf on this dude and *he cried*. And then when I tried to make latte art the first time, it was supposed to be a heart but somehow it looked like a little dick in a cup. So you'll do way better than that, I can feel it."

"Did you serve someone the dick in a cup?" I ask.

Margaret throws her head back and laughs. "No, I drank it myself. Consumed that little dick energy."

Margaret shows me the basics of the espresso machine and even has me pull shots for the next drink that comes up. It's more physical than I expect; you have to tamp down the espresso with the right amount of pressure, and then swivel the portafilter into place in the machine with just a little *oomph*. It makes it all the more satisfying to watch the dark liquid pour out into shot glasses.

"See? You did it!" Margaret beams at me and tips the shot glasses into a paper cup branded with Grounds Control's logo. "Should I make a fern or a heart?"

"Fern," I say, and watch as she tips the milk from its steaming pitcher back and forth into the cup. It's like magic to watch the fern appear. I'm decent at a lot of artistic things, but this feels like something else entirely. "I'll never be able to do that."

"Believe in yourself," she says. "Do you want to call the drink at the counter?"

"Is it hard?"

She cracks up. "No! You just call out the person's name and the drink. Phil, double latte. Easy breezy beautiful."

"Phil!" I call out. "Double latte!"

"That was a hypothetical name," Margaret says, through giggles. "I'm sorry. I should have made that more obvious. It's actually for—"

"Fran." A girl pops up near the counter. "Thanks."

"Sorry for calling you Phil," I say. "I'm new."

"Don't let it happen again," the girl—Fran?—says with a smirk. Her reddish-brown hair's tously up top and really short everywhere else, and she's also in jeans and a T-shirt. Everything looks worn in a really broken-in way, like her clothes would be soft to the touch. I can tell she's no-nonsense, the kind of person my parents think they are and are emphatically *not*. And I'm not sure why I can identify this quality in a girl I've known for approximately seven seconds, but it radiates from her.

"I might be back later," Fran says. "If more people want drinks."

"That's why I didn't know it was your order," Margaret calls over. "It's so small."

"I'm mysterious that way," she says, though she's looking at me. "See you later."

"She seems cool," I say once she's gone, though I realize I'm embarrassed the second it's out of my mouth.

"We went to high school together," Margaret says. "Fran's a *player*."

I want to ask follow-up questions to that, but I can feel that the shop is growing busier, and it's time to focus on drinks. Margaret's so fast at everything that I mainly just keep pulling shots of espresso and then getting out of Margaret's way as she dashes around steaming milk and whisking in cocoa powder and splashing in ferns and hearts. By the time the pace lets up, I glance at the wall clock to see it's already ten.

"Sorry for slowing everyone down," I say.

"Go check the self-service station," Grace tells me. "Take a rag because it's going to look destroyed."

"People are monsters," Margaret says. "Gross dirty monsters."

"Only some of them are, but they ruin it for the rest of us." Grace smiles and hands me a rag. "You're doing great. I've got a feel for this stuff."

"What stuff?" I walk out to the front of the shop and make a face at the messy counter space. "When to use rags and when not to use rags?"

"She's really funny," Margaret tells Grace, and I feel myself smile practically involuntarily. I can tell Margaret is a Cool Girl, and a Cool Girl thinks I'm funny. It's probably the first time in the history of my life that this has happened.

"Employees!" Grace calls out to me. "You're gonna be a good one, Lydia. Whether you believe me or not."

Chapter Three

I thought I'd be exhausted after my first shift, but I'm not, and it isn't just all the free iced Americanos I drank, though those probably play a factor. Grace needs to stay longer for all sorts of backroom paperwork things, so she sends me home with a spare key. I don't need cash for lunch because Grace gave me my share of tips from the tip jar, and it's more than enough to grab takeout from the pizza place down the block.

Mom and Dad never wanted Penny and me to have jobs because they wanted us to be able to focus on school and our extracurriculars, but I feel *good* today, way better than I expected.

And I barely thought about boys. Hardly any time spent on Ben's hair at all.

"Look at me!" Penny practically dances through the front door, holding up a name tag on a lanyard. "A real business professional."

"That's your thing that makes you a business professional?" I ask. "A lanyard?"

"My face is on it." She shoves it at me and we both laugh. Penny is the type who looks cute on her goddamn driver's license, so of course her work lanyard photo is great, too.

"How is it?" I ask.

"I have cracked the code to avoid boys all summer." She sits down next to me on the couch. "There are no boys there at all. Everyone is old, really old."

"Hey," Oscar says, walking through the room.

"Well, *you're old,*" she says, and we crack up.

"You'll be old before you know it!" he calls from his and Grace's bedroom.

"What about you?" she asks.

"Boys? No boys, nope. Cute delivery boy, but we only cross paths a little."

"I meant the job," she says. "I assumed you could make it one day without boys, though maybe I shouldn't have."

"The job is good, even if it starts in the middle of the night," I say. "I learned how to make espresso. And soon I'll learn ferns and hearts."

"I'm going to come up with a naming convention for all the archival paperwork I'm scanning," Penny says with a gleam in her eyes, and even though I have no idea what that means, I'm happy for her. I know it's the kind of thing she can write about when she applies to undergraduate business schools next year.

Business school. *Business school.* I can't imagine how Penny's mind works that it sounds fun to her, and considering how often she sends me links with headlines like "A Degree in the Arts Might As Well Be Throwing Away Your Money!," I know she doesn't get me, either. The things that have always united us are teaming up against Mom and Dad—a no-brainer for most siblings, I assume—and boys. This summer we're not going to have either, and for the first time it hits me that maybe Penny's well-researched plan missed a vital element. Without boys or our parents, how do we make any sense to each other? Maybe more importantly—how do I make sense to Penny?

"I saw a cool ice cream place earlier," I tell her. Ice cream might not be as solid a commonality as boys or our parents, but who doesn't love ice cream? "I can treat, from my tip money. Want to go?"

"I might just do a sheet mask and read until dinner," she says.

"We could go for dessert?"

"Maybe tomorrow." Penny gets up from the couch and walks to our room. I try not to feel completely rejected and pick up my phone like that was my plan to begin with. There's nothing exciting going on, though, even when I go against the rules I've set for myself and pull up Tate's profile, and now I feel even more rejected. I knew he was headed across the country to North Carolina with his family, but he's bad at photography, so he could be at any random beach for how his posts look. I teased him about it constantly when we were together. *Tate, take a photo of me, but ignore all your instincts or I'll yet again look like a troll that lives in a bog.*

I still don't actually know what went wrong. How can someone tell you they love you and then…*not*? Tate's hardly the first boy who broke my heart, but he was the first one where it felt like a hit-and-run, like I could chronicle the events of our relationship over and over and still not make sense of it. It shouldn't matter now—even without pledging to Penny that this summer would be devoid of boys, it shouldn't matter. He's taking shitty pictures of the Crystal Coast and I'm in LA trying to fit in at a space-themed coffee shop. And, despite what I want, we're over.

I just wish that it was what I wanted, too.

~

Yesterday at Grounds Control might have been great, but it turns out I'm no better at getting up the next morning. Grace has to physically shake me from my slumber again, though I do force myself to put at least ten percent more effort into my clothes and hair. I might never master something like Margaret's braid crown, but I coax my hair into little space buns, which are cute and also on-theme.

"What do you want to learn today?" Grace asks me as we walk over. I'm sleepy enough that I only now remember Ben and his big box of pastries. If I dab on lip gloss, will I look cute like Margaret or more like I fell asleep with a lollipop in my mouth? I assume the second.

"Can I learn the register? I know you have to go superfast, but I feel like I'll learn more of the drinks before I actually have to make them that way."

"That's a brilliant idea," Grace says, and she doesn't sound sarcastic. It makes sense, because Mom is rarely sarcastic, and even though Grace is about a thousand times cooler than Mom, the more I'm around Grace, the more I can already see how they're sisters, too.

Ben is leaning against Grounds Control with a pastry box when we get there. I've never thought that punctuality was hot before, but one person can change an entire quality for you.

"Hi, Five Days a Week Pastries Benjamín," I say, and he grins.

"Hey, Niece Lydia. How was your first day?"

"Good," I say, even though it was more like *great*. Boys don't have to hear everything; some mystery never hurts. "How were all your deliveries?"

"All good too. See you ladies tomorrow." He waves and heads to the Kia parked at the curb. I try to casually follow Grace inside, but she's still shooting me little looks.

"I never promised not to flirt with any boys this summer," I say, even though that *was* exactly one of the things that Penny and I promised each other. It's not at the heart of the agreement, though, because flirting itself isn't the problem. It's the stuff that flirting leads to, the way we both find ourselves caught up in emotions that take over.

Honestly, I don't one hundred percent get it. Songs are all about loving someone until there's nothing else left, and romantic movies have these sweeping epic moments where everything but your love interest is thrown to the wind. But when you feel like that in real life, stuff goes wrong, like your grades or your goals or your focus backstage. (The backstage part is probably just me and not a universal thing.)

Hopefully the summer off from boys, even boys like Benjamín with long lashes that would brush your eyelids if you kissed, will reset something in me that needs resetting. And then, senior year, I can get back into good graces with everyone else on REACT, apply to colleges where I can theoretically study theater tech, and still fall in love with someone hot and smart and nice enough for Mom and Dad to not worry.

Ugh, listing it out, even just in my head, feels like it's a lot to ask for. College in particular seems impossible, especially if Penny's sharing her opinion of theater degrees with Mom and Dad on the regular and not just with me. I'd love to worry about college *more*, actually, but I'm a little afraid that college is for Penny and people like her, people with solid plans and experience, not people like me who're still figuring things out.

But if Penny's including me in this whole scheme of hers, I must not be completely hopeless.

"Are you OK?" Grace asks me.

"Just thinking of everything I have to figure out senior year and it sounds practically physically impossible," I say. "Should I start the coffee?"

"Do you need help?" she asks, and I shake my head and start measuring out coffee beans to grind. We did this so regularly yesterday that it already feels like a routine I've got down. Maybe it's silly, because Grace knows she only hired me because I'm her niece, but I still want her to be glad I'm here.

"I feel like there's a lot of pressure on kids now," Grace says as she sets out all the pastries. "We had way less of that, and I think your mom and I turned out fine."

I know that Mom worries about Grace, because she has these private conversations with Dad that aren't private at all. Why isn't Grace married to Oscar yet, why does Grace ignore the fact that nearly sixty percent of restaurants fail in the first three years, why doesn't Grace seem worried about the fact that she's in her early forties and certainly by now her eggs have just about run out and will leave her childless and sad. But Grace *does* seem to have turned out fine. Grounds Control seems like it looks *exactly* like Grace must have dreamed it up, and it stays pretty busy, and I know that it's only been open a year, but I can't imagine it not making it at least another two. And it's true that she's childless, but *sad* seems the least accurate word to describe Grace.

"What?" she asks, and it's like she can read my thoughts, and we both laugh.

"You do seem like you turned out fine." I try to make it sound like the fact isn't a little surprising. "I mean, Mom's a huge goober, though."

"Yeah, that's nothing new."

When I unlock the front door, the same guy is out there glaring at Waze. Grace is already working on his drink, but he still exhales several times as I slowly ring him up.

"I'm new," I say as I screw up the next-to-last screen for the third time.

"I can tell."

Grace hands him his cup and leans over my shoulder to show me the right button to hit. I manage to take the guy's credit card and swipe it through with no further screwups, but of course he's still muttering about freeways when he leaves.

"You know that's just him, right?" Grace asks.

I do, but I'm grateful she thinks so, too. "Well, sure, but I still set him back at least seven seconds, so that much is on me."

Margaret's there before long, and she lets out a little *oooh* when she walks by me. "Supercute hair, Lyds. Do people call you Lyds?"

"No one has ever called me Lyds," I say.

"I'm the first!" She watches me as she ties on her apron. I realize the top part's embroidered with her name, and I wonder if two and a half months employment is enough to garner a personalized apron with my name in the Grounds Control font. "How's the register going?"

"That Waze guy hates me, but OK otherwise."

She practically cackles. "Oh, Waze guy hates everyone."

I've never been on the house side of the stage, only behind, wearing all black as a member of tech crew, but right now I feel like I'm playing a part. *And it's great.* The girl who hits it off with a Cool Girl, who gets a nickname, who gets hair compliments. How did I earn this role?

"You're doing great, I'm sure," Margaret continues. I try not to beam, but I could beam. This *thing* that's always felt so hard before is just *happening.* A summer without boys sounds a lot easier if I suddenly have people to be friends with. That feels exactly like the kind of person I should be turning into, the girl with friends who's good at her job and never, ever gets distracted when someone tall leans over her and gives her *that look.*

"Grace would pull you if you weren't. Even as a niece."

"It's true." Grace opens the pastry case. "I'm going to make this brown butter apple croissant mine. Do you guys want to split it with me? We could even split two, if we're feeling wild."

"Ugh, I'd be so fat if I ate pastries here," Margaret says while she organizes the steaming pitchers. Like it's nothing. Like I'm not standing right there. "I like picturing Ben carefully slicing all these little apples, though. Lyds, I assume you met Be*n.*" She draws out the *n,* and it's enough for us all to understand it means he's hot.

"Yep," I say, and then luckily three customers walk in at the same time, and I get caught up enough in mastering the cash register that I can forget about Margaret for moments at a time. The line gets steadier, longer, but I maintain my focus. Honestly, there's something like relief in my chest, a lightness that I don't have to wait to find out how I don't actually fit in with the Cool Girl at all. It's a clichéd reason, but I guess that's how clichés work.

If I'm being honest with myself, knowing how other girls—smaller girls—feel about bodies like mine is a huge reason I'm not friends with girls, that I profess not to understand girls, even though I'm a girl myself, even though being a girl isn't like some set-in-stone thing. Still, it feels like there are plenty of things I *do* understand about girls, things like that even if I'm a girl who's happy, a girl who's kissed lots of cute boys, I'm still a nightmare—their worst-case scenario.

Who wants to be friends with people whose biggest fear is looking just like you?

"Hey there."

I glance up at the next person who's made it to the front of the line and grin. "Hey, Phil."

Fran laughs. She's in another perfectly faded shirt, effortlessly effortless somehow. I feel like I don't always make enough of an effort, but it's completely different. Her hair is askew from product or maybe her own hands running through it, and yet it might look even *better* like this.

"Glad to see that's gonna stick," she says with a grin. The light blue shade of her T-shirt practically makes her coppery tan skin glow. "How's your morning?"

"Too early, OK besides that. Your usual? Double fern latte?"

I have no idea why I remember Fran's exact drink and I also have no idea if it's weird I remember it or not, so I just hope it's not.

She holds up a chain of five Post-its. "I have a whole list today. You ready for this?"

I make a big show of flexing my hands before holding them in position at the iPad. "I was *born ready*."

Fran goes over the list patiently, even as the line grows behind her. Every drink has to be rung up separately for a different name, so it takes some time, but I only have to call for Grace's help once, and if I'm going to spend any extra time on one customer today, I'm glad it's Fran, patient and smiling and tall.

She's still waiting when I get through the rest of the line, four out of five drinks sitting in the carrier in front of her.

"Thirsty?" I ask, and she laughs.

"Parched. Nah, I'm—well, I'm supposedly a PA for this indie movie, but it turns out PA manages to stand for Beverage Getter."

"More like BG," I say. "An indie movie is cool, though."

She shrugs. "Hopefully I'll start seeing some of it."

I watch her as Grace brings over her final drink. Fran is not a Cool Girl, but she's definitively cool. Margaret did scoff a little when she called Fran a player, but a player feels like such a better word to be called than the one that gets directed at me more than I'd like. And what makes one girl a player and another girl a slut anyway?

"See you," Fran says to me with a nod. This sounds ridiculous, but there's some sort of level of respect I feel I've earned to get that nod.

"Bye, BG Phil."

"This one," Fran says to Grace, "is full of jokes."

Grace laughs. "She's full of something. Thanks, Fran."

"Lyds!" Margaret pops up over the espresso machine. "Switch off with Grace and I'll let you try to make a heart on my latte."

I don't feel so much like Lyds anymore, but I join her anyway and hold the pitcher as she directs me. I actually watched some YouTube videos on latte art last night in bed while Penny was rewatching her favorite TED Talks or whatever, but it's nothing like painting or drawing. I could *paint* an amazing heart.

"Hey," I say, having an idea while I swish steamed milk around. It looks less like a heart and more like an explosion. A heart attack, at best. "What's something cool my sister and I could do tonight that we could walk to?"

"From here? Hmmm." Margaret makes an intense thinking face that makes me laugh even though I don't want to like her anymore. "What's your sister into?"

"I dunno. Brené Brown?"

Margaret snorts. "Ooohkay. Well, if you just want to get food or something, there are, like, a million amazing restaurants and taco trucks."

"Getting food doesn't really seem like *doing something*," I say. "It's just dinner."

"I happen to think exploring the vast landscape of LA cuisine is *totally doing something*." Margaret giggles. "But your plans, your rules. You could also take the train downtown. If you're into bands or whatever, there are some cool all-ages spaces, but I'd have to ask my friend Tara for more specifics because I'm such a dork about music, I don't know anything cool at all."

"You seem cool," I say, a statement I regret immediately for multiple reasons.

"Oh, shut up," she says with a laugh. "If you met Tara you'd know what I mean. *Oh I got into this secret show under a staircase,*" she says, switching into an extremely affected deep voice, *"and I bought a seven-inch record they only printed eleven of on zebra-striped vinyl. The lead singer is an Amazon Echo."*

I crack up as she dramatically shrugs and takes a sip of the heart attack latte.

"Your art might suck now, but it's still a good latte," she tells me, and there's such kindness in her voice that it would be so easy to erase what she said earlier. People say things like that all the time, all the things they do or don't do so that they don't end up fat. So that they don't end up anything like me.

Also I really wanted to split that stupid brown butter apple pastry, and now there's no way I'm going to.

Chapter Four

"So I have four ideas to propose." I hold up notecards to Penny so she'll know I'm serious. "For Friday night, if you're free."

I don't add *please be free because if you somehow already have plans I'll be more than a little worried that our relationship can't withstand having all the boy drama extracted from it.* Margaret helped me during our downtime today—I'm learning the rhythm of the shifts—and we used Yelp to invent four cool but different Friday night scenarios, a whole two and a half days ahead. My sister loves notecards, research, and timely planning, so it is no coincidence at all just how in her wheelhouse my presentation is.

Penny looks up from the living room armchair with none of the excitement I'd been picturing on her face. "Sure."

"So, option one, we could—"

"Whatever you want to do is fine," she says. "Just tell me that morning so I wear an appropriate outfit to work, in case I don't have time to change after."

"I worked really hard on my notecards." I hold them up, fanned out, like a magician. There's only four of them, so I guess it's not really that impressive.

"I told you notecards were helpful," she says, but she's already looking at the book in her lap. I can tell from the bold type on the cover that it's some powerful guide Glennon Doyle told women to read, so

I don't wait for her to wave her hand to dismiss me. I just leave Pen to it.

"Hey, Lydia," Oscar calls from the kitchen. "Did Grace mention when she'd be heading home?"

"Nope," I say. "She's a mystery."

"Tell me about it. How's it going at the shop? She says you're catching on well."

"I hope that's true," I say. "It's a lot to learn, and everyone else has got it down."

"Grace got her first coffee shop job back in the nineties or something," Oscar says. "She's had time. Give yourself a break."

"Well, sure, but I think Margaret is about my age and she's a goddamn whiz." I'm not sure I should curse in front of upstanding Oscar, but he doesn't flinch. Mom and Dad would have probably had something to say about that. "Is Penny a whiz already?"

"Eh, Penny's limited by my office's technology. Or lack of, I guess. She's doing great, but she's been assigned to this ancient copier and printer so that she doesn't tie up the main one with the scanning project, and that thing got replaced for a reason. But, yeah. Your sister's smart, you obviously know that."

"She's the smart one," I say.

He laughs. "No sympathy. Do you know my brother is an actual literal rocket scientist?"

"Oh shit," I say, and laugh, and it sounds pretty silly but it's like all at once someone took some pressure off me. Oscar has a job and a cool girlfriend—though I may be biased there—even if he's not the sibling who's good at everything. I don't think I would have characterized my future as hopeless, exactly, but at this moment I'm feeling a lot more of what I can only describe as hope.

"Maybe I don't try to figure out dinner and we just order pizza once Grace is home," Oscar says. "That sound OK to you?"

I give him a thumbs-up and head to my shared room to safely stash my notecards for a later time. There's no way I made my penmanship that good for nothing.

This whole idea had been Penny's, but I trust Penny's ideas. And I want it to work. I want this big reset where my brain spends time thinking only about the right stuff or at least enough about the right stuff. I wanted Penny to look as excited about time with me as she is about time with tomes about empowerment and success. But only a few days in, and nothing feels new between Penny and me at all.

~~~

"What did your sister pick?" Margaret asks me the next day while I'm again attempting to create a fern in a latte. "No, more like—" She gestures, and when I guess I don't catch on, she takes the pitcher from me and shows me. "Make sense?"

"It all makes sense. I just can't control the milk with my mind."

"Ooh, imagine if you could! I'd burn all my haters. Scald 'em in their eyes."

I hand off the latte to the very patient man waiting on it and apologize for the state of the latte art with my new requisite "I'm new!" and the shrug I hope is at least a little cute.

"Anyway," Margaret continues when I'm back next to her at the espresso machine, "did your sister pick one of the notecards yet?"

"Ugh, she didn't even care," I say, even though I really want to keep more from Margaret, who I emphatically do not trust now that I know how she really sees me and people like me. It's as if I can't resist her Cool Girl allure. This is how Cool Girls do it!

"She said we could do whatever, and she didn't even look at the cards."

"No!" Margaret pauses her work at the espresso bar to clasp her hands to her heart. "Your handwriting looked so perfect! You better save those cards."

"I save everything, don't worry." I start espresso shots for the next order. "Why do we only make ferns and hearts? It's not exactly on-theme."

"That's a very good point." Margaret looks over to Grace, who has no one in line right at this moment. "Why do we only make hearts and ferns?"

"They're the two easiest latte arts," Grace says. "And also the only ones I learned at The Roast Of, where I worked up until opening this shop."

"It would be cool if we had a rocket ship," I say.

"Hell *yeah*," Margaret says, and does a blasting-off sound effect. "Saturn and its rings!"

"David Bowie's face!"

"OK, you two, reel it in." Grace turns from us as a customer walks in, but I can tell Margaret's mind is still whirring, too. We get the next drink started, and she raises her eyebrows at me.

"What are you doing after work? You want to come over and watch YouTube videos of how to invent latte art?"

I'm completely of two minds about Margaret, on only our fourth day of knowing each other, but I agree anyway. I can't even completely figure out why. Is it only the allure of the Cool Girl? Maybe it's easy to think I've had tough standards for friends in the past, considering that someone like Margaret has never given me the time of day before. But also…*do* I have standards for friends? How do so many people have entire social circles when I find every single aspect of this confusing as hell?

Margaret also lives within walking distance to Grounds Control, but in the opposite direction. Her house is tucked back a bit more, and even from the front walkway I can tell it's bigger and nicer than Grace and Oscar's.

"Thanks for nerding out with me on this," Margaret says as we walk inside. "I'm leaving for college in two months and I kept thinking, I gotta leave a legacy at Grounds Control! This is gonna be it."

"Where are you going to college?" The possibility is only a year away for me, but it really seems further than that, impossible even. If college is for smart, driven people, I'm not sure I'm together enough to even start thinking about it. But also it's way too late to not be thinking about it yet, so why even bother?

"Take your shoes off before you go any further into the house," she says, and laughs. "Oh, gross, I sound exactly like my mom. But, seriously, take your shoes off. And Vassar, 'cause I couldn't get into Brown."

"Vassar's like a really good school though, right?" I should definitely know more about colleges already. I honestly *want* to know more, but it's too overwhelming, and since neither of my parents went away to college, I can tell they don't know how to be overbearing about this upcoming part of my life. They stayed nearby, got the minimum requirements to become CPAs, and that was it. That means that I'm on my own and even mild googling makes me feel like I'll never sort it out.

"Yeah, it's good, and the campus is really pretty. I'm excited when I'm not terrified." She grabs my wrist once our shoes are off and pulls me through a bright and open living room down a hallway to her bedroom. It is *exactly* as I could have pictured it, cool pale pink vibes, Instax photos sprinkled liberally around the empty wall space, a bed with tulle as light as cotton candy threaded through the canopy top.

"I know, I know," she says with a shrug. "It's such a pink princess room, but I can't help what I like!"

"No, it's good," I say. "Way better than my room."

"I feel like if a boy came in here he'd shrivel up *and die.*"

"No way, a lot of boys secretly love shit like this," I say. "The good ones aren't afraid of pink and fluffy stuff. My last boyfriend—"

I cut myself off, because if I think of Tate buying me a Pusheen plush that was eating a little stuffed cookie, I might cry. I had joked I was just like Pusheen, round and obsessed with snacks. It had only been a throwaway comment, and so when I'd seen him with the little stuffed cat under his arms, I felt it. *This might be it. He might be the one.*

Except it wasn't and he wasn't, and I had to donate Pusheen to a children's charity because I couldn't look at her without bursting into tears. Hopefully the child in need who ended up with her couldn't sense the heartbreak that had cast her out of my home.

Margaret pokes my arm with her index finger. "Are you OK?"

"I had a dramatic breakup," I say. "I wish I was OK already."

"Do you want to talk about it?"

I shake my head. "If it's all right."

"Oh my god, Lyds, of *course* it's all right. Let's just watch YouTube weirdos make beautiful foam art."

We both have giant iPhones, so we take turns pulling up videos and watching experts. There are actually only a few ways to start foam art into a latte, so that's why most cafés do the standard hearts and ferns and tulips. It's all about the height and angle of the milk poured into the cup, and once you're good enough, you can get a little creative and make those basics look like—well, not *anything*, but definitely beyond the basics. David Bowie's face probably isn't possible, but a rocket seems potentially doable.

"This is going to take some time," Margaret says with a sigh.

"I mean, I can't even do the easy ones yet," I say. "You deserve a better partner in your legacy."

"No, no one else would be excited about this," she says. "Even *Grace* was, like, whatevs."

I wonder if I should bring up another video on my phone. This is the exact kind of situation that terrifies me: the open-ended, one-on-one friend hangout. What are we supposed to do? Are there cool conversation topics? Since I have to ask that question, I assume I shouldn't even attempt to figure it out.

It was easier with boys, because in lieu of talking, there was always kissing, etc. But also that kissing convenience meant I didn't get so nervous with them. If I always had the backup ready, who cared if conversation got awkward for a moment? There were always methods to get things back on track.

With friends, though? I have no idea.

I mean, it isn't like I've never had friends. But they tended to be activity-related, either in my classes or also involved in the theater department. I tagged along to group stuff, sometimes got invited to parties, and mostly that felt like enough.

"Oh, I just remembered, so since you and your sister didn't pick a place yet, I have an idea for you," Margaret says. "But it's totally self-serving. A bunch of us are going out for KBBQ on Friday night, but two of Tara's friends canceled, so if you two came it would be a perfect six. I know you think dinner isn't *doing something* but I'm gonna prove you wrong."

"What's KBBQ?" I ask.

"Korean barbecue," she says. "Have you never been?"

"Sorry," I say. "I'm such a boring suburban white girl."

"OK, well, only one question, but it's important: Do you like meat?"

"Lots," I say. "So does Penny."

"So come! You can meet some of my friends, and we'll eat so much meat you'll smell it in your hair the next day."

"Is that supposed to be appealing?" I ask as she mimes sniffing her own hair, then mine. We both crack up, and I text the idea to Penny. It's hard to say if this is really friendship or not. Maybe Margaret thinks I'm gross, just a fat girl she'd hate to be anything like. And maybe it'll be weird to eat a meal with someone who feels that way, plus all her cool friends. But, also, there's nothing else in how she's acted to make me think that. Everything else honestly feels like the kind of friendship I've never managed to find, and so easily at that. It was just the one thing said. If I ignore that one thing, everything's perfect.

"So why are you staying with Grace this summer?" she asks.

"My parents are on a cruise," I say, because it's true but a lot easier to explain than the full truth. "It's my dad's dream thing."

"Aw, that's cute. Is it cute? Or is it just weird?"

"Both, honestly. Anyway, it worked out OK because I guess someone just quit—"

"Jenn," Margaret fills in. "She was good but less fun."

I try not to look overly excited that Margaret think I'm fun. More
fun than Jenn, at least. "So I get the job until school starts, and
Grace's boyfriend—"

"Oscar," Margaret squeals. "Dreamboat. Nerd heartthrob. Business
casual hotshot."

"Whoa, small smart men are your type?" I ask, and she pretends
to swoon.

"Completely. All I want to do is show up at Vassar and run right into
a sexy geek exactly my height." She snorts with laughter. "Not that I'd
know what to do if I did. I am *hopeless* about boys. Should I admit that
only a few days into knowing you?"

I wasn't sure what to do with this mess of feelings, these mixed
signals that I was someone Margaret wanted to impress while also
being Margaret's worst fears. Situations like this were exactly why I'd
kept to myself in a lot of ways. Well, not specifically *situations like this*.
Someone as fun and smart as Margaret had never befriended me so
aggressively before. It was all new.

"I should probably head out."

"Oh no!" Margaret laughed even harder. "I knew I shouldn't have
said that."

"No, obviously not because—"

"Good. So you'll come with us on Friday. You and your sister?"

I look around again at the perfect room and feel how it isn't me,
doesn't accommodate someone who's style-less and big. So what
does it matter? I might as well say the big scary thing, after all. Work

might be a little more awkward, but for me it's already awkward. I might as well be honest.

"Yesterday you said a thing about not eating the pastries because you'd end up fat," I say, sort of backing toward the door. I'm ready for escape. "So I guess I don't really think I should go out to eat with you on Friday."

Margaret clasps her hands to her mouth, and I don't know what it means but I should probably go.

"Lyds, no, hang on." She's suddenly across the room and pulling me back from the hallway. "You know that I didn't mean—"

"No, I know," I say, shoving a loose lock of hair back into one of my buns. "You didn't mean *me*. But, like, I *am* fat, so also you *did* mean me when you said it."

She watches me for a few moments, and I want to leave even more.

"I'm just going to—"

"No, hang on. I'm trying to think of the right thing to say and my ideas are all terrible. I guess I should just say sorry, though."

I shrug, because I hadn't made some big plan to be honest. And now I've got nothing.

"It was really thoughtless of me and even though it's not how I meant it—look, I'll totally understand if you don't want to hang out with me, but also, give me a chance and I promise that Friday night will be super fun, enough to distract your sister from TED Talks or whatever."

I can't help laughing at that. "You have no idea what it takes to distract Pen from a TED Talk. I'm not sure a bunch of meat will be enough."

"Lyds, I'm willing to try."

I guess I am, too.

Chapter Five

On Friday morning, everything happens at the same time.

I'm at the cash register because this morning was busier than usual, and I'm still not fast enough on the espresso machine to handle it once we're at peak business. It's OK because I like it all, the satisfaction of watching shots pull or saying hi to a regular who's here every single day. I'm not someone who's ever had a thousand interests or hobbies, so I didn't expect that I would like *this*, of all things.

It's nice to realize there's more about yourself that you don't know yet. Maybe I'm being way too optimistic, but it seems like a good sign for the future. To be fair, I'll take all I can get right now.

My phone buzzes while there's a lull between customers, and I glance down at my lock screen to make sure it isn't an emergency. Not that I've ever had an emergency in my life, not *really*, but you never know. But, no, it's just Penny. *Sorry, people are socializing after work and I feel that it's appropriate I go. You understand, right? We can go out to dinner any time.*

"Ugh," I say aloud. "Margaret, my sister can't make it. I'm sure she's doing some business casual evening with a bunch of old people where they talk about their favorite pantsuit brands or something."

Margaret laughs, and I'm grateful because it's better turning this into a funny moment than dwelling on my sister choosing other people over me. "I mean, Lyds, it's her Ann Taylor Loft dream, let her live it. You'll still come, right?"

Fran walks in holding a neon orange Post-it chain that stretches nearly two feet long. I barely know her, but I can tell from her posture and the way she trudges up to the counter that she's exhausted. Even her plain black T-shirt looks tired.

"Too much BG, Phil?"

"Way, way too much. Is it easier if I just hand you these?"

"I mean, maybe?" My hand brushes hers as I take the chain carefully enough not to let any of the Post-its separate. I know it exactly right then, though it's possible it was already something simmering in my subconscious.

I try to hurry through the orders, even though no one's in line behind Fran, and even though maybe she'd like the break from her boring duties. I want to seem competent, to Grace and Margaret, and to Fran, too. To everyone, really, but these three especially.

There's still no one else in line once I get everything rung up, and I glance back at Margaret. The plan's brewing in me, even if part of me can pretend these are all separate, detached actions.

"So is it bad that Penny canceled?" I ask Margaret.

"Well, our reservations are for six people, but it's not really a big deal if there are only five of us."

"BG Phil," I say, and Fran looks up from her phone. "Do you want to go with us for Korean barbecue tonight? We have an extra spot."

I can tell Margaret's giving me a funny look, but it's fine. I was never going to master Cool Girl friendship anyway.

"Where?" Fran asks. "The SGV?"

"Genwa," Margaret calls. "'Cause they take reservations and I *hate* waiting for anything if I don't have to."

"Uh, yeah," Fran says. "I can go. When?"

"Seven." I take my phone back out of my pocket and hold it up. Fran takes it from me and types in her number. I text it right away. *Sorry there's so much BG today.*

A message pops up right away. *It's all good. There are worse places to spend time.*

Do you want to carpool tonight? Since there's six of us I don't know if I can ask Margaret. She's probably in a carful of people already. I'm the interloper.

WE'RE the interlopers, and, yeah, I can drive. Pick you up here at six?

"It takes an hour to get there?" I yelp, accidentally aloud. "Why is LA traffic so stupid?"

Grace brings over two drink carriers packed with beverages. "Our traffic is very stupid, but we're still the best city in the whole country, if you ask me. Fran, would it improve your day if I treated you to a pastry? Any pastry?"

"Yeah, definitely," she says. "Any pastry's good for me."

Grace studies the whole display before carefully taking out a pistachio croissant and sliding it into a paper bag. "My best friend started out as a PA. And she's a producer now. It's going to work out fine."

Fran smiles at Grace. "Thanks for that. See you later, Lydia."

Whoa, I like hearing her say my name. I didn't even know she knew my name.

"Grace, let Lyds come back to drinks duty since it's slow." Margaret gestures for me to join her. Grace nods, so I squeeze by her to switch places.

"What's going on *there?*" she asks in a whisper.

It's not news to me that I like girls, in general. But this—a specific girl—is news. Is *new.* "I have no idea."

Getting ready is like a whole journey.

As I sort through everything I packed, I know I won't be dressed right for Margaret and her friends, but I also know that even if I were given free rein to a store that had nothing but cute plus-size clothes, I wouldn't be able to assemble a look that *would* be right. It's not in my blood—just look at Mom and Dad's cotton suburban looks. At Grounds Control it's easy to look close to some version of... well, *right.* Jeans and T-shirts practically seem like a uniform already, and my boots are sensible supportive footwear, and not this thing I like that might just look clunky and awkward in any other setting. But now Margaret will learn the truth, which is that my off-hours look is just about the same thing as my on-hours look, only swapping out a T-shirt I wouldn't want to spatter with espresso and foam and jean shorts instead of jeans.

Plus there's Fran. There's nothing *real* about Fran, I know—I think? But, still. There's Fran.

There wasn't this magical moment when I was filled with this knowledge that I didn't only like boys. It was the sort of thing that snuck up, dawned on me over time. I'd notice a girl while we were out and have a little pang. The first few times I brushed it off, but then I'd catch myself listening to Demi Lovato on repeat while thinking about Kristen Stewart's jawline, and before long the whole thing felt pretty nailed down.

I've tested out the word in my own head, bisexual, the label that felt right, genders like mine and genders not like mine, but it always felt like it's only that—a test. I wasn't living it for real, and I guess since I kept falling in love with boys, I thought I might never know for sure. Not that you need to even kiss people of other genders to be bisexual, of course. You can be fully *living it* with nothing on the surface changing. What was below the surface was all that mattered. Still, I guess *I* wanted more before I said anything. I wanted to before I even really *thought it*. I wanted to kiss someone else, fall for someone, let myself get swept away by daydreams of a future with someone else. Then it would be something I'd talk about.

Fran, though, is not a test. Fran is real as hell, and so I catch myself as I'm going through rituals. Perfume oil I dab behind my ears before dates, even though this is not a date. Black lacy bra instead of my very supportive pink one, even though in no world is anyone seeing it tonight. Time taken to blow out my hair, even though normally I'd rather be doing just about anything else. Also, of course, the whole no boys for the summer thing, but Fran's no boy and so why am I even thinking about that?

Of course there's a part of me that wonders how Fran will look at me when I get into her car, but I'm also preparing myself for Margaret and her Cool Girl friends. I can't trick them into thinking I'm someone or something I'm not, but I can do everything possible to seem at least slightly cooler than I actually am.

It's hard for me to guess what Margaret really thinks of me. Maybe she only invited Penny and me out of pity, since the notecards went over so poorly. But I want to be less pessimistic, because if I'm mostly having so much fun hanging out with Margaret this week, maybe she feels the same way. Maybe being honest with her about how her words had hurt me had been the right move.

This is my no boy summer, after all. Anything could happen.

I walk back to Grounds Control and arrive at the same time a pickup truck pulls up to the curb and rolls down the window.

"Hey, Lydia." Of *course* Fran drives this old beat-up thing, because she's no-nonsense and salt of the earth and genuine. A heartthrob from another time and place. "Ready to go?"

"I was born ready," I say, even though I definitely said that to her the other day. Why am I now saying this all the time? Is this how I *flirt with girls? Like a dad?*

"Yeah," she says with a grin. "So I've heard."

"I'm just making sure everyone knows how ready I am," I say as I climb into the truck. It's taller than I expect, so I really have to hoist myself in.

"Sorry," Fran says. "I forget, I'm so used to it. It was my dad's before it was mine."

"Your dad must be cool," I say, a really uncool thing to say as soon as it's out of my mouth. Now there are definitely no date vibes, because, truly, I am better on dates than falling into a car and then immediately complimenting someone's dad.

Fran laughs and pulls the car into traffic. "Oh yeah, Arnie Ford, cool as all hell. Nah, he's a landscape architect so he goes through trucks like crazy. I'm the oldest, so I got the oldest car available when I turned sixteen. My younger brother made out slightly better."

"How old are you?" I ask. "Are you in the same class as Margaret?"

"Eighteen, and I am," she says. "What about you?"

"Seventeen, and I'll be a senior in the fall. I guess I'm a senior already, but it doesn't really feel like it yet. Are you going away to college soon?"

I hope that she says no, even though it's silly. I've known her—if you can even call it that—for four days now. What she does in the fall has nothing to do with me.

"Nah." She shrugs. "My parents don't want me to take a gap year, so I'm going to take some classes at PCC while I try to get more on-set experience."

"Do you want to be a director or something?" I ask.

She shrugs. "I don't know. Probably not."

"Oh, you totally *do* want to," I say.

"In a perfect world, sure. In this world, where it's hard for female directors and screenwriters to get taken seriously, who knows."

"Ugh," I say. "That sucks."

"Yep. What about you?"

"I'm only a senior. I don't have to know anything yet," I say. "Well, for real, I want to go into a theater tech program, do something behind-the-scenes. I like building sets and managing props and designing lighting . . . I mean, all of it, really. The stuff no one sees that makes all the magic happen onstage."

Oh shit, I definitely didn't mean to say that all aloud. I barely try to think it, because wanting it so much is ridiculous. If college and futures are for people like Penny, where does that leave me? Daydreaming about lighting and scenic design while I take over at my parents' accounting office?

"That's awesome," Fran says.

I shrug. "My sister says a degree in the arts is just throwing money away."

"No offense, but your sister sounds terrible," she says, and I laugh. "Do you go to school around here?"

"Nope. Up in Rancho El Aderezo," I say. "I'm here for the summer because my parents are on a cruise. I get to work with Grace, and my sister is working with Grace's boyfriend scanning documents and making spreadsheets and whatever."

"How'd you manage that?" Fran asks.

"Oh, Penny thinks she has the better job, that she'll learn a ton about business and parlay it into an amazing essay to get into whatever undergraduate business program is currently ranked the best."

"Lydia," Fran says very seriously, "I am not joking. Your sister sounds *terrible*."

"She's not," I say, even though she blew me off tonight and I know the thing about arts degrees sounds really mean. It's just how her mind works; she wants the best for me. Well, the best in Penny-adjusted terms. "What's your brother like?"

"This'll sound biased, but, seriously, that kid's the greatest," she says. "He's just this total do-gooder type, volunteers and brings in our elderly neighbor's groceries."

"Are you the bad kid, then?" I ask. "I mean, I'm the bad kid. And I'm barely bad!"

"How are you bad at all?" she asks.

"Nothing fun! Just like I don't already have a business school picked out and my grades aren't amazing and whenever it's my turn to unload the dishwasher I forget."

"Oh shit, I didn't know I was in the presence of a non-business school selector with OK grades and dishwasher issues."

"Shut up," I say, and laugh. "You know what I mean! I'm not the one they brag about."

She holds up her hand to high-five me. "Yeah, me either."

We're the first to arrive at Genwa, so we wait outside, on the sidewalk next to a busy street. This really feels like LA for real to me, but I don't ask Fran if it is, because I can hear how suburban and naive I'd sound. There are plenty of people in school with me who don't feel the way my family and I do about the city, how far away it is, how unknown it seems, how much harder and more difficult life here must be compared to the ease of our town. I know that Darren and his parents have season tickets to different theaters in LA, but the Joneses don't live that kind of life. We keep LA at a safe distance.

Right now, as cars drive as fast as traffic allows, I don't feel any of that, though, and it dawns on me that I don't mind LA. Maybe I even like it. What's safe about accepting Margaret's invitation, about roping in Fran, about already thinking about our drive home and what else we might admit to each other in the pickup truck's cabin?

"Lyds!" Margaret appears on the sidewalk, walking down from a smaller side street. She's in a simple black shirt over perfect white denim shorts and sandals. It's cuter, more delicate than my outfit, but I don't feel off base. I take in the girls with her, though—three more girls to worry about. "Everyone, this is Lydia." And then, almost as an afterthought, "Hey, Fran."

Fran just nods, in this effortlessly cool way that all at once I wish I could steal and that also melts something inside me.

The other girls are Ava, the previously mentioned concertgoing Tara, and Su Jin. Ava is blonde and the sort of pretty where she *almost* looks like a bunch of actresses, but I can tell from the pattern and material that her dress is vintage—and not, like, hipster vintage, *vintage*. Polyester vintage. Tara's wearing a black jumpsuit that is this level of badass I can barely even comprehend. Her thick nearly black hair hangs over half her face, though you can still tell how intensely perfect her heavy black eyeliner is, with the little wings on each end. Su Jin is tall and willowy with her black hair in a super-short pixie cut and is wearing a shapeless floral maxi dress and dewy makeup that's probably all from Glossier and would just make me look greasy. Literally all three of them are intimidatingly cool in different ways, but I remind myself that Margaret invited me and I'm taking chances these days.

Plus then Su Jin opens up her buttery leather bag and points it in our direction. "Do you guys want, like, candy? I get so hungry waiting for dinner."

I pass it up because even after the apology I have no idea what Margaret might say about what eating too much candy could lead to. But Fran digs around and pulls out a pink Starburst.

"Ooh, you're lucky, pink's the best one," Margaret says. "I got an orange and I spit it out the window."

"Orange is the best flavor by far," Tara says, and even though this opinion is objectively wrong, I can tell we're all worried she's too cool to disagree with. Is orange secretly cool and we just don't know? The only thing that's clear is that no matter how cool Margaret and her friends are, there's a hierarchy and Tara's at the top. "Hey, Fran."

"Hey, Tara," Fran says, and even though I have no idea who anyone is to each other, really, suddenly I'm extra alert. Maybe if I had more experience—well, more *girl* experience, specifically—I'd be able to decode that moment. But while I'm, like, ninety percent sure that Fran's into girls, I don't really have a read on Tara. I definitely don't have a read on the way they looked at each other.

We're taken back to our table, which has a grill right on top of it. My family is a family of chain restaurants, so this is already all-new territory. I mean, being at Grounds Control versus a Starbucks is kind of all-new territory.

"Sit next to me, Lyds," Margaret commands, and everyone else files around the table accordingly. Fran's on my other side, which is both perfect and nerve-racking. "Is everyone good with everything? I feel like I've gotten very good at ordering."

"She's legit really good at it," Tara says. "We tried to go without you once and Su Jin panicked and ordered, like, ten people's worth of pork belly."

"Honestly that seems like a true quality problem," Margaret says. "Ava! Put your phone away, we have rules and decorum when we all go out. Phones only for food porn photos."

"Just another three minutes," Ava says. "I'm making sure I win this auction."

"Oh no," Su Jin says as Tara raises her eyebrows.

"What for this time?" Margaret asks. "You guys, she was so excited for this package she was getting but it was just like this old piece of paper."

A couple waiters stop by with water and tea as well as what seems like a couple dozen little bowls of different foods I can't identify.

"This is banchan," Margaret says to me. "All these amazing side dishes, and you can get free refills of all of them. Are you good with spicy stuff?"

"I actually am," I say. "I know, it's shocking to me, too."

"It wasn't just an old piece of paper," Ava says. "It was a blank piece of letterhead from the first corporate McDonald's office. Anyway, this is for a vintage Del Taco sign to hang in my dorm room. I'm going for this old-time fast-food vibe."

The rest of us all burst into laughter at the exact same moment, and Margaret starts serving sides onto my plate.

"Are you her *mom*?" Su Jin asks, and we all keep laughing.

"I'm her guide! She says she's only been to, like, a Chili's and a Red Lobster before." Margaret laughs even harder. "I'm teasing! We love having a suburban friend. You're like our exchange student."

Fran leans over while everyone's scrambling to serve themselves banchan, and before I know it has taken a tiny piece of broccoli from my plate with her chopsticks. "This is so much easier."

"You thief!" I glance around and realize how *safe* this all seems. I might be like an exchange student to LA girls, but that's not actually what it feels like right now. I'm just part of this night.

"So what kind of stuff do you guys do up in the suburbs?" Tara asks, and I feel a prickle of defensiveness. These are the moments I hate, when I'm sitting in a group where everyone knows each other better than I do, and each question is an opportunity to prove just how not part of things I am. It's never been that I couldn't see those social systems in place; I've just never really sorted out how to be part of them. Other people seem like they're born with this knowledge, but to me it's like watching one of those complicated jump rope routines and understanding when they'll swing my way but still knowing I'd never be able to just jump in.

Watching Tara, though, and hearing her tone, I realize that she isn't trying to poke holes in me. This isn't some opportunity to show how different I am from everyone else. I'm pretty sure it's just a question.

"I mean, not much," I say, because even without the poking of holes, I still want everyone here to think I'm . . . well, I can't manage cool. But at least not exceedingly uncool. "I do a lot with the theater department at my school."

"Ava too," Margaret says. "I mean, she did. Now she's going to study sociology and become a brilliant professor but leave the stage cold and empty of her talents."

"Oh, I don't act," I say quickly.

"Well, and I don't think the stage will be cold and empty without me," Ava says, "so I think we both understand how to take things that Margaret says."

"How dare you," Margaret says, and we all laugh, even chill and cool Fran.

"Do you run tech?" Ava asks me.

"I guess I've done everything at some point but mainly set design and construction," I say, feeling everyone watching me and wishing I hadn't said so much. If vintage-cool Ava is leaving theater behind for a more responsible-sounding future, is it embarrassing that I have no plans to do so?

"That's amazing, how have you not told me any of this yet?" Margaret pouts dramatically but then her face shifts abruptly into glee. "Oh my god, the meat's coming!"

The server with the immense tray of raw meat actually swerves and arrives at another table.

"You guessed wrong," Tara said, which somehow strikes all of us as funny, or at least we all laugh at it.

"Wrong about meat!" Su Jin and Ava say at the same time, and now all of us are laughing even harder. I can't remember the last time I laughed so much.

"*You* guessed wrong and thought *my* name was Phil," Fran whispers in my ear, before swiping seaweed salad from my plate. I clang my metal chopsticks against hers and the seaweed flies across the table. Everyone is still laughing, and I see from the looks of the diners around us that we have turned into the annoying table. Su Jin and I exchange a look, and even though I barely know her, we somehow band together to try to quiet down the group. Margaret shows me how to get better photos of our sides and then the trays of meat that the staff cooks on the grill right in front of us so that later we can post good photos on Instagram, and while *of course* I'll do that, it hits me that I haven't thought about the world outside this table in a while.

Chapter Six

The drive back is quiet, but it's not uncomfortable. The roads and freeways have emptied out, at least a little, and Fran jams a cassette tape into the ancient stereo. It's all sludgy guitar and moody vocals, very 1990s, and I wouldn't have guessed it for Fran's soundtrack. People surprising you is one of my favorite feelings— even better than surprising yourself.

We've been on the road for a bit when a thought bubbles up and then I can't let it go. The truck feels safe, though. Even safer than the table.

"Were you and Tara...?" I let the question end there. Sometimes saying very little is actually saying all you need. The words feel enough.

"Well, sort of, sure." Fran shrugs. "It was sophomore year, I think. Maybe junior. A long time ago, in high school terms."

"Were you guys...serious?"

Fran kind of snorts. "Who was serious sophomore year?"

Me, I almost say. Brian, Jace, Jordan, and Henry were all sophomore year. They all felt big, world-shifting at the time. I lost my virginity to Jordan—though I hate how it sounds to *lose* it and *to* someone, like money in a poker game gone bad—at a party at Aysha Gorman's house. I still remember how even though we were giddy from sneaking around and taking the tiniest sips out of Morgan Flores's flask earlier in the night how *serene* I felt right afterward, how I looked at Jordan and wondered if he might be my forever.

I mean, he absolutely was not, but there was a time where that felt real enough.

But then I remember Margaret saying *Fran's a player*. Was that because of Tara? Or because of more? More...girls?

I realize that Fran's slowing down, and suddenly we're parked next to Grounds Control, which is dark at this hour.

"Is this OK?" she asks. "Or do you need me to drive you home? And where's home?"

"This is fine," I say, and I fumble with the old sticking seatbelt buckle. When I look up, Fran's there, right in my space. Her eyes are fixed on me, like she doesn't have to say a word to tell me what's going to happen. And I let it; I let her. She slides off my glasses and I hold still. Her face finds mine, her lips find mine. She kisses me, and I let her, I let her lead this moment as my body hums in hunger for this, to be discovered and explored. To be Fran's someone new.

"Was that OK?" she asks, still in my space as I gasp for breath, as my body seems to throb everywhere. It's not a real question, of course, and I know it. Could I seem more OK?

I wait for more, but it was just that, one kiss. I can always read these moments. Early on, at least, I get this all right. I slide my glasses back into place, open the door, and look back at Fran, who's still right here. "Thanks for driving."

"Thanks for inviting me. See you soon, Lydia."

I hop out of the truck and wave, a casual wave to let her know I do this all the time, I'm devoured and then I'm off on my way. I'm just as casual about this moment as she needs me to be.

I expect the house to be dark when I walk inside, but Oscar's up in the living room watching some HBO show with a lot of expletives and crime. All guys are different and I hate reducing any gender to stereotypes, but a lot of them seem to spend their time exactly this way. I wave and leave him to it, and then I find that the light is on in my room, too.

Penny looks up from her laptop. "Thank god you're home. Lydia, I'm sorry I bailed on you."

I wasn't expecting to have an actual conversation right now, and to be honest I don't know if I'm up for full sentences yet. Being so freshly kissed is its own reality.

"No prob," I manage to say.

"*Really*," she continues. "I thought it would be an amazing opportunity to learn more about corporate life. Instead it was just a bunch of Oscar's coworkers drinking and talking about how they're still disappointed by the *Game of Thrones* finale, a million years later."

I can't help laughing. "This is your future, Pen."

"Well, when I'm old I probably won't mind," she says. "But I'm not old and I should have gone with you."

I try not to think about that possibility too much. She *should* have gone with me, this should be the summer of us, away from boys, away from everything we've messed up. This summer's to get our shit together, but it's also for us being connected in a bigger way—or at least I had hoped that it would be.

But also if she had come tonight, I wouldn't have asked Fran. I wouldn't be standing here so freshly kissed.

"So did you have fun?" Penny asks.

I manage to only smile a little. A non-kissed amount. "Yeah. I had fun."

"Is Korean barbecue good?"

"Oh my god, Pen, it was *so good*." I grab my phone and climb into Penny's bed so I can show her all the photos I took with Margaret's guidance.

"Take off your boots!" she yells, and I laugh but do as I'm told. "This looks amazing. Can we go another time?"

"Sure, but you need a big group. It's like . . . so much meat."

"Seriously," she says, which is funny because Penny's basically always serious. "I'm sorry. This summer was all my idea, and I probably threw off all the plans you'd already made, and then I blew you off for the most boring night out possible."

I wave my hand at her, even though it means something that she's saying this. "Since when do I make plans?"

"No, Lydia, really." Penny takes one of my hands and squeezes it. "You didn't condemn yourself to a boyless summer. That was all me. And maybe you think it's a good idea but really I think you're doing it *for* me, and it means a lot. I'm not going to take you for granted."

It's a lot right now, the hand-squeezing and direct eye contact and the sharing of emotions. This is not how boring girls from the suburbs act, as far as I knew. Are we already no longer boring girls from the suburbs?

"I do think it's a good idea, though," I say, despite the fact that I just kissed someone less than a half hour ago. I didn't kiss *a boy*. Is that why I let it happen? "When Tate dumped me . . ."

Penny squeezes my hand more tightly.

"I mean, it was terrible. You know it was terrible." I sigh because it's unpredictable when it'll all flash back, but instead of Tate's voice ringing in my ears (*This just... isn't working out for me... at all*), I'm thinking about tonight. If I was still Tate Shepard's girlfriend—which for a solid month is all I wished I'd become again—I wouldn't be out on a Friday night with five girls. I wouldn't have a table full of people laughing at my jokes and making me laugh even harder with their own.

"Anyway, taking a break from boys is good," I say, and I've never believed it so firmly since Penny hatched her scheme. "It's good to think of other things."

Other things might include Fran's eyes when she leaned over me, but it doesn't count. I only promised a summer of no boys, and Fran's not a boy. I'm only even in LA another two months and one week. What can happen in that time? Fran's a player, after all, right? So I'm just in it for the game. I'm not neglecting the other stuff, the time with Penny and the part-time job and figuring out what else is out there. I'll be home and emotionally refreshed before I know it, even if I manage to keep kissing Fran in the meantime.

"Sometimes I worried I was losing myself," Penny says, and it doesn't even make sense to me, because I don't know anyone who's more *herself* than my sister, who keeps a motivational bullet journal and always has a plan. "It's not who I want to be."

"At least you had yourself to lose," I say, and in some ways it's more ammo than I want to give Penny, that I'm aware she's someone and maybe I'm no one. But I don't want to miss out on whatever this is tonight. We might be turning some corner in our relationship where we talk about more than boys and why Mom and Dad are so annoying.

But even if we aren't, and it's just tonight in this room, I don't want to miss any chances. "Like all my plans are vague and sometimes I really don't know who I am."

It was easy being Tate's girlfriend that way—it gave me a role. Before him it was Jason, and that made sense too, just like it had with Danny, and all the boys before. It hits me that I was twelve when Kevin Butler asked me to be his girlfriend. Have I just been some boy's girlfriend for the last five years? Not Lydia Jones?

"You're not tempted by that cute delivery boy, are you?" Penny asks. "It's so much easier for me, since I'm in this boy dead zone."

"I'm not tempted by Ben the cute delivery boy hardly at all," I say. "I'm not tempted by any boys right now."

It's not even close to a lie.

"It means a lot to me," Penny says. "Our no-boys pledge and working on ourselves and getting work experience and all of this."

"Me too," I say, and it's still technically just as true, but am I lying? No, of course I'm not lying. Ben might be extremely cute and skilled at winking, but he's barely warranted a spare thought from me. I'm absolutely keeping to the no-boys pledge.

"I saw a really good speech on women needing to put themselves first." Penny reaches for her phone and pulls up YouTube. "Want to watch it with me? You're going to feel *so* inspired, Lydia."

Penny doesn't usually include me in this part of her life. I've always assumed she didn't see me as being as worthy of self-fulfillment as her, so there was no need to co-watch intense ladies giving intense speeches. There's a rush of competing feelings in my heart right now, relief and sisterhood and guilt. So tonight we split her earbuds and, for the first time, we watch together.

I'm on a group text when I wake up the next morning, fifty-four messages already. I don't have to work on the weekends, so this is the latest I've slept all week by hours, and I'm not sure I've ever felt so refreshed.

Margaret's is the only contact I already have, but I quickly deduce the other three are Su Jin, Tara, and Ava. Su Jin's easy to figure out because she relies strongly on her Bitmoji to express her thoughts, and it's really accurate, way more than mine is. Ava uses GIFs of things I've never heard of and that look old-fashioned, and Tara uses a minimal amount of words—why does that always seem so cool?—and invites us to an all-ages show at a club downtown that everyone else turns down immediately. I wonder if Tara has a second group text going with people who go to all-ages shows downtown.

"Hey." Penny walks into the room with her hair up in a towel. I'm very jealous of her silky blonde princess hair but not of the whole routine that goes into maintaining it. "Oscar told me about some nearby hikes that sound fun. Do you want to go?"

This feels close to another first, an invite from my overly scheduled sister who usually has more ROI-friendly (that's "return on investment," something I know only because, of course, Penny told me) ways to use her precious free time. Am I suddenly a strong return? But Su Jin's already suggested we meet for coffee and donuts this morning, and I've already texted back *SEE YOU THERE!* because I'm still working out the nuances of my group texting-persona. I don't think I'll ultimately stick with ALL-CAPS, VERY EXCITED, but it's what I've got now.

For a moment I think about inviting Penny along, but only a moment. For one, I may have painted Penny in way too broad a brush when describing her to Margaret. Yeah, she falls asleep to TED Talks and once did a report on Elizabeth Holmes *after* she was revealed to be a huge liar and scammer, but she also swoons for boys and is really good at helping our parents cook and knows the words to every BTS song. Unlike Fran's conclusion, Penny's not terrible. The other side of her personality just makes for a better story.

And while I don't think the rules of our no boy summer are necessarily guaranteed to come up in conversation, I don't feel like risking my new friends hearing about it. Plus it's not like I think Fran and I were subtle last night, even though no one said anything. There could be questions, and then even though, again, I'm not breaking any agreed-upon rules, would that be how Penny sees it?

"I can't now, but I could do something tonight," I say. "Dinner or whatever? A movie? I don't know what people do."

"Dinner and a movie sounds great," Penny says. "I'll do some research on Yelp and Rotten Tomatoes to find our best options."

"Actually." Guilt bangs around in my head, and I know what I should do. "I can hang out with them some other time."

"You're sure?" Penny asks. Her tone makes me happy that I let guilt get the best of me.

"I'm sure. Do you still want to go on a hike?"

A huge grin breaks open across her face. "Do I!"

"No, never mind. You have to tone your hiking enthusiasm down or I'm not gonna do it."

~

Oscar loans us his car, and Penny drives us to Ernest E. Debs Regional Park. We're quiet as we start out, making a big loop through a lot more greenery than I expected to find in Los Angeles. We haven't even been here a week and I already feel it, how LA isn't matching up with what I'd expected. I think about saying this, but Penny, I presume, will eviscerate those expectations with sourced and cited facts and figures.

I actually don't know what I should be talking about with Penny. A lecture always seems so nearby, things she knows that I don't, careers that would be bad news for me, ways I could improve myself. Obviously, it's stuff like this that cause my descriptions of Penny to make people like Fran assume that she's a monster. Penny's not a monster, though. Penny believes everything she says, and if she knows better than me, why shouldn't she share it?

Boys weren't part of that, though. Boys were—are?—something we sorted out together. Last night had felt different, but I'm not sure that's for good. Just like this hike, I still feel like I have to watch my step. I don't want to feel stupid or worthless, and I don't want to risk making Penny certain that I'm either of those things, either.

"You didn't have to cancel on your friends," Penny says, a little out of nowhere, as we're making our way through the trail.

"They're not *my friends*," I say, though I don't actually know this. Last night hadn't felt like them and me. Last night was just *us*.

She waves her hand. "You know what I mean. It's good to cultivate a social group."

I couldn't help laughing at that. "What a normal way to talk about it."

"You know that I haven't had a group of friends, and even when Mr. Hockseye tells me I should 'think about expanding my social group,' I don't—"

"Why is our guidance counselor giving you social advice?" I accidentally yell this, and more than a few people turn around to see why a loud teenage girl is ruining their scenic nature moment.

"Despite his limitations, he's what I have. He has this 'image' of an ideal college applicant," Penny says. "And I'm doing what I can."

"Oh, I'm aware."

"Friends are hard, though," she says, and I feel it then, the thing that means that my sister isn't a monster. We're both so bad at this.

"Yeah." I try to give her a look that tells her I understand this, that I've always felt kind of outside of social things, too. It's a lot to expect from a look.

"Are you OK?" she asks. "You should really get prescription sunglasses."

"I was trying to look empathetic," I say, and we both laugh. It's safer around Penny than I give her credit for. Why is that so hard for me to remember?

"Want to go over your college action plan?" she asks, and I laugh more, because maybe it's safer but Penny's still gotta Penny. "By this point, you really should have already started your—"

"Can we just enjoy the scenery?" I ask. It's absolutely a technique to shut down this line of conversation, but I mean it, too. The lake, the trees, the peeks at Downtown LA, looming in the horizon. I love that I didn't know to expect this; LA has been like that a lot.

CHAPTER SEVEN

Monday morning feels like a flashback to the week before. I barely get up in time, I flirt with five-days-a-week-pastries Ben, and I pale in comparison to Grace as we open the shop. Waze-anger Jeff is our first customer of the day, as always, but I guess I'm getting used to him and his panic.

It's not exactly the same, of course. I sort of know what I'm doing, even if I'm not nearly as good as Grace. Why would I be? This is her life's work. I'm just here for the summer. And the flirting with Ben isn't real, it's just fun. Plus today I'm extra sleep-deprived because I got a late-night Sunday text that said *What are you up to?* And suddenly I was going through the McDonald's drive-thru for hot fudge sundaes and then kissing Fran in her pickup truck. Last week I worried I was too fat and uncool to fit in at Grounds Control; now I'm still worried a little about these things in the way I'm always vaguely worried about them, but I'm fitting in anyway. I guess that's progress?

"Lyds!" Margaret walks in with her arms outstretched. I'm afraid I'm expected to hug her, now that we've hung out socially—twice if I count watching latte art videos last week—but I realize she's holding something.

"Margaret, you're amazing for getting that done," Grace says, and I realize it's my own Grounds Control apron, with LYDIA neatly stitched at the top right edge, just like everyone else's.

"Wow," I say, and my voice sounds way too eager for an apron, so I attempt to really coolly switch it out for the plain one I'm wearing.

"You look amazing," Margaret says, which makes me laugh.

Grace sighs. "I can't believe I'm saying this, but you two are way too excited about that apron."

"Oh, go take your Gen X world-weariness outside, Grace," Margaret says with a cackle. "Lyds and I love these aprons."

I give a thumbs-up for some reason, which is even dorkier than my *wow*, and Margaret and I burst into laughter. It reminds me of how I used to make friends during my little kid afterschool and summer activities, or how I'd pick up friends while a theater production was going on. A friend at work is the same thing—situational. It's the bleed into the rest of my life that I feel less sure about. But Margaret—and the rest of her girl gang, honestly—make me want to try.

Business picks up, and I assign myself to the espresso machine, where I feel the least detrimental to the flow of things. Pulling shots is so straightforward and satisfying. I keep busy there, even when Fran comes in, because I know that Fran wants to play it cool, and so even though what I'd like to do is leap over the counter and fall into her arms, I just look over my shoulder and nod.

My phone buzzes in my pocket while I'm making drinks for Fran's film crew, and I take advantage of Grace's lack of rules and get out my phone.

Why are you hiding back there?

I'm on espresso duty. It's VERY important.

What are you doing tonight?

Nothing, I type, even though Penny and I had discussed walking down to the other main street in Highland Park to see what was there.

There's something kind of comforting about this tiny part of Los Angeles proper having only two main streets, like where we live, even if nothing else is the same. Anyway, the thing with Penny isn't definite, and Fran is very hard to refuse when she's *right here*.

There's no response or even dots that Fran's typing, so I shove my phone back into my pocket and get back to drinks. Grace doesn't seem to notice that I make a point of bringing all of them over instead of leaving the job to her and Margaret, and Fran grins when I reach the counter.

"I like your apron."

"Right?" Margaret pops up next to me. "My aunt owns the embroidery shop so I told her to put a rush on Lyds's apron and to make it extra perfect."

"It's quality embroidery work," Fran says. "If you didn't know, I have a real eye for quality embroidery work."

Margaret elbows me, like we're friends and she knows my secrets. I guess we are and that she knows at least a few.

"See you guys," Fran says, and Margaret elbows me harder once she's out the door with all her beverages.

"Spill," she says, and I don't mean to but I give Grace a little glance, and I see in her eyes that Margaret gets it. "Later."

Later, though, there's still no responses from Fran. I go back to Grace's after my shift and try not to watch my phone too much. If Fran texts, I'm nearly positive I'll agree to whatever she asks, no matter what my tentative plans are with Penny. Which is not good, of course, and I know that. And Penny's not stupid—Penny is the exact opposite of stupid, obviously—and if I'm acting weird like I was the other night, she'll notice. Why do I have to have a sister who notices everything?

I've probably spent more time discussing boys with Penny than any other topic. Not boys in general, though, mainly specific boys. How Tate could seemingly change his mind out of nowhere, could look at me like I meant nothing anymore. How Drew could be so jealous when Penny talked to Miguel, and how it got hard to sort out what was a fair reaction and what was dumb boy ego. It's been like this since Penny kissed Christian Bower in sixth grade and told me about it and I realized I could tell her about my seventh-grade boyfriend, Liam. Before then, we'd occasionally banded together over something annoying our parents did, but boys unlocked something new for us.

This is it, it hits me, as I try to distract myself with one of Penny's books that's lying around the room while mainly staring down at my phone so that I know the exact moment Fran texts. If Fran texts. *This is why* Penny's decreed the no boy summer, and I know it. If there's more to life than relationships and, well, obsessing over them, I need to try another version of things for this summer. For more than a week, at least.

When Fran texts—if Fran texts—I'll tell her I actually already have plans tonight. If I hang out with Penny and get good at latte art and read books that aren't assigned for school, there's nothing about Fran that's breaking any rules. It'll just be about fitting her in. And it's how the beginning usually goes anyway. You don't want to come on too strong and scare someone. You don't want to be too available or you seem lonely or desperate, especially with someone like Fran. I'm good at all of that already. This I can handle.

Once Penny's home, I agree to head over to Figueroa Street. I'm sure I would have done the exact same thing if I'd already heard from Fran, though since I have not heard from Fran, that's easy to say. From the outside, it probably looks like I'm dangerously close to falling into old patterns, but nothing about Fran feels old or part of a pattern. And it's not because she's a girl; there's something about my life here that just already feels freer and more open and full of connections I could never make at home.

"How was your day at work?" Penny asks once we've set out from the house in search of the strip of shops and restaurants. Oscar's recommended we eat at a sports bar that he says will let us in if we promise we're only there to eat buffalo wings and watch the Dodgers. I'm way more into wings than I am sports, but I love that Oscar has ideas for us, and so I know it's our plan for later.

"Good, I finally have my own apron," I tell her, and she wrinkles her nose.

"What were you wearing before?"

"No, like my own personalized apron. My name's embroidered on it." I can tell this doesn't impress Penny, so I elbow her. "You were *swooning* over like lanyards and file-naming conventions! I am allowed to love my apron."

She waves her hand at me. "Sure. Congratulations on your apron."

"We all get it," I say, though the *we* is just *me*. "Your things are great and my things are all dumb. You could at least be polite about it."

"I don't think that—" Penny stops and studies me. "Do you think I think that?"

"*Don't* you think that?"

"No, I just don't care about aprons."

"Do you think I care about your files?"

"A new filing system, though—" She notices my expression and stops herself again. "Fine. This may only be a *me* topic."

We see that the main strip is just ahead and pick up our pace. This part of town is crowded and noisy, and the stores and restaurants are a mix of old and modern, hipster and crumbling old-fashioned places and chains, all squished together. It's nothing like where we live, where everything looks shiny and new and has room to breathe.

I try to gauge if we look out of place or not. Penny has a very set look, normally a no-nonsense blend of Madewell and internet brands that she pulls together to look a little preppy and a lot *to be taken seriously*. She's in a perfectly cut pair of jeans with a blue top that's kind of buttoned-down but pretty all at once. I'm more boring, always, but I do like how my hair looks up, like there's at least something intentional about me. My standard jean shorts and T-shirts looked more thrown together than intentional—because they were.

"Let's check out this bookstore," Penny says, and pulls me in before I can agree or refuse. I'm not as big a reader as she is, but I see right away that this isn't a regular bookstore but one that specializes in art, design, photography, all sorts of visual stuff. Penny's frowning, but I see how everything's arranged beautifully, gorgeous books in a gorgeous setting. I don't always feel like the thing that I do is art; theater for me is also construction and heavy lifting and teamwork. But it's not *not* art, either.

Penny doesn't complain as I look around, but we both realize the books are marked up ridiculously, and an employee seems annoyed that teenagers are touching these stupid expensive books, so we head back out, barely managing to contain our laughter until the door swings shut again.

We keep wandering in and out of shops until we reach the Greyhound, and Oscar is right, we plead the case for buffalo wings and we're waved inside like magic. It's my first bar, but it just looks like a restaurant with way more TVs on the wall. I start to comment on this to Penny, but it seems like a miracle we had such an honest exchange earlier, even if it was about something as stupid as aprons. Aprons were just the thing that gave me the chance to tell Penny she acted like my stuff was dumb and her stuff wasn't. So I'm definitely not ready to go back to setting myself up for being the stupid one for not knowing things like how bars were different than restaurants. Maybe Penny just loved reciting lists of facts she knew and I didn't, but it was hard not to take it personally. It's so much nicer when she loves files and I love my apron and those two things can coexist equally and no one (i.e., me) is a dummy.

Penny offers to place our order at the bar, so I use the time alone at the table not to watch the Dodgers play baseball on what seems like three dozen TVs of various sizes but to sneak a glance at my phone. The only notifications on my lock screen are some likes for my Friday night KBBQ photos.

"It's strange not hearing from Mom and Dad at all." Penny drops back into her chair and sets a large plastic number 13 on a stand on the table so that the waitstaff will know where to drop off our food later. "If their phones worked at sea I can't imagine how many poorly cropped photos they would have already sent us."

" 'Guess what this is!' " I laugh at the memory. *Memories*, really, because they do it all the time. "I don't know, some blurry vaguely green thing?"

"I guess we'll get all the photos at once, when they dock somewhere," Penny says. "It's easier then. A simple, 'wow, looks fun' should suffice, and it's much easier than, yes, blurry vaguely green thing identification."

The entire room erupts into a booming moan at the same time, and for just a second I'm worried something truly terrible has happened, like a national disaster, but then I realize the reaction is to whatever terrible baseball thing just happened to the Dodgers. More than one of my exes loved baseball, but I never really got the feel for it, just a long slow game that didn't seem much more exciting than gym class. Who wanted to watch that for four hours instead of making out? Lots of people, it turned out, but never me.

"Sports are a great way of forging connections with groups you might not otherwise share commonalities with," Penny says, of course, and I moan like a person who's disappointed in baseball.

"You can just dislike baseball," I say. "It doesn't need you to defend it and its connection-forging superpowers or whatever. You can agree with me and not die."

"I agree with you plenty," Penny says, looking past me at the biggest of the TVs. "I actually don't know how I feel about baseball. I'm going to find out. That's what this summer is for."

"Oh, *god*," I say, and Penny bursts into laughter at that. "No boys *and liking sports?*"

"No boys and figuring out who we are anyway," she says, and I like that *we* so much that I keep an eye on the game, too.

$\sim$

Penny and I have been back home for hours before Fran texts. I'd love to say I'd forgotten about her by then, but that wouldn't exactly be true.

wyd

I make a face. *That's all I get?*

It's been a long day. That's all you get.

This is exactly the time I'd normally call down the hallway to Penny and ask her what I should make of this. But now Penny's right here in the room with me, reading a book about leadership, and yet the very last thing I can interrupt her with is relationship drama. Well, not *relationship* drama. This is a few kisses in a pickup truck.

OK, more than a few. But still.

I try to guess what Penny would tell me to do, if it were a few months ago, if Fran were the latest boy. *Ignore him,* I can imagine her saying. *He can do better than that.*

Imaginary Penny is right, so I do. And it works, because Fran's back a few minutes later. *The shoot went late. My job was to reset this pile of pebbles. It was exhausting and boring at the same time.*

Pebbles are serious business, BG Phil.

Look, if there's anyone who's extremely aware of the serious nature of the business of pebbles, it's me.

The little typing dots keep appearing, then disappearing, then appearing again. I don't do anything with my time except stare at them.

Finally, a message appears.

For real, Lydia, I don't know what I'm doing. If this is film, why do I want it so bad?

This isn't film forever, though, right? Not that I know anything about movies but this is just getting started. They don't make directors move pebbles around or whatever.

The whole thing's just different than I expected. I don't feel inspired.

When DO you feel inspired?

I know it's a personal question, but that's the thing about texting at night in your bed. It's like you get to skip steps.

I'll show you sometime.

I don't know if it's real or a line *or a line*, but I still smile. *Sorry your day sucked.*

Me too. My family was out this evening. I wanted to bring you home and put my hands all over you.

I sit up with a start.

Penny looks up from her guide to teen leadership. "You all right over there?"

It would be, I realize, a good time to say something. *Technically I'm not breaking our code because* or *Nothing's really happened yet but* or starting from the very top with *Hey I'm pretty sure I'm bisexual and maybe I should have told you that already.*

"Sorry, yeah, I'm fine" is what I say, though. And then, for some reason, I hear Margaret's voice again. *Fran's a player.* I know that it's true and I realize that makes me part of the game, and still the only thing I'm currently concerned with is sending back the perfect response. And so Penny will have to wait.

Chapter Eight

Su Jin stops by Grounds Control the next day, and I realize it's the first time I've seen any of them there—besides Margaret, of course. I'm at the register partly so I can get more experience and get faster at it, and also since it's around the time Fran comes in and this gives me more of an opportunity to talk to her.

"Lyds," Su Jin says, because they all picked it up from Margaret like it's what everyone calls me. "Are you free tonight?"

I basically am, but I still pause because what if Fran texts and says her family's out again and *tonight* is when she puts her hands all over me?

No. Seriously, new friends and new experiences are the point of the summer, right? Not Fran's hands. Not any other parts of Fran. Things besides boys and Fran. How did Fran derail everything so quickly?

"You have to be free." Margaret darts over and throws an arm around my shoulder. "We're taking you to Joy."

"That Chinese place across the street? Big outing."

"Oh, stop." Su Jin rolls her eyes, but I know it's just for her no-bullshit affect. "It's Taiwanese and it's amazing and you'll love it. And we know you're from Whitegirlsville so you don't have to do anything but show up and enjoy and we'll handle everything. You know Margaret loves to order for you and practically put food in your mouth like a baby bird."

"Can you meet at six?" Margaret asks. "I know that's, like, when old people eat, but if it's much later, the line's out the door. Chrissy Teigen Insta'd a photo there once and it blew up."

"So annoying," Su Jin says. "It was already our spot, we didn't need all these non-neighborhood randos. So you're coming, right?"

I agree despite Fran and feel strong and good, because Fran's not the point of the summer. But then I start to have doubts. It's actually hard to tell if friends are the point or not, because there was never any part of the deal about *no friends* the way the *no boys* rule is so firm and absolute. Friends haven't ever been a problem—well, not in the way boys were, at least. If the summer is for *more*—life beyond boys—then hanging out with friends is the right thing to do. But if the summer is truly supposed to be about connecting with my sister, making plans with anyone else might not be the best idea.

It's surprising that Penny didn't formalize this somehow, but without that official decree I guess I'll take advantage of all those open loopholes. Friends: yes. Kissing people—well, *person*—who isn't a boy: yes.

Grace lets us make Su Jin a free latte before she goes. I practice fern foam art and—let's just say it's good it was free.

"Lyds, I'm glad you're coming tonight," Su Jin calls on her way out the door.

I'm still getting used to the idea of a group of friends, much less a sudden and cool one, much less a no-bullshit type like Su Jin including me so earnestly. It's like a super trendy earthquake struck me. But I just smile. "Me too."

"Your ferns suck, though. Later!"

ᴍ

If I'm being completely honest, I haven't had Chinese food that isn't PF Chang's or Panda Express, but I genuinely love every single thing I eat at Joy, and not just because I don't want to embarrass myself around my new friends. Spicy shrimp wontons, super-flavorful pork over rice, a savory pancake stuffed with egg and cheese that I could eat just about literally every day, and dan dan noodles. I've actually had dan dan noodles at PF Chang's, but I don't bring that up. It's one thing to be the inexperienced suburban girl; it's another thing to call too much attention to it. Plus, this is so much better. The flavors taste so fresh and rich and real.

Eating crowded around a table with friends feels different, too, though REACT ended up packed around plenty of tables over plenty of meals during my time in high school. I'd always felt this layer of separation with REACT, like everyone else had been given the secrets to successful group hangs while I was trying to remember what memes were still funny to bring up and how hard to laugh at jokes. It isn't like I've suddenly gotten some guide to groups wisdom; it's more like I feel I have very little control over my inclusion in this group, and this earthquake of friendship is just keeping me rolling along with it.

"So what's up with Fran?" Su Jin asks while we're finishing the tiny remaining amounts of food in each bowl.

"And don't say *nothing*," Margaret says. "I practically have to douse you guys with half-and-half when she's in Grounds Control so you don't melt down the place with all your steamy tension."

I glance at Tara, and she shakes her head. "It was a long time ago. It's nothing. For real."

"Hey, it's more than OK that it wasn't nothing," Ava says with a smile that seems completely for Tara's benefit. It strikes me as such a true moment of split-second kindness, pushing for truth while making sure you're not being a jerk. "Back then, at least. After all, that was the year I dyed my hair black and stopped wearing color, so that I could really devote myself *to my craft.* That's so much worse than being sad about a girl."

Tara rolls her eyes, but I can tell her spirit's not in it because she's also smiling at Ava.

"I don't really know what's going on with Fran," I say, accepting the last wonton half from Su Jin. "It's ... fun though."

I realize that I'm talking about Fran, a girl, like this is just part of my life and not something to hide. It hits me that the possibility that I was intruding on whatever because of Tara was scarier than being a girl who dates girls. The friendship earthquake didn't even give me a chance to get nervous about ... coming out.

Wait, is that what's happening? Coming out always felt like a big speech I was supposed to give while Mom and Dad cried and we all learned some very special lessons. Love, Lydia. Nothing could sound further from my life, and so while there had been boy after boy ... after boy, it had been so easy to never discuss. But maybe coming out is this too, just talking about a hot girl who might be a player but also a really good kisser.

Obviously, there are queer kids at home, too. I know a lot of them who are also part of the theater department, but even after that realization that I was one of them, I also ... didn't feel like one of them, somehow. Everyone is so sure of themselves, with enamel pins proclaiming their identities to anyone who can see their backpacks or denim jackets, proudly supporting the Rancho El Aderezo LGBTQ+ Club at school events, knowing exactly who they are. None of them seem like a messy bisexual who people already whisper is a slut without even knowing I don't just like boys and don't just kiss boys. I can't imagine the LGBTQ+ Club rolling out the rainbow carpet for me; it just seems like it would cement my reputation as a slut instead.

"Have you had girlfriends before?" Margaret asks me.

"No girlfriends," I say. "A lot of boyfriends."

Maybe I shouldn't have said *a lot* but this perks up the table, and I answer all their questions about the boys.

"I wish I'd met you sooner," Margaret says, sounding pained. "I'm so terrified to talk to boys. I'll be the only one at college who's never even maintained eye contact with one. You probably have really good advice."

"I mean, not for maintaining eye contact," I say, and we're all laughing again. "Boys aren't that hard to look at, right? They're just people. And if they make it hard for you, they're not the right person anyway."

"Sometimes, to be fair, they're very handsome and hard to look at directly," Ava says. I feel like Ava's always making space for people to be themselves, and I make a note to make more of an effort to do that myself, if I can figure out how. "I'll give you that, Margaret."

"Just be careful," Su Jin says, and I assume she's addressing Margaret until I realize she's looking right at me. "There's a trail of broken hearts and tearful girls wherever Fran Ford's concerned."

Tara looks up. "Hey."

"Not you." Su Jin mouths, *Of course her.* "Just, like, in general."

"Lyds can handle herself," Margaret says. "She's obviously, like, a full-on relationship expert."

"I wouldn't go that far," I say, but also Margaret's not wrong. My ex-boyfriend Jarrod, for example, never had a girlfriend until I came along, and not because girls weren't trying. I don't know why I can figure this stuff out, but I can. And it's fun when someone's keeping you on your toes. Last night all I could think of was Fran the player, but now I just feel like I'm in the game, too.

She texts as we're leaving the restaurant. By now a line halfway down the block has formed, and we all giggle smugly at how full we are and how we didn't have to wait at all. It's like I'm in a TV show with this big group of friends and a semi-romantic message waiting for me. I don't push the night to end early so I can escape to return the text and maybe find a way to meet up with Fran, but when Ava says she should probably get home, I'm one of the first people to agree and say good night.

Sorry I got so hopeless doom and gloom last night. The pebbles just about broke me.

It's completely OK. Today was better?

Definitely better. Not amazing but no pebbles today. I'll take it.

I want to ask where she is and what she's doing, but I know that's exactly one way I could scare off a relationship-averse person, so instead I let the moment breathe. I let hers be the last text sent.

Penny's not home when I get there, but Grace and Oscar wave me into the living room where they're watching some reality show where rich women yell at each other. Shows like that can make you feel like that's the inevitable climax of friendships, but I can't imagine any of my new friends calling each other a beast nonironically. Something dawns on me about what feels different here than back at home, and it's that even with all the honesty and messiness—and whatever once upon sophomore year happened between Tara and Fran—I didn't have to hold my breath tonight. Nothing felt like a trap, no one felt poised to make me feel unwanted. I just *was*.

"How was dinner?" Oscar asks. "Did you get the pancake? The pancake's the best thing on the menu."

"We did. We got almost everything."

Grace glances over at me with a raised eyebrow. "You had fun?"

My heart thuds a little. What's Grace getting at? "I'm fine, why?"

"I'm worried your feelings got hurt last week at work—or at least it seemed like perhaps that's what happened—and even though I noticed, I didn't even do anything about it and—"

"I talked to Margaret," I say, feeling like a mature person, particularly in comparison to the TV right now. "We're fine."

It's also a relief that Grace's concern has to do with Margaret and her friends and not Fran. Since Grace knows about my promise to Penny, it wouldn't be great if she'd sensed anything was going on. Plus, while I might have successfully come out for the first time to my new friends, I wasn't exactly ready to have that discussion with anyone else tonight.

"You're sure? I feel like I'm not parenting you that well."

"She seems fine, Grace," Oscar says, though it seems mainly like he's just trying to get the room quieted down so he can focus on the reality ladies. I'm fine with that, but the ladies are only a couple more points into the argument when my phone buzzes.

Wyd

This again?

This again. For real, are you free?

I excuse myself from Grace and Oscar and go out to the porch, waiting. The way to maintain power in a ... whatever this is right now is probably *not* to be so available, but I'm only human. Staying away from her feels futile. And I'm allowed to use my power however I want.

Penny walks up, and I do my best not to look like I'm counting down the minutes to kissing. Hopefully that's not a specific expression I have.

"What are you doing?" she asks, though her voice sounds free of suspicion.

"I'm going to hang out with a friend," I say, which practically isn't a lie.

"What friend? How do you have so many friends here?" she asks, and while she doesn't necessarily sound happy, she still doesn't seem suspicious. *Too* suspicious, at least. I still hope she goes inside immediately and doesn't see the truck pull up. Even if Penny thinks I'm straight, I don't know how someone could see Fran and the way we look at each other and not assume something's going on. None of it feels subtle, and I'm grateful somehow Grace has no idea. Maybe middle-aged people lose their sexual-tension detection abilities.

"Fran," I say.

"*Fran?* Is she eighty?"

"Penny, we are both named after grandmas, what is your point?" I say, because that's where our names came from, Mom's grandma and Dad's grandma, both of whom died long before either of us was born.

Penny and I both laugh, and whatever had made the air between us feel tight and heavy seems to have been zapped away.

"Why are you asking me all these questions? You've been out, too, and I have no idea what you were doing. Don't I get to interrogate you?"

"No, I know," Penny said quickly. "I should trust you more."

I try to keep my expression neutral at that.

"Anyway, I wanted to see if I liked sports on my own, without boys, like we were discussing," she says with a shrug. "So since you were going out with your other friends, I went back to the Greyhound after work with some of Oscar's coworkers."

"And?"

She smiles—as Fran's truck pulls up. Why did I encourage this conversation? "Maybe. Did you know there are a lot of statistics in baseball that could be interesting to study? I'm going to start reading the e-book of *Moneyball* tonight."

"I have to go," I say, with what I hope is only a vague nod at the truck and not a sexually charged one. "But I'm glad you were able to Penny-up even sports."

"I was hoping we could hang out now," she says, and I open my mouth to respond. "No, I should have told you when I'd be back. It's fine."

"Tomorrow night?" I ask.

"Perfect."

I back away and wait for her to let herself into the house before opening the door to the truck.

"Hey," Fran says as I climb in.

"Hey," I say. "Where are we going?"

I worry it's too eager a question, but then she smiles at me and says, "Wherever you want."

"Can we see the ocean?" I ask, and she laughs.

"Don't you live just north of here? You don't think we're close to the ocean...do you?"

"I'm bad at geography," I say. "And most useful things. How far's the ocean?"

"Traffic shouldn't be too bad right now," she says. "If you want to see the ocean, let's go."

So she drives us there with the old cassette deck going. We're quieter tonight than last time we drove across town. It's OK because the music fills the gaps, and because I like watching Fran. Her eyes are so focused on the road ahead that I get a chance to study her face, her nose that tips up at the very end, the curve of her jawline, her top lip that's a little fuller than her bottom one. I feel an ache for her, to have my hands in her hair, my lips on her lips, my body pressed up against her body. But instead I'm all the way over here, across this very wide truck, thinking of how her fingertips felt on the small of my back. Has she even touched me there or am I just imagining it? There hasn't been that much physical contact, not really, the kiss after Korean barbecue, and the moments after our sundaes, wrapped up in each other's arms, kissing like it was breathing, like there was no other way to stay alive. But then those times end and we can breathe just fine on our own.

"What are you thinking about?" she asks, and I laugh, and I know that she knows. Why bother to hide this anyway?

"So are the pebbles done?" I ask. "Unless you never want to talk about pebbles again. Just pretend I never asked."

"The pebbles are done," she says. "I guess I shouldn't complain. I know people would be grateful for this opportunity, and it's not like I'm learning nothing."

"Have you ever tried to make your own thing?" I ask.

"I have, and ... yeah. I've made a few things," she says. "But it's like no one likes what I'm doing. They all have this idea of what I should be making, and my actual work doesn't line up."

Fran's so tough and take-charge, so it's hard for me to imagine a world where her work doesn't just speak for itself. Whatever that work is. It's weird to hear the tone in her voice, how maybe she doubts herself because of how people react.

"That sucks," I say.

She sighs instead of agreeing, and somehow I find myself understanding that sigh.

"Oh my god," I say, as we fly past more and more of Los Angeles. "How are we still not there?"

Fran laughs. "I told you it wasn't close!"

"I thought you were exaggerating," I say, which makes her laugh harder.

"So can I see them?" I ask. "Whatever you've made so far?"

She shrugs, and maybe I asked for too much. "I don't know. Maybe."

Then we're quiet again, until Fran pulls off the freeway and finds an open spot in a parking lot near the ocean. The air's different when we get out of the truck, all wind and salt and sea. I follow her to the sand, and we both shed our shoes to walk out farther. There's hardly anyone around, and I think very hard about kissing her right now.

"I have this idea," she says. "For a short film. My teacher last semester warned me if I didn't do it well, it'd be too cheesy, but I think I could pull it off. I hope I could, at least. Even if it's just another thing no one wants from me."

"I want it from you," I say.

"Stop," she says with a grin. "Anyway, I thought about making it this summer, when I don't have homework or anything else to worry about, but this PA work's taking up a lot of my time, which I guess was stupid not to realize. Not that I thought it'd be easy or—I just thought..." She sighs. "Sorry. I'm complaining so much."

"Complain all you want. Could you make it with your extra time at night?"

"Maybe," she says. "I don't know. I couldn't shoot outside, so I'd have to figure out lighting and a set—"

"I'm great at that stuff," I say. "Well, I know how to do it, at least. For theater, but it probably has some overlap. I could help—if you wanted me to."

"Maybe," she says, but a smile sneaks through her expression.

"Just let me know. It'd be fun to try. At my school, the film and theater clubs are, like, completely separate territories, so it'd be a chance I won't get next school year."

"You're amazing." She pulls me in close. "Lydia, I should be honest with you."

Good moments never start this way, with honesty as a warning and not a promise.

"I like you a lot," she says, and I can see right away how this is a rehearsed and practiced speech. Hell, a *performed* speech. This is the speech girls get before Fran Ford breaks their hearts. "But I'm not really a . . . relationship person. Not right now. Who knows, maybe never."

"Oh," I say, keeping a careful handle on my tone. "Did it seem like that to you? I'm not right now, either. I had a super painful breakup last month, and that's the last thing I need now." *I also have a complicated pledge with my sister and even though I haven't technically violated even one term of it, I should keep myself in check.*

"Thank god." Fran presses her lips to my cheek, at the corner of my mouth. I think about how I'm exactly the girl she needs me to be right now. "I really want to have some fun this summer."

"Well, good," I say. "I'm super fun."

I turn my head just a little so our lips line up, and we kiss as if we aren't standing on a public beach, like the whole world is just the two of us. Our hands keep moving, holding each other's faces, cupping the back of her head, sliding around my waist. I lose track of her body and my body, we feel so connected. I don't know how long this lasts, our lips parting and coming back together, the waves lapping against the sand, our breath coming faster and heavier, but I know that all at once it's all I need and also not enough.

"Let's go back to your truck," I tell her, my voice stretched and raw. "I—"

"Yeah, me too." She dips her head down to kiss my neck. "But not here. We'll have my house to ourselves sometime soon. I don't want you with anyone else around."

That's where we're different because right now, I don't care. Right now I have no reasonable thought left in my body. But I catch my breath and I watch the ocean find the shore again and again. Maybe this is where it normally goes off course, when the person I'm kissing isn't like Fran, is willing to forget reason, too. This time will be different.

∿

Penny's still up when I get back, even though it's late and I was hoping to escape her. Not in general, just that I feel I'm so obviously post-kissed and hazy from desire. What if she wants me to talk about the seven habits of highly effective people? I couldn't even list them; right now I'm not sure I could even list seven people who aren't Fran.

"Where were you?" she asks, looking up from her book. "I mean, not like Mom and Dad, *where were you, young lady*, just . . . I'm making conversation."

"You're so weird," I say. "Just hanging out with Fran, like I said. We went to the beach."

"Oh," Penny says, a note of disappointment in her tone. "I had the beach on my list of things we could do this weekend."

I wave my hand. "There are lots of beaches. We'll just go to a different one."

"What one did you go to tonight?"

I pause. "Honestly, I have no idea."

"How do you not know?"

"I dunno, there was sand and the ocean," I say, and now we're both laughing. I turn from her and pretend it's because I'm changing into my pajamas and not because if she looks at me too closely she's got to see that I spent a large portion of tonight kissing someone. How would I explain that? Were there even words for what was happening with Fran?

"I should get some sleep. Work is way too soon."

"Did you know sleep deprivation was a factor in some of the biggest disasters in recent history?"

"Oh my god, do not tell me that story about Chernobyl again. The worst thing that happens if I'm tired tomorrow is I make a weak latte. People will live, Pen."

CHAPTER NINE

Penny asked me to meet her at Oscar's office right when she got off of work the next night. Even though it's technically walkable, and even with last night's talk still fresh in my head, I take a chance and text Fran.

I know you're probably filming late, but is there any way you can drive me somewhere pretty close at 6? Well, at like 5:50 to arrive at 6. No pressure.

I obviously regret it as soon as I send it. Of course this isn't the text to send less than twenty-four hours after the no-relationships warning. The text to send is no text at all! Plus there was no need for so many specifics, and the *no pressure* at the end isn't fooling anyone.

Sure, I'm pretty free for a while actually.

I wonder if it's an invitation. I start typing *wyd* only partially as a joke and then delete delete delete. What am *I* doing?

But there's over an hour before I'm meeting Penny, so I *do* send it, and before long, Fran's parking outside of the house, the house that's empty except for me.

"Hey," she greets me once she's standing at the front door. I'd opened it as soon as she'd texted that she was parking, but she'd taken her time, walking casually down the block and up the front path. Her hair glowed golden in the sun, and her skin looked tan and warm, and it hit me that I'd never seen her outside in the daylight before.

"Come on in," I say, as casually as I can manage. Given how badly I wish we were already kissing, I'm thrilled it's not just a squeak. There's nothing casual or sexy about a squeak.

"Cute house," she says with a nod to the front room.

"It's Grace's and her boyfriend's," I say. "I'm just here for the summer."

"Yeah, I know," she says with a smile. "It's still a cute house."

"I'll give you a tour," I say, but all I really do is take her to my room. Penny's and my room, that is, but right now there's no Penny to be found, just Fran and me and this twin bed.

"No one's home?" Fran asks me.

"Just us," I say with a shrug.

"Interesting," she says, sitting down on my bed and leaning back on her elbows. It feels like an invitation, a dare, a game of chicken. I stay standing.

"I do need a ride at five-fifty," I say, and a grin draws across her face. "It wasn't a line."

"Oh, yeah, girls are always trying that ride at five-fifty line on me," Fran says. "C'mere."

I start to climb onto her lap, but I stop myself. I've made out with plenty of guys who were skinnier than I was, but Fran's so wiry and lean. I feel inexperienced again, like I'm going into freshman year and not senior, like I've never even been near a bed with someone before.

This stuff is all instinctual, or at least it has been for me. Sex—well, sex and the things surrounding it have never been scary to me. Even when it's new, it's not like it's something you know. It's something you *know*. And it's something you're figuring out with someone else, and even though my whole social life and much of my family life has been built around worrying about saying or doing the right thing, it's just not been like that with boys. Not in this way, at least. Staying in a relationship, sure. But never what comes first.

Fran leans forward. "You OK, Lydia?"

"I've only dated boys before," I admit. "I don't want to squish you."

"Do you think I'm weaker than *boys?*" she asks, and somehow manages to pull me on top of her in one move. I suspect she's per-fected this move with some practice. We're both girls with practice, and I realize that comforts me. The truth about my experience—and lack of—being out there in the open comforts me, too.

"I like your body, you know," she says, right into my ear.

"I like my body, too," I say quickly. "I don't know why I think of boys as stronger. Or—I mean, it's not like a boy's never been on top of me before. I don't know. I—I feel—"

"Yeah?" she asks, kissing me gently.

"I'm *flustered,*" I say, even though I've never used the word *flustered* before, much less while lying on top of someone. "Also, thank you. About my body, I mean. I like yours, too."

"We don't have to do this," Fran says. "And by *this* I mean anything. You were the one who sent the text so I—"

"I wasn't feeling flustered then," I say, and we both laugh. I slide away from Fran and turn to lie with my head on my pillow, and she joins me, her face inches away from mine, the longer parts of her hair brushing my cheeks and forehead.

"What's your favorite movie?" she asks me, and I laugh. "Why is that funny?"

"I don't know, I thought you were going to ask something..."

Fran grins, sliding her hand over my waist, slipping beneath the hem of my T-shirt to touch my bare skin. "Something about your body? Something about my strength compared to that of boys? Please, could boys lift pebbles all day? I doubt it."

"Well, no, not some of the boys I've dated," I say, and we're both laughing now. "I guess some of this is new to me. I didn't think I'd feel that way."

"I mean, everyone's new, at first," Fran says, and her lips find mine again. She's right, though, because it's true that no matter how many girls' broken hearts are in her past, I'm new right now. There's plenty for both of us to figure out, and not just me with my lack of girl experience.

I reach for my phone as the kissing intensifies, as the space between our bodies disappears. "I'm going to set a timer, because I have to leave in—"

Fran laughs and sits up. "No offense, Lydia, but I'm not going to have sex with you *on a timer*."

"I didn't say—" But I was also laughing again. "Fine, I didn't *not* want that."

"You always put me in these impossible scenarios," she said, her voice low in a way that makes my heart speed up. "The beach. On a timer."

"Those are two scenarios," I say. "Not *always*."

"Feels like always," she says. "How's this weekend? I think my parents are going out on Saturday night, and my brother's always out. We won't have to set any timers."

I love how straightforward this is, that Fran of the vague texts and the sexy over-the-counter looks is making these specific plans with me.

It's no one's power move right now, just an open spot on the calendar that's what we both want.

I'm less flustered already.

Fran drops me off a block from Penny's office, exactly where I pointed her to, no need to mention how I'd already gotten good at directing Fran to park a little bit down the block from things. I was running a minute or two behind because Fran had tried to ask me about movies again, but I got distracted by the empty house, and so we'd spent the time kissing instead of talking. Plus the girl who didn't need relationships didn't need a ton of talking anyway. I was *nailing* being that girl.

"Sorry I'm late," I say, walking up to Penny who's right outside the building looking at her phone.

"Only a minute," she says, and looks up at me. "Everyone at the office says that in LA as long as you're not fifteen minutes late, you're considered on-time. Which seems a bit inconsiderate to me, but what do I know?"

"Everyone says LA is laid-back," I say. "You should probably move somewhere ... less so."

"That's the goal," Penny says with a sigh. "Come on, let's go. I planned out our whole evening."

I follow her down the sidewalk, while thinking about that sigh. Obviously I knew that Penny dreamed about business undergrads and MBAs, but for some reason it hadn't quite hit me that wrapped up in those dreams was the dream of getting away.

"Here," Penny says, and takes something out of her bag. "I went at lunch to get these so that it would be easier tonight."

I examine the shiny card that looks like a credit card but isn't.

"It's for the LA Metro," Penny continues. "If you didn't know, Los Angeles has a subway system, and we can take it from just about a block from the Greyhound."

This *is* all news to me, and it sounds a little exciting and dangerous all at once. Today's been a lot of that, actually.

"Where are we going?" I ask. "Or is it a surprise?"

Penny smiles at me. "It can be a surprise."

We arrive at the subway station, and Penny expertly guides me through swiping my card and following her to the track. I'm surprised that it's aboveground, nothing like images of the New York subway. It also doesn't feel dangerous, just a mix of people all sitting quietly as the city flies past the windows, but these are more things I keep to myself in order not to sound like an idiot in front of my sister, who planned all of this just for me.

"So can you, like, not wait to leave California, then?" I ask, and I watch as Penny frowns at my terrible sentence structure. "Imagine a smart person asked that same question."

"I'm looking forward to college, yes," she says. "And, also yes, none of my Match or Reach choices are in California. But that part isn't intentional, I just selected the programs that made sense, and got some advice from Mr. Hockseye."

"I feel like Mr. Hockseye has too much say over your future. Remember when the journalism club did all those interviews with the administration and he said his favorite food was sandwiches? Not, like, one specific sandwich, just *sandwiches?*"

Penny actually laughs. "Yeah, that was weird, and I obviously doubt his overall abilities. But he's really specific about college plans, and he's all I have. It's more than Mom or Dad can do, and they also refuse to hire me a college admissions counselor."

"Like you need one! You know everything about applying to college, and you're not even technically a junior yet. You have a perfect GPA and extracurriculars and volunteer work."

She waves her hand dismissively. "So does everyone who has the college lists I do. And they also have parents who understand the process and people hired to help them. Mr. Hockseye might be my only hope."

"I don't want to live in a world where that's true," I say. "Look, I know I'm an idiot compared to you, but if there's anything I can help with, just tell me."

Penny makes a gesture as if even the thought is impossible.

"Seriously. I'm not using my money from Grounds Control for much, besides getting meals out sometimes. Will the rest help you hire an admissions person whose favorite food isn't sandwiches?"

"No," Penny says quickly. "Get yourself into college first."

"I thought you said that a degree in the arts was like throwing your money away."

"This is our stop," Penny says, getting to her feet. I follow suit, stumbling but not falling as the train lurches to a stop, and then clambering out the door behind her. We're suddenly downtown, and I can't believe a short train ride was all that separated us. There's a magic, I realize, to living where Grace and Oscar do, how so many things are practically at your fingertips in ways you don't even see.

"This is amazing," I murmur, looking around at the skyline, the freeways and train tracks all around us.

"Come on." Penny grabs my arm and yanks me out of the subway station. "To the library."

"Oh my god, seriously?" I have to laugh. "Our big adventure is the library? No, of *course* it is."

"You'll like it," she says. "I promise. If you don't, I'll pay for dinner."

"I'll pay for dinner," I say. "Save your money for that college person."

"OK," Penny relents, and I smile. "Anyway, I didn't mean that you shouldn't get a degree in the arts. I was talking specifically about the ROI of different degrees, and you're more likely not to reach earning potential to match—"

"Now you're just saying the same thing with bigger words."

"I'm not," she says, and then tugs me down another street, where a huge building with a beautiful pointed tile roof comes into view.

"Is this the *library*?" I ask, and when Penny confirms, I find myself hurrying right along with her to get inside. Inside there seem to be staircases everywhere, high ceilings, tons of light streaming in, nothing like what I'd expect from a library. Libraries are not typically a place I hang out for any longer than a school project has required, but this building feels nothing like the dusty stale air at our school library.

"I'm sure you're wondering why I brought you here," Penny says.

"Well, I was, but not now. This place is *gorgeous*."

She waves her hand. "No. I have an idea for us, for the summer. I thought maybe it might not be enough just to steer clear of boys. It's not *doing* something; it's the absence of doing something."

I snicker at that, and Penny elbows me.

"I didn't mean—anyway. I thought we should each have a project. Like I discussed with you, I'm interested in learning more about statistics in sports. Maybe there's something you want to research, too."

I'm ready to complain that of course Penny's taking our summer and not just putting limitations on it but now making it more like school. But then I remember something from the other night.

"OK," I agree. "I'm going to learn about set design and lighting for film and how it compares to theater."

"Interesting," Penny says.

"I might help a friend with a project this summer," I say quickly, whether or not that's true. The *might* makes it not a flat-out lie. "So I'm already doing something. Not just *not* doing boys."

"Lydia," Penny says, but ends up laughing softly. Making my perfect sister laugh in a library feels like a huge victory.

Of course Penny's already looked up where the sports books are, and she helps me locate the film section, which is unsurprisingly huge here in Los Angeles.

"We're really just allowed to be here?" I ask her, examining titles on the shelves. Is it going too far to research on-camera lighting when nothing's confirmed besides the hot girl I'm doing whatever with mentioning a film she'd like to make? Probably. But it'd be nice to know this stuff regardless.

"We can't check out the books but we're completely welcome to stay here and use them," she says. "So don't overload yourself."

I laugh because she's hanging onto a stack of what looks like a dozen volumes.

"I know what I'm doing," she says.

I never really doubt that, so I grab a couple of books that look interesting and follow Penny to a section of tables so we can read. She's brought an extra notepad, composition-style, speckled black-and-white cover, for me, and I feel like someone else as I scribble ideas into it.

Penny's always been like this, books and research and time spent in libraries on purpose. REACT is my favorite part of school, but I guess I feel the same way about it that I do about the kids in the LGBTQ+ Club. I'm the messy one no one takes seriously, not the girl who arrives with neat stacks of research in her enamel-pinned backpack.

Suddenly I don't know why I think that. I'm *good* backstage, strong enough to hammer set pieces together, opinionated enough to make decisions about color choices and prop selections, knowledgeable enough to yell up at the lighting booth when some cues lagged. Even now I realize that this new world—cameras instead of a live audience—doesn't intimidate me, it's just new rules and results. So why do I still feel like a messy disaster?

We stay at that table until our stomachs are growling loudly, and then Penny directs us to a restaurant she looked up on Yelp for the right balance of "ratings, prices, and wait time." I'd make fun of her, but we get a table right away and the mac and cheese is amazing.

"So even though it's our summer without boys, you're doing a sports project?" I ask her, and she twists her face up in what I know is offense.

"Boys don't *own sports*, Lydia," she says. "Not even baseball."

"You're right," I say quickly. "It's weird I even thought that. It's just always been—"

"Well, of course," Penny says. "For us, sports haven't been like that. That's why I'm seeing now if they could be."

I like that. Baseball's still not something I ever would have guessed she'd be interested in, yet there's something about that that makes me feel that we are more connected this summer than we normally are.

"Let's just split this," Penny says when the check arrives. "Both of us should be worried about college."

I smile when I realize that's true.

"Want to come down again this weekend?" Penny asks as we head back to the subway. I think about New York, how there are a lot of colleges there and also a lot of theater. Could I end up there next year, riding their subway and navigating their sidewalks?

"Sure," I say.

"Saturday?"

A flush of panic overtakes me for just a moment. But, no. I can handle this.

"I'm helping my friend with her project on Saturday," I say, which is definitely one way I've never referred to sex before. "Sorry."

"Oh," Penny says.

"I mean, probably not until the night. I could do something before."

"Sure," she says, but as we swipe our Metro cards I already feel us moving backward, and I'm mad at myself for making plans with Fran without considering Penny—but also how could I say no to Fran?

It turns out things can still be complicated even when boys aren't involved at all.

CHAPTER TEN

My guilt, which has been humming along at a nice low level ever since I turned down Penny's invite for Saturday night, ratchets way up before I've even opened my eyes on Saturday morning. It's unfair; I get only two days to sleep in and instead of staying cozy under the covers, I'm wide awake while my emotions fight: excitement and nerves for tonight with Fran on the one side, my sisterly guilt on the other.

So I get up and take a fast shower. Penny's in the kitchen with what looks like a sensible breakfast and the newspaper, because why not act fifty years old instead of sixteen when you're perfect Penny Jones?

"You're up early," she says.

"You're up *earlier*," I point out.

"Relatively speaking, I meant."

"Instead of your digestive yogurt or whatever you're eating, do you want to walk down to Grounds Control? I get a discount on coffee and pastries, and you can see how cute it is."

"Oh," Penny says, and frowns at her yogurt. "Yeah, that sounds great. This is kind of terrible."

"Let me guess, you read an article that this is the best breakfast for high-income earners," I say, folding up the paper for her.

"Something like that," she says with a smile.

We walk out into the bright sunshine, and it feels good to, for once, be the one leading the way. There's nothing we can walk to at home; everything requires a car, so Penny and I share Mom's old Prius, an arrangement that works out more than it doesn't. Model UN and the fall musical are rarely on the same time lines.

"This *is* cute," Penny says as we walk inside. Grace waves to us from behind the counter, and it hits me that she works here seven days a week, no mornings to sleep in. She must truly love this place.

I don't recognize anyone but Grace behind the counter, because the weekend crew is completely different, and the line is different, too. During the week, people are rushing to their jobs, but now the shop's filled with groups taking their time to examine the menu and pastry case.

"What can I get for you two today?" Grace asks when we finally reach the counter, and then she shakes her head when she sees me get out my wallet. "Oh, please. Just go grab a table while you can, and I'll bring something out."

"Ooh, special treatment," I say, which makes her laugh.

"Don't get used to it," she calls, and Penny scopes out a good table near the back.

"Mom and Dad are right that restaurants are risky investments," Penny says. "But this does seem to be doing well. Is it always this busy?"

"Basically, yeah," I say. "It's different during the week. People are in more of a hurry and they almost all take their stuff to go. Also, Grace isn't doing this as an *investment*. She loves it."

"Hmmm," Penny says as the door swings open and a frazzled-looking Fran plods in, a trail of Post-its in her hand. I didn't know she had to work on weekends, or maybe I wouldn't have invited Penny here, which is probably terrible of me but it's just easiest to keep everyone separate. I look right at Penny and avoid any potential eye contact with Fran, as my heart decides to start beating what feels like one million times per second.

"You look weird," Penny says. "I really think you should get your eyes examined."

"I think you should get *your* eyes examined," I say, and we both laugh even though it's the stupidest joke ever, and hopefully that's that. Hopefully, Fran stays focused on her Post-its. Hopefully, Grace doesn't do anything like direct Fran over to me or yell at me to say hi to her. It doesn't sound like a thing Grace would do, but the dangerous possibilities of this situation are making my brain overfunction.

It's also just really difficult *not* to look at Fran, the way she stands, the way she runs her hand through her hair to push it back from her face, the way she bites a corner of her lower lip in concentration. She could be doing all of those extremely hot things right now, only hours away from our plans alone in her house, and I have to sit here and avert my eyes. It seems like half the reason I'm even dating Fran—or whatever we're doing—is because I couldn't look away from her. Once she's standing inside Grounds Control, it's hard to focus on anything else.

I mean, yes, in some ways it *is* always like that for me, a boy comes along and then it's all *him*, hopes and thoughts and plans and intricate daydreams of kissing, etc. It was always easy to get caught up, because what else was there? Mom and Dad had work, Penny had school and other boys, and friends were part of my extracurriculars—well, *extracurricular*—and that was that. Boys made it easy not to change anything.

But I'd promised to set that aside for this summer for my sister, who—historically speaking—has rarely asked much of me at all. And I could have done it, I'm sure, except that Fran and the way I feel around her is different, and not just because she isn't a boy. The way we feel drawn to each other feels like something brand-new.

My phone vibrates in my pocket and I'm afraid it's Fran and she'll somehow hear the buzz in the bustling café, and things'll get weird, fast, but it's just the group text. They're all out for donuts and coffee again, which would have sounded appealing if not for my sisterly guilt.

"Something important?" Penny asks, and I legitimately can't tell if she's being sincere or passive-aggressive. Either way, shoving my phone in my pocket is the smartest plan of action.

"Nope. Do you want to go back to the library after this? I'm free all day long."

"What about your friend and her project?" Penny asks.

"That's not until this evening. Come on. You love the library!"

She agrees, just as, amazingly, I hear the door swing open and shut and then glimpse Fran trudging to her truck carefully with two trays of drinks. Grace appears with pastries and lattes for us, and everything's safe again.

"Did you get to say hi to Fran?" Grace asks, right after I take a giant bite of a muffin.

"Fran was here?" I ask innocently, though my mouth is full of muffin and I'm not sure if that adds to or detracts from suspicion.

"She was, big order. I'm surprised you didn't see her waiting."

I glance at Penny, but she's blissfully sipping the matcha latte Grace brought to her.

"This is amazing, Grace," Penny says. "You must be so proud of this café."

Grace grins, and I realize I'm smiling, too. I have nothing to do with Grace's success, of course, but I still feel a little ownership of this place. Penny's a tough crowd, and yet she sees that Grounds Control is special.

"I am, Pen." Grace gestures to the counter. "I need to get back to it, but I'm glad you two stopped in. Big plans today?"

"Central Library," Penny says with a scholastic gleam in her eyes.

"Oh, I love that place," Grace says. "If you need ideas for where to eat or get snacks downtown, text me and Oscar. We have a lot of thoughts."

So we retrace our steps from the other evening, and I spend my time reading about movies and theater and wondering if there's a future where I could be doing this for real. I have no doubt Penny will do whatever she sets her mind to, whether it's whatever Oscar's office does or whatever Wall Street people do or wherever baseball statistics lead a person. I'm still more than a little convinced I'll stumble through the same local degree program Mom and Dad did to become a CPA and do people's taxes for the rest of my life, even though I'm not great with numbers or with people. That's how doomed I am; even my backup plan feels tenuous.

Sitting here, though, next to Penny, my notepad open and my mind going a million miles an hour, nothing feels that hopeless. Not that there's anything wrong with my parents' lives—they seem really happy—but it's not what I want. And acknowledging that, even if it's just to myself, feels kind of new and maybe even exciting.

Penny figures out a late afternoon lunch spot for us via research, even though I want to text Grace and Oscar for ideas.

"If we ask them we only have the insights of two people," she says as we walk back into the bright sunshine. "This way we're using the insights of thousands of people. There's so much less risk."

"I mean, it's to get pizza or whatever," I say. "There's not that much risk involved."

"But why have *any* risk if you don't have to?"

I don't know how to answer that.

By the time we're back at Grace and Oscar's, Fran's texted *7?* and I've agreed to that. It's tough getting ready and I should have planned ahead better, because Penny's settled in the room, sitting on her bed and reading one of the books she brought from home. Is it suspicious to change into a slightly better outfit to supposedly go help a friend? Probably not. Is it suspicious to change into cuter underwear? Yes, absolutely, so unfortunately Fran is going to see these floral print nightmare underpants that Mom gave me for last Christmas and are infuriatingly comfortable. Putting them on this morning was a real rookie mistake.

Penny looks up as I fuss with my hair. "I thought you were working on your project tonight?"

"Yeah," I say quickly. "We'll probably get dinner out first or something. I don't want to look sweaty, OK?"

"You don't look sweaty," she says, but stands up. "I can make your hair look neater, though."

I let her brush it out and wind my hair back into buns. It feels deeply dishonest to pretend this is for looking appropriate at some nonexistent restaurant when all I'm hoping is that Fran's fingers are soon unwinding my hair, letting it loose as we—

My phone buzzes, and I flip it over when I see Fran's name.

"You're acting weird," Penny says, patting my hair and nodding. "Much better."

I checked the mirror. She's right.

"I've never helped with a movie before," I say, which is true both literally and metaphorically. It seems to satisfy Penny, and she heads back to her book. My phone is safe to look at yet again.

Bad news: parents are staying home tonight after all. We can still hang out if you want, but no pressure.

I respond right away. *I'm still in if it's actually OK.*

Yes, I want assurance from her. Yes, I want it to actually be OK because Fran feels the thing between us too, knows that it isn't just physical chemistry too, wants to get to know me too, secretly wants to rethink that no-girlfriend stance.

I say goodbye to Penny and decide to wait in the living room, since Grace and Oscar are busy making dinner in the kitchen. I guess I need a moment to adjust my expectations for the evening, to tell my body that nothing is happening, that my grandma underpants are going unseen, that in front of Fran's parents I'll have to—

I actually don't know how I'll have to act in front of Fran's parents. Does she just invite girls over all the time? *Fran's a player.* Back home, I could get away with it, I realize, a girl in my room and the door closed and no suspicion from Mom and Dad. But Fran—well, Fran doesn't look straight. I'm sure her parents know she's queer. Still, though, what am *I* to Fran? Just a random girl? What would she have to tell them anyway?

Normally, these are exactly the topics I'd take to Penny. Well, not *exactly*, the specific stuff about dating girls is all brand-new. But the parsing out meaning from texts, from invitations—we thrive on that stuff! Maybe Penny and I are finding other things to talk about—well, at least we're finding ways to hang out quietly. But it isn't just that I worried relationship talk is all Penny and I have, it's that I'd forgotten how much that relationship talk helped. I miss her insight, even when it's couched in TED Talk risk-averse language.

My phone finally buzzes. *Cool, see you soon.*

I'm not sure what I was expecting. But it turns out that even without assurances from Fran or advice from Penny, I'm still ready to go. Fran pulls up at seven, and I'm getting used to getting into the truck—well, not *gracefully*, but less gracelessly, at least.

"You're far away," she says, and so I guess we've passed some invisible mark where now I get to slide over and sit close to her. I watch her focus on driving, how she shakes her hair out of her face when the air conditioner blows it that way, how even though she's lean and wiry how strong her forearms look, one hand on the wheel and one on the stick shift. I think about her hands on me instead, even though I know that's no longer what tonight's about. Should I be surprised there's still a tonight when sex is off the table? No assurances, but no canceled date, either.

"Sorry," she tells me. "They normally don't change plans so last-minute, but I guess they've both had busy weeks and both secretly wanted to cancel, and I did my best to convince them that a party was exactly what they needed, but I don't think I was that persuasive."

"It's fine," I say.

"Have you had dinner yet? They're cooking, at least. If you don't mind eating with my parents. There's not really any getting out of it. Shit, I should have warned you of all of this sooner."

I laugh because nothing Fran does or doesn't do feels like an accident. "It's fine. I'm great with parents."

That much was true. Two ex-boyfriends' moms still followed me on Instagram. Tate's parents had said I should come with them on vacation this year—before the breakup, obviously, before he'd decided whatever he'd decided.

"It doesn't really matter how you are with them," Fran says. "They're like human golden retrievers with the affection and the attention."

"That sounds nice," I say, and she laughs. "It does! My parents have this amazing, happy marriage and they run a business together. They're kind of neutral on people outside of the family."

"My dad asked my mom to help run his landscaping business, and she laughed him out of the room. He had to hire someone," Fran says. "Which is good, because my mom's a lot of things but not office manager material. For a while she wanted to be in charge of family finances and our internet got turned off because she forgot you have to pay for it."

"Oh my god, I'm afraid that's what I'm going to turn out like," I admit, and Fran bursts into laughter. "Seriously, being an adult always felt so far away, and now I'm turning eighteen in a few months, and just . . . what?"

"Ugh, tell me about it. It seems like everyone's moving away and I'll still be here living with my parents and going to school nearby like nothing changed. It came up fast."

She pulls into a large driveway, huge compared to the house behind it, just an average house lit up brightly. There are three pickup trucks, including Fran's, and a red Prius that's just like my parents' except a less boring color.

"Hey," Fran says, and I turn to her for whatever important information she's about to give me, but instead her lips find mine. I'm glad I sat close.

She lets us into the house that smells just flat-out *amazing*. "I'm back," she calls, and it warms my heart that Fran's part of *a family*, that this tough girl lets her parents know she's home even though she's probably been gone for all of fifteen minutes.

"Honey, does Lydia like—" A woman, obviously Fran's mom, walks into the room and laughs. "I guess I could just ask her myself. Hi, you must be Lydia. I'm Daniela Morales, but you can call me Dani."

I have never managed to call a parent by a first name, but I smile and shake her hand anyway. Her hair's darker than Fran's, but they have the same smiles and the same complexions.

"So how are you with spicy foods, Lydia? Fran's dad's making his usual chili, but he goes a little overboard so I'm giving you a chance to get out of this now," Fran's mom says with a smile.

"I can handle spice," I say, weirdly now a theme of my time in LA.

"I told you it'd be fine," Fran says. "We're going to my room until dinner, OK?"

"Can I get you something to drink?" her mom asks me. "Honestly, we don't have much to offer. Fran didn't give me a lot of warning."

"I'm fine," I say.

"What about a snack?" she asks. "Fran's dad's going to be fussing with this pot of chili for way too long."

"Mom, we're fine," Fran says, and tugs me toward the hallway. "Call us in for dinner."

"Are you sure you—"

"Oh my *god*," Fran says, and I laugh, following her down the hallway. "See? Relentless."

"It's nice," I say. "She's nice."

Fran opens a door and flips on the lights as we walk in. Her four walls are all different colors, a mix of tans and blues, and little stuff is tacked up all over. Photos, stills from movies, those little strips of paint samples from hardware stores.

"I like your room," I say.

She shrugs. "I used to have a ton of movie posters but I decided I wanted stuff that inspired me and looked like how I want my own work to look someday, instead of just other people's stuff. Like in my room it should be about figuring out what I want to do, not what other people have already done. I'm not sure it's working, though."

I sit down on the bed but Fran stays standing. Is it weird I sat down? The bed somehow seems less intimate than her desk.

"I saw you earlier," Fran says.

"What?"

"At Grounds Control." She grins, shoving her hands in her pockets. "With a cute girl. You were too busy with her to notice me."

"Ew, Fran, that's my sister."

She laughs. "Shit, sorry. You can hang out with whatever cute girls you want but—"

"But you'd be jealous if they weren't my sister?" I ask, and she shakes her head.

"No, I'm not like that."

It's good that she's not—there are so many things going on here, like the fact that I'm only here until August and that probably I shouldn't be dating anyone per my agreement with Penny or at least not *seriously* and of course this is what I've agreed to—but I guess I do wish Fran already wanted me all to herself. I know that jealousy isn't healthy, and I'm glad she's not like that. I've seen how jealous boys have treated me and Pen at times, and I never want to be in that situation again. I just want to be *enough* for her. It doesn't all necessarily make sense together, of course. I should be keeping some distance and not falling too hard and honoring my pledge to Penny and taking Fran at her word and also I want to wrap myself up right here in Fran's world and let it crowd out everything else.

Fran pushes the door almost shut with her shoe and walks over to the bed, dropping next to me and finding my mouth with hers. Instead of worrying we have nothing to talk about and there's no hope in making this *more*, I kiss her back.

"I don't want to get you in trouble," I whisper, and she laughs.

"I won't *get in trouble*," she says, and cringes. "It makes me feel like I'm twelve saying that. My parents are cool. Mostly. You see I follow the law of *door's technically open.*"

"Yeah, you're a real rebel," I say, and she laughs again. I love how often I manage to make Fran laugh. This connection I feel tugging us together doesn't feel like something I invented; it seems so solid and *real.*

"Like I've said. I just thought things would be different." She shrugs. "I keep thinking I should have just gotten a job or worked with Dad for the summer so I could earn money and have my own place. But I also made the mistake of looking up how much an apartment would be, and it's definitely more than Dad's gonna pay me. All of it just makes me feel like a kid in the worst way."

"I know what you mean," I say. "College feels, like…insurmountable. I feel like I should have started taking it seriously at least a year ago and maybe it's too late now."

"No, definitely not," Fran said. "My mom keeps pointing out that there are a lot of different paths and that's why I should just take classes locally and figure things out, and even though I wish I could just take the next year off completely, I know what she means. I'm sure you're fine, Lydia. More than fine."

I kiss her for saying that and I kiss her again because it's not just that she said it but that it seems like she really believes it. Did I know before it could be so hot to simply have someone believe in me?

I lie back and pull her down with me. She raises an eyebrow but doesn't struggle.

"You're really pushing the limits of that *door's technically open* law," she says.

"Well, you're really cute and I heard the chili takes a while," I say, looking up at her.

"I mean, don't get carried away and set a timer," she says.

"The timer was a good idea," I say, as her lips graze my neck. "It was practical!"

"Careful, you sound like your hot sister," she says, and I pretend to be offended, even though I love everything about right now, in Fran's room, on Fran's bed, under Fran's hands and mouth. We make out until we hear footsteps down the hallway, and luckily her mom only calls and doesn't walk in on us springing away from each other—like that's ever fooled anyone.

I still probably need a moment to look less flushed—a danger of being an extremely pale person—but Fran strides down the hallway and so I follow. Her brother's apparently out, so I take his seat at the table, next to Fran and across from her parents. Fran's dad looks just like a dad version of her, same reddish-brown hair, same eyes, same casual smile. They're even dressed the same, T-shirts and jeans that look a little vintage, and he's got her posture, or I guess she's got his.

"So, Lydia, do you go to school with Fran?" her mom asks. "Well, *did you,* I know you've all graduated now."

"I don't," I say. "And also I'm going to be a senior, so I'm still in high school."

"That's great," her mom says. "See, not everyone's going away, Fran."

Fran sighs. "Lydia normally lives, like, an hour away. And I know not everyone's *leaving* leaving. I'm fine."

I touch her hand under the table, even though I'm not sure what my role is as far as her family's concerned. Or I guess at all, really. Do I get to comfort her and worry about her, or should we stick to making out first and foremost? Ideally it's all of it, but if Fran professes not to want a relationship, maybe I shouldn't be acting like her girlfriend.

She squeezes back, though.

"Hope you're all ready for this chili," her dad says as he serves it into bowls for each of us, making sure I get the first one.

"It's spicy, but not as bad as he acts," Fran tells me, even before trying it. "He loves doing this whole spiel. You'll be fine."

"I'm offended by that," he says, in a way where I can tell this is their normal family routine. It's cute that someone tough like Fran also has routines and a dad who looks just like her and regular family dinners. My parents have learned that keeping longer hours means a lot more business; apparently a lot of accountants keep hours like banks, which means it's hard for anyone with a job with standard hours to make it to appointments. So they stay open late and rack up a ton of evening tax returns and whatever else they do. This means we don't have a ton of dinners together, though Mom does lots of meal prep on the weekends to make sure we at least eat balanced meals most of the time. I never feel unloved or anything, but I do like sitting at this table, soaking up someone else's family's energy. My parents seem so happy, but every once in a while I get a little glimpse of a life I might like to have instead when I grow up.

The chili is great—spicy but not painfully so—and Fran's dad tells us about some giant lawn he started working on today. A landscaping business originally sounded boring to me, but as he talks about planning out the plants and the layout of the yard, I actually think about theater and filling a stage and how so many things in life aren't that different. I'm not sure why that hits me as special, but by the time Fran's mom sends us on our way with dessert—chocolate pudding with little wafer cookies—I'm feeling kind of blissed out from everything. And that's before I even start eating the pudding.

"Your parents are great," I say, and she nods.

"It's true. I'd love to complain about them but..." She shrugs. "What about yours?"

"I don't know. They're really happy, and they love us a ton, and we don't actually fight that much. Penny's so perfect, though—I mean, you saw her! Sometimes I feel like the practice kid, you know? The thing about the first pancake or whatever? Penny's the pancake they got right."

"Lydia," Fran says, "you are a very good pancake."

That's the most romantic thing I've heard in a very long time, but right now Fran's door is wide open so I just smile and eat my pudding.

Chapter Eleven

Sometime later, Fran comes back from taking the pudding bowls to the kitchen with a gleam in her eyes.

"You look dangerous," I say, and she laughs.

"Guess who decided they want to go out to a late-night movie," Fran says, and the air in her room shifts, and I find myself flustered again even though this is exactly what I woke up thinking about. Well, this plus sisterly guilt.

"You get that I haven't before, right?" I ask. "With a girl, I mean."

"If you don't want to—"

"No, it's like all I want right now," I say, even though the truth's that I want a whole bunch more. But this is a good start.

"Me too," she says, sitting down next to me on the bed and kissing me like we're still in the middle of it, like there was no hour-long break to eat dinner and dessert. "Also we can slow down or stop at any point, you know."

"Of course," I say, but I do like that she says it and that I feel safe here. We fall back into kissing, back onto the bed and each other, and our clothes come off and we slip under the covers. I forget to be nervous because—well, it's just *good,* not just Fran's hands and mouth on me, but mine on her, too. It feels like discovering something together, and I guess it is, figuring out what feels good for someone else as they figure you out. It's teamwork. Sexy teamwork.

"I'm glad your parents went out," I say afterward, and we both laugh.

"Yeah, me too." She shoves her hair back from her face and sits up a little. "Do you need to get home?"

I laugh. "Are you trying to get rid of me?"

"Definitely not, just trying to be considerate."

"Yeah, you've been pretty considerate tonight," I say, and she grins. "But, no. I'm good for a while."

"Good," she says, settling back next to me. "Can I ask you something?"

"Of course. What's up?"

"Why wouldn't you tell me what your favorite movie is the other day?" she asks, and I burst out laughing. "What's so funny?"

"Again, I just thought it was going to be something . . . you know, sexual?" I keep laughing. "I feel like I'm really disappointing you in my lack of movie talk in bed."

"There's nothing disappointing about you in bed," Fran says, and *oh yes* this is a line, but it's a good one. "I'm just curious. I love movies, and hearing what other people like, I dunno. It's interesting."

"Yeah, but you're, like, a film person," I say. "I just like stupid stuff, Pixar movies and superheroes and sometimes old musicals."

"None of that stuff is stupid," Fran says quickly. "I'm not that kind of film person, Lyds. Do I seem like that?"

"I don't know, maybe? I thought all film people were like that."

"Yeah, trust me, a lot of them are. You're expected to love all these serious directors—and they're all male, of course—and anything fun or lighthearted's crap. Believe me, I'm not like that."

"What kind of movies do you want to make?" I ask her, and it's funny how personal it still seems after the night we've had together and considering we're lying naked next to each other still.

"I love movies where everyone's really sharp and funny and it's still romantic as hell," Fran says. "Like if I could make movies like Nora Ephron did but they're about queer people instead."

"Who's Nora Ephron?" I ask, and Fran makes a horrified face. "See? Film people!"

"No, sorry, I'm just surprised. *Sleepless in Seattle? You've Got Mail?* Any of that sound familiar?"

"I feel like my mom loves those movies," I say.

"Yeah, exactly. That's how people treat me when I say it, like that's not what serious filmmakers should aspire to. And then I think, shit, are they right, am I wasting my time?"

"Just because I'm a movie idiot doesn't mean you're wasting anything," I say, and she smiles lightly.

"Come over next week and watch movies with me?" she asks, and I nod. "I promise I won't be a film jerk."

"I mean, you might need to be, a little. I really am pretty stupid."

"You say a lot of things like that," Fran says, sounding serious. "And you know that you're not. I know your sister's some overachieving type, but—"

I kiss her because I don't want to talk about Penny's or my flaws, but also because there's something in Fran's voice that's so warm and kind. Even if we're never serious, even if whatever this is between us is as fleeting as the summer, I love that she sees me this way.

~

The house is dark when Fran drops me off, but Penny's up when I get to our room.

"How'd your project go?" she asks.

"Great," I say, and manage to laugh at that only a little. "How was your night?"

"Grace and Oscar took me out for ramen," she said. "I knew it was a common dine-out cuisine in Japan, but I didn't realize it was so different from those blocks of instant noodles at the grocery store. I feel like my life's been changed by a soft-boiled egg."

"Oh my god, Penny Jones admits to not knowing something!"

"What do you mean?" She puts down her iPad and frowns. Penny, unlike me, wears contacts for her terrible vision, but I've learned this summer that she switches out at night when she's reading in bed, so she's peering over the tops of her lenses like an old-fashioned disappointed schoolteacher. "I don't know everything."

"In no way is that true," I say. "I'm afraid to even say what I don't know because you're always ready with a whole cited source."

"I am *not*," Penny says, though she continues to frown. "Is that what you think?"

"It's how it *is*," I say, and it's funny to me that I'm being so honest right now, because normally all I want to do around Penny is protect myself at every given opportunity. I tell myself it's because it's been a night of honesty and vulnerability in a lot of ways, definitely not that I'm being extremely dishonest about one specific thing in my life right now and a little honesty with Penny elsewhere couldn't hurt. Definitely not that at all.

"Name an example," Penny says.

"Do we have to fight right now?" I ask, getting under the covers. All I want to do is close my eyes and think about Fran.

"We're not fighting. I just don't think this is something I do, and you're saying it is, so—"

"Pen, you're like this about *everything*. Except when I'm feeling, like, extra optimistic, I've decided against even trying to figure out what I want to do in college because all you do is tell me how what I want to do is throwing my money away. The other week when—"

"Lydia, I never meant you shouldn't study whatever you wanted in college. I assumed you were only considering theater tech programs. It was just interesting information I thought I'd share with you."

I sigh. The truth is that I know this. Penny's never out to hurt anyone, or I wouldn't be here sharing this tiny space with her. Penny, of course, means well and wants everyone to succeed. But it's not as if her words don't have consequences, haven't made me assume my future plans are stupid and that I should give up now. No matter what she intends, when she tells me these things, sometimes I have to wonder what I'm even doing. More than sometimes. Who am I to think I can defy the odds? It doesn't matter if Penny's not trying to kill my dreams when it seems obvious that maybe some of my dreams should be put out of their misery.

Ugh, I could kill my sister for somehow getting me to this mindset and not the one I planned on falling asleep with tonight—the one where I replay tonight at Fran's in my head over and over on a loop. Then I remember that if I wasn't sneaking around and could actually talk to Penny about Fran that everything would be different.

But no. When I think about tonight, all the moments where it was only Fran and me, even if this were a normal night, back home, with no rules in place about who we didn't date, I wouldn't share tonight with anyone else anyway.

ᐯᐯ

Penny wakes me up early the next morning, my only other day to sleep in. What is happening to my summer.

"I want to do something nice for you," she says.

"Letting me sleep would have been a great start."

She waves her hand dismissively. I'm too sleepy to wave mine back. Penny's determined, though, and it must be because of what I said last night, because to Penny being nice isn't letting me do what I actually want but instead some kind of arranged activity she thinks is good for me.

Luckily all she's seemed to have arranged is a walk to get breakfast tacos, and she explains that Grace and Oscar told her if we didn't go early we'd have to wait in a long line outside in the hot sun. I think of going to Joy with my friends the other night and wonder how everyone keeps track of what time you're supposed to eat where. But once I'm eating fresh flour tortillas stuffed with eggs and beans and cheese and potatoes, I find it hard to be annoyed about anything.

"Fine," I say between bites of tacos. "This is better than sleeping in."

"Sometimes I'm right," Penny says, and then laughs, and I crack up because it's like something's different now. I think the no boy summer might actually be working. We walk back and borrow Grace's car, and Penny drives out to the beach, which takes longer than it did the other night, even though it's a Sunday and why is there traffic on a Sunday? I have no idea if this is the same beach or a different one because I'd been pretty distracted that night, and today it's easy to sit on a towel on the sand and stay present. I don't even look at my phone until we're back in the car, a little sunburned and sleepy, and it's fine that Fran hasn't texted. It's casual and it's nothing that would interfere with the goals Penny set for us.

Everything's somehow going perfectly.

Chapter Twelve

When we have downtime at Grounds Control on Monday, Grace heads to the back to do some paperwork, and Margaret gives me a very serious look.

"Did you get those videos I sent you last night?"

Margaret had clearly spent her Sunday evening going down some kind of latte art rabbit hole on YouTube, but the good news is that it was a really safe topic so I sat next to Penny and watched them all with her once we were home from the beach and slathered in aloe.

"Sorry, I meant to respond," I say. Friendship maintenance still feels new to me, and I'm not always sure, given the rhythm of the group text (very all or nothing), what the right one-on-one friend vibe is. It is possible I'm overthinking this part, but I don't want to take any chances.

"Want to try while it's quiet and while Grace can't laugh at us?"

I agree, and we pull some shots and foam extra milk. Margaret tries first since she's got way more experience. It's still pretty magical for me to watch an image emerge from just the careful tipping of steamed milk into a mug, but as the lumpy drawing appears, I can't help but laugh.

"Well, *you* try, then," Margaret says, though she's laughing so hard that she wipes her eyes on her apron.

I run a Google image search for rockets and take a stab at it. Margaret's so much more natural at it, but the physics of it are starting to make sense to me. I've built sets out of practically nothing, formed castles and city skylines starting out of scraps. It feels right that I should be able to uncover the shapes possible in espresso and foam.

"Do you know about this street festival early next month?" Margaret asks, as we laugh at my sad attempt. It's worse than hers by a lot. "I know there's always a thousand things going on here with food trucks where you can't tell if it's a festival or not, but this one is legit."

"I don't know anything about it," I say.

"We go every year," she says. "There's a ton of food trucks and little booths from local vendors, and local bands play. And even though stuff like that can get, like, super clichéd and hipstery, it ends up not being like that too much because old people come, and families bring little kids."

"Sounds fun," I say.

"Oh, yeah, you're totally going with us, no way out of it," she says. "Anyway, I need your advice, though!"

"What do you need *my* advice on?" I ask, and she turns bright red. "Wait, is this about a boy?"

"Ohmygod," she says in a whispered rush. "There's this boy from school I always—well, he's really cute. We had a lot of classes together and I always hoped one day he'd look at me and say, 'Margaret Kim, I find you very smart and cute.'"

"*And?*"

"I ran into him yesterday when I was running errands with my mom after work—I know, so embarrassing—and for some reason, the festival came up—oh my god, now that I remember, *my mom* brought it up? Anyway, he said something about hoping he'd see me there."

"That's a good sign," I say.

"I was hoping you'd say that," she said, her cheeks flushing. "I trust your boy judgment. I mean, it would have been better if he'd said the smart and cute thing—well, maybe not if my mom was there!"

"It's a good sign," I say again, genuinely. "Also you *are* very smart and cute."

I worry immediately it's a weird thing to say, but she beams.

"So I was thinking of asking him to come with all of us," she says. "Not like a date, obviously, it's all of us. Is that weird? It's not like he and I have talked that much, but we were always friendly in school. And he's going to college in San Francisco, so I know we're not going to end up dating seriously or—whatever, I just want to have a date and kiss a boy before I go to college. I'll feel better if I do."

"You should totally ask him," I say. "And we can help take the pressure off. I could, like, invite Fran or something, too."

I say it way too casually and it comes off as calculated as it is. This is the thing about having friends, I'm realizing. They see right through your normal tricks.

"Mmmmhmmm, sure, you could just, like, invite Fran," Margaret says. "What's up there?"

I shrug. "We're just having fun, remember? So we're having fun."

I mean, we are having *a lot* of fun.

"Is that what you want, though?" Margaret refills the frothing pitcher and begins foaming more milk. "Pull some more shots. I feel like we're getting close."

I tap out the used grinds and tamp in fresh ones. The whole routine of it is so regular and already has become comforting. "I like having fun. And I know what I'm doing. There was this guy I went out with the other year who never had girlfriends, but I knew how to handle it."

"Ohhhh, you think you're the girl who's gonna tame Fran Ford." She grabs the mug from me and tips in the milk. "It *is* good to have goals!"

"I'm not stupid," I say. "If that's what you're thinking."

"Oh my *god*, Lyds, never. You're the one with all the experience who knows everything about handling romance. I just think that Fran in particular is . . . a lot to handle."

I can't help but grin at that, and Margaret catches me.

"Guard your heart, Lyds."

"My heart's fine." I think about what it would have been like, working with Margaret, being friends with Margaret, when Tate dumped me. Penny was there for me, of course, but this is different. It's extra backup, and heartbreak can use as much backup as it can get. It would have been better.

"But thank you," I add. "It's nice that you're looking out for me."

"Always! It's kind of fun to worry about your potential drama. We've been kind of a drama-free group for a while."

"What about this boy?" I ask. "Potential *good* drama lurks there, right?"

Margaret blushes even more. "Don't jinx it!"

"Can you ask him to do something that's sooner than next month? It's so far away."

"No, I'm good with the wait," she says. "I need some time to prepare."

The door opens, and somehow it's Fran. Margaret elbows me and grabs the cleaning supplies to tidy up the self-service station.

"Hey," I say.

"Hey." She runs her hand through her hair, though it flops right back over her forehead, almost over one of her eyes. I haven't seen her since Saturday night, since we kissed goodbye in her truck at the end of Grace and Oscar's block, the easiest spot to pull over to let someone out, and also to make out with no one noticing.

"How many Post-its do you have today?" I ask, casual, definitely not like the last real conversation we had was while we were underneath her covers.

"None right now," she says. "I'm running some errands, but I thought I'd come by and say hey."

"Well, mission accomplished," I say, and we're both grinning. It's very cute that Fran can look so cool and laid-back, but her smile is so *real*. It doesn't look forced or perfected, it's just *hers*. And it's for me. Just like her being here.

"I can make you a drink," I offer. "Whatever you want. I mean, don't go crazy or anything."

"Practice a rocket in her drink," Margaret calls.

"Is...that a euphemism?" Fran asks, and we all laugh. Even Margaret.

The drink doesn't turn out very well, but Fran still smiles when I give it to her.

"Is this the rocket?" she asks.

"I think when you don't have to ask, that's when it's the rocket," I say. "See you."

"See you," she says. "Oh, I was thinking..."

It's a really bad fake casual tone, and I love everything about it.

"If you want to come over some night this week to watch movies, it should be good with my schedule." She shrugs, messing some more with her hair. It's extremely cute. "Just text me what's best for you. If you still want to."

"Obviously I still want to," I say. Maybe that's too eager, but I feel caught up in the moment and I think for Fran this is eager. She's started to feel safer to me, I realize. I don't have to be so careful with every single emotion in front of her.

"Great, text me later then," she says, and heads out. I feel pretty good for how I'm handling everything but then I make eye contact with Margaret, who cracks up, and I feel messy and lovestruck and so painfully obvious about all of it. And it's not at all how I promised Penny I'd behave, but I really love all of it, right down to the unrecognizable rocket.

"You're hopeless," Margaret says. The truth is, though, that I feel like I'm the opposite—so full of hope I could burst.

$\sim$

Penny wants to hit up the library again early in the week, and even though I have yet to do anything with my newfound filmmaking knowledge, I agree because—well, a lot of reasons. I like riding the train next to my sister, watching the landscape shift and feeling like it's shifting something in us. I like sitting with a notepad and a stack of books, like I'm cosplaying as a smart girl. I like afterward when Penny consults Yelp and figures out the perfect place for food. It doesn't matter that much to me if I never get up the nerve to ask Fran about her movie or if she never shares it with me. It doesn't feel like a lie when I'm still learning.

But, also, if I'm honest, I'm trying to make something up to Penny. No matter that Fran's not a boy, it's not like I believe in my heart that I'm respecting the rules of the summer. And the group text is setting up some big Friday night hangout, and even though friend group stuff is still new and vaguely scary to me, I want to go. And of course if Fran's serious about watching movies, that's another night where I'll be busy. Penny and I never said explicitly that this summer wasn't just about avoiding boys but about *not* avoiding each other, but I'm pretty sure it's supposed to be baked in. And here I am, sometimes doing every single thing *but* hanging out with her. So whatever Penny asks, if I can, I'll do it.

"Grace and Oscar sent some restaurant recommendations," I say as we leave the library for the night. "Do you want to pick one? Or I can pick. I know you love Yelp but—"

"I don't *love Yelp*," she says, and I laugh at her impression of me. I don't feel like a specific enough person that anyone could even *do* an impression of me, and it's kind of delightful. "It's just the safest way to choose."

"You don't always have to completely cut risk out of your life, Pen," I say. "Aren't those blonde women you listen to always saying stuff like jump over a wall and cut through the clouds and break the ceiling?"

"I think part of that is a Carly Rae Jepsen song, but, yes, point taken." Penny folds her arms across her chest and sighs. "Sure. You pick lunch. From the curated list sent to us by Grace and Oscar."

I'm not actually ready for this level of responsibility, but the two of them intensely messaged about Grand Central Market, so we make our way east with the help of our phones. It turns out to be a food court and market, dozens of restaurants and delis and produce stands all jammed into this huge building, and people crammed all over. We get into line for falafel wraps and carry our trays outside back into the lingering evening sunshine. Up in the suburbs I spent a lot of time in the air-conditioning, but in LA I like it outside, with the heat and the noise and the smell of the city, even though I know it's just from cars and pollution or whatever. Home no longer feels clean in a real way—there's something sanitized about it. And I guess I'm starting to like how LA feels *real.*

"I like it here a lot," I say, after we're stuffed from lunch but still waiting in line to get coffees from a stand. Coffees from a stand! I had no idea I wanted this, all the fun stuff about city life. "Not just this market. LA. I always thought it sucked, but it doesn't."

"It definitely makes me want to live somewhere with a good public transit system," Penny says. "Do you know there's one top theater tech school in LA, and one in between here and home?"

I shrug, because at one time I *had* known that, before it got realer and more impossible. "Wait, did you do research for me?"

"There are good schools all over the country, though, not just LA," she says once she's ordered and we're waiting to pick up our drinks. "I'm sure that given your background, if you can do well on your SATs and maybe add another extracurricular this fall before applications go out, you'll have a shot at plenty of them."

"Penny, are you like a clone? Like the opposite of an evil clone? I want to talk to the real Penny."

"Clones are identical in DNA, so I'd still be the real Penny if I were a clone," she says, but then laughs.

"You're such a nerd."

"Yes, *obviously,* Lydia." She smiles at me. "I never thought you needed my support or blessing or anything, you know. No one in the family is like you."

"What's that supposed to mean?" I ask, because, sure, Mom and Dad are fun to make fun of, but if I ever thought of the whole family as separate units, it was us v. them, not everyone else v. me.

"Creative," she says. "We all like numbers and situations where things have a right or a wrong answer. But you're someone who goes into an empty theater and knows what to add to create a whole show."

"I don't create *the whole show*," I clarify.

"You do a lot, from nothing," she says. "So you didn't seem like someone who was looking for support from me for college. Not to say that you were asking for my support. Just that—"

"I know what you mean," I say. "Pen...you *do* say things all the time that sound mean or like you think I'm an idiot or that my whole life's a joke."

I can't believe I just *say this* to Penny, but instead of getting visibly mad or crying like I probably would if someone said something like that all at once to my face, she calmly collects our coffee milkshakes from the bar (recommended strongly by Oscar) and walks by my side as we roam back through the building.

I have no idea what she's feeling, but it makes me realize something. It wasn't just that boys were all Penny and I had before, it was that boys felt *safe*. Penny could scoff at my interests and life goals—well, she seemed to, at least, though maybe I was off base there—but she was never like that about boys, even when I did objectively stupid things. If I was able to be honest with Penny right now, she wouldn't reprimand me that I'd been warned that Fran was a player and I was setting myself up to get hurt. She'd ask about the invitation to watch movies, about the way Fran looked at me every time I sat down in her truck, how I'd felt a connection from the first time we met.

"Penny," I say while she's examining a display case of fancy cheese. Yes, I'm very worried she's going to hold up the rules of the summer to prove I can't keep seeing Fran, but maybe the risk is worth it to *talk* about this, and not just with Margaret but with someone who knows my history. Someone who's *safe*. "I should tell you—"

"Don't apologize," she says quickly. "It's good that you said how you feel. I think that we've both made a lot of assumptions about one another, and I've realized that's very easy to do with the person you've known the longest. I never assumed you needed or wanted my approval about anything, so I didn't think much of how I—anyway. I'm sorry if I ever kept you from pursuing something important to you."

I run right into a pole I'm so stunned by her words, and then I'm double-stunned because I *ran into a pole*. Penny manages to help me without laughing (much) and we get back outside and laugh together until we cry, though luckily my very organized sister has some ibuprofen in her bag because I'm definitely going to have a headache later. And the giggly ride back to Highland Park is worth more than any relationship advice I could get from Penny.

Chapter Thirteen

Margaret is standing next to me when I check my phone during some downtime, and so she sees me tap frantically to my newest messages from Fran once I see her name on my home screen.

"Oh, Lyds," she says, practically cackling.

"Don't," I say, though it's mainly just because Grace is nearby and because it's a little fun being teased like this and I want to do my best to play my part. I guess I'm not trying *too* hard to be someone else. After all, sometimes it hits me how being myself has worked fine so far with Margaret and her girl gang.

"Wait, *what?*" Margaret's eyes are huge, and I realize she's reading my messages, and I elbow her. "Sorry, it was too tempting. But *Fran Ford* is asking you over to watch *Sleepless in Seattle* and *You've Got Mail?*"

"Yeah, she's into the filmmaker or whatever," I say, because I'm trying to be a less-obsessed person this summer, and I have consciously not googled every single reference Fran's ever made, unlike when I started going out with Tate and, knowing he loved the *Fast & Furious* franchise, made Penny watch every single one of those car movies with me over one weekend.

"*Lyds,*" Margaret says and literally throws her hands in the air. "Those are *super romantic movies.*"

"It's about *filmmaking*," I say, and Margaret practically collapses into giggles. Luckily, the door opens and we've got customers again, and it keeps Margaret from teasing me too much.

We end up walking over for pizza together once we're off, and I notice how easy it's been to be friends with Margaret. I'm glad I was honest with Margaret the other week, because there's less and less about hanging out with her that puts me on edge. It feels comfortable crammed into a little booth across from her, eating as much pizza as I want.

"Lyds," Margaret says, shaking a bunch of red pepper flakes onto her slice of pepperoni, "I think it's possible that Fran Ford actually *likes* you."

I smile and tap back to my texts. "I really think this is just about movies. If you like romantic movies, it doesn't make every situation about those movies romantic, you know?"

"Sure, sure. But. Fran's not stupid, she knows how it comes across to invite you over to watch movies about true love."

"Yeah, but Fran also comes *with warnings*," I say.

Margaret leans forward in her seat. "Wait, what warnings?"

I give Margaret the rundown of Fran's little speech on the beach, the stuff I would have told Penny before, and it's nice to finally have some of this out of my head.

"Yeah, whatever, she's a player," Margaret says. "But she does seem to actually like you. And I know *you* like her."

"I'm fine with whatever," I say quickly. "I mean, yeah, of course I like her. But I'll be an hour north at the end of the summer and—I don't know. It seems OK not to worry about any of that too much."

"Ugh, you're so mature," Margaret says. "Meanwhile I'm getting up the nerve to see if a boy will go to an outdoor festival that thousands of people will be at. Hundreds? I don't know, a lot."

"This stuff's just always been..." I shrug. "Easy? I hope that doesn't sound conceited. I didn't know what it would be like with a girl, but I guess it's actually about the specific person, not just their gender. Which makes sense, if gender's not some exact specific thing that applies to everyone, it's not like people are, either."

"See? So mature. Meanwhile, I'm like, how long is it safe to look at someone's lips if you're not sure you're ready to kiss them yet, but also to let them know if they did want to kiss, it'd probably be fine."

"Five seconds," I say, in my most serious Penny-like voice, and Margaret's eyes widen. "I'm kidding, don't write that down or anything."

"Hang on, I'm going to look at your lips for five seconds and let's see how weird it is," she says, and opens the stopwatch app on her phone. It's definitely weird, and we try not to shriek with laughter in the very small space.

I'm so caught up in our conversation I stop thinking about—well, anything other than whatever we're talking about. But on my walk back to Grace and Oscar's, I start to wonder whether maybe if my focus hadn't been so much on boyfriends once boyfriends were possibilities that—I don't know. Is it a coincidence that once I was completely single in this completely different way that I ended up in an awesome friends situation? Not like I stayed *completely single* for long, though that feels different too, and like I told Margaret, not because Fran's not a boy.

My brain feels overloaded with thoughts, so I take advantage of the empty house and turn on one of my playlists, loud, and flop down on my bed. But it's hard for me to hang onto this *regret* or whatever it is for too long, because there are a lot of things that are more fun to think about. College in a year, maybe right here in LA. Staying in touch with Margaret and everyone else once they're all scattered around the country in the fall. Watching romantic movies with Fran, no matter the reason. Actually—

I text Penny first. *I was going to work on some film stuff with Fran tonight, but I wanted to check in with you to make sure you didn't have anything planned for us.*

I'm technically not lying at all.

Thanks for asking. I was actually thinking about watching a Dodgers game at the Greyhound after work with some coworkers. Good luck with the film!

So Fran picks me up around five, and I slide over to sit right next to her for the short ride to her house. We're the only ones home, but she still leads me to the living room and pulls DVDs off of the shelf. I guess I'm more than *technically* not lying to Penny.

"Thanks for coming over," Fran says as she's getting everything set up, the sound system on, the lights dimmed a little. "I can make popcorn, if you want."

I grin at her.

"What?" she asks.

"You're really cute," I say, and she sits down next to me on the couch. "Wait, where's my popcorn?"

Fran laughs and leans in to kiss me before getting up. "Butter? Salt?"

"Yes and yes," I call as she walks into the kitchen. Is this what it would be like, I wonder, if Fran becomes my actual girlfriend? I guess I still feel like it's not something to even hypothesize about. Fran's speech worked on me, even if she was just doing her *no relationships* thing, and even if I'd also been playing a part to win her over. The speech combined with the player comments from Margaret—it was a lot to ignore. But now that I'm here on her couch with popcorn popping in the microwave and movies she wants to share with me, things feel different.

"OK, I know you think these are movies for moms, so I'm glad you're giving them a chance," Fran says, walking back into the room with a bowl of popcorn and sitting back next to me on the couch. "At least I hope you're giving them a chance."

"I'll totally give them a chance," I say. "And I didn't say they were *movies for moms,* just that my mom liked them. And I guess it did surprise me since I always feel like film people are so serious. No one in REACT—that's the theater tech club—even talks to the film people; they're all terrifying."

"I believe it," Fran says. "I stopped doing much with the film club at my school because the guys seemed to run everything, and they didn't respect the kinds of movies I cared about and wanted to make."

She laughs and looks away. "I mean, and I stole all of their girlfriends."

"*Fran,*" I say, feeling weirdly proud. That can't be the healthiest reaction.

"Well, not *all* of them," she says, looking back to me. "Plus girls aren't property and they can hook up with whoever they want. And who would want to kiss someone who won't shut up about Christopher Nolan when I'm around instead?"

"You're my hero," I tell her, and she laughs and leans in to kiss me. "So are those the kinds of movies you want to make? Romantic comedies?"

"Someday, maybe, yeah," Fran says. "I don't feel ready yet, and not just because I haven't really had a big love story yet."

I don't mean to but I let out a bit of a snort at that, at the note of longing I don't miss in her voice. Her super casual voice.

"What?" Fran asks.

"Fran, you don't *want* a big love story!" I say, even though I know we sort of have this unspoken agreement not to talk about this stuff. She was honest with me, I've never pushed back or even hinted I wanted something else—if I even *do* want something else, which I'm not completely sure of—and I might be risking something to say it.

"That's not true," Fran says quickly. "It's not like relationships with rules and whatever are what makes a real love story. I'm not shut off to that."

"You kind of are," I say, even though *why am I doing this?* Things are really good, especially this afternoon, the sofa and the popcorn and the movies on-deck. "You do your whole no-relationships speech right at the beginning, stopping stuff like as it's starting."

"I didn't stop anything with you," she says with a little grin, and I can't help kissing her. Honestly, I can't help much around Fran.

"Anyway, it's not just that I haven't had some huge love story yet," she says. "I can tell I'm about to nerd out hard in front of you about Nora Ephron, but something I love about her movies is that the characters feel like they've already had whole lives before we meet them, really specific lives with private jokes and things they already love. And I'm eighteen and have never really left my hometown, so I feel like I have... more life in front of me before I can do something like that."

"Yeah, but...your hometown's *Los Angeles*," I say. "You're not stuck in the middle of nowhere, not experiencing anything."

"Sure, but there's a lot more I hope is in front of me," she says. "The thing is, these guys at school, and probably at all the film schools I didn't get into—didn't even apply to—they talk about the films they love in terms of how important they are, you know? And I guess I just don't know what's more important than who you are and who you love."

I watch her as she talks, her eyes wide, her hands moving.

"And these movies...they get that. She got that, you can tell in the writing and directing, how people matter more than the rest of it. And I can know that but also know I'm not ready to fully *do that*, because her work has this confidence about it. I'd kill for confidence like that."

"Me too," I say.

"They're not perfect," she adds, pushing her hair back as it flops into her eyes. "The movies. Everything's all really white and straight and cis and rich, but in some ways that just inspires me more. If I could find a way to talk about people like me, show how it can all still be really smart and moving and funny..."

I realize I'm staring at her, but it's getting harder and harder to look away. She obviously realizes this too, the staring part at least. Maybe the difficulty in focusing anywhere else as well.

"What?" she asks with a smile.

"I mean, Fran. You were just this cute girl who showed up at work and ended up being a really good kisser. I didn't know you were— you're—I just feel like you're really amazing."

"No," she says, her cheeks flushing. "Enough of me. First movie? Popcorn?"

"Sounds perfect," I say. Fran starts *Sleepless in Seattle,* and at first I wonder how I'm supposed to get too wrapped up in middle-aged people from thirty years ago, except all of a sudden I just *am,* I want everyone to fall in love the way I want to fall in love, big and a little messy and forever. And, like Fran said, *specific,* I realize. I want someone to like all the dumb things about me, not just that I'm cute and good at kissing and kissing-related activities. I want someone worth flying across the country for, someone worth embarrassing scenarios and enduring your friends knowing exactly what you're up to.

It was easy to call Fran out on shutting down relationships before they could even start, but I wonder if I'm any better. What's real or honest or *specific* about hoping every single person is the one without giving them any time to actually *become* someone to me?

"Next movie, or do you need a break?" Fran asks once the credits are rolling and I'm pretending I'm not crying from the happily ever after of it all. I guess really it's just a *happy right now,* which is more honest and hopeful. The two of us might be bad at that—Fran shutting down so early, me trying to skip to the finish—but sitting on the couch together feels right in the middle. It feels like a happy right now.

"I don't need a break," I say, and Fran laughs at the tears in my voice and gives me a kiss before getting up to change the discs. The front door opens almost as soon as Fran hits play, and her mom walks in and waves to us.

"Oh, I love this one," she says. "Hi, Lydia. Did Fran tell you I'm the one who got her hooked on movies to begin with?"

"Mom loves taking credit," Fran says, but she smiles.

"Did you two eat yet? And where's your brother? I think your dad's working late."

Fran pauses the movie. "No, we haven't eaten, and I have no idea where Alex is. Should we go finish this in my room?"

I try not to smile at how cute it is watching cool-as-hell Fran get snippy with her mom. To be fair, though, is there anything about Fran I *don't* think is cute? Doubtful.

"I could order Thai, sound good? Lydia, I know you're good with spicy."

"Yeah, I'm good with spicy," I say, feeling like I've passed some kind of test.

"Thai's fine," Fran says, and I laugh at the impatience in her voice, though it does make me miss Mom and Dad, sitting on my own couch, figuring out dinner, getting a little annoyed. Home seems as far away as Mom and Dad do. But also Fran feels so comfy, so easy to be with, just a girl with things she loves and a family that gets on her nerves and time she's set aside just for me. It's hard to feel too homesick when I'm next to her.

Fran starts the movie again, but her mom keeps asking questions about what she's ordering via an app on her phone, so Fran pauses again until the order's submitted. Her mom hangs out with us and laughs and gasps at all the same parts I do, so it doesn't feel weird to have her there like it does sometimes when parents don't give you any space. Plus no matter what Margaret thought about the movie selection, Fran isn't showing me these movies for some romantic reason. She's showing me what matters to her, a guide to understanding the art she wants to make herself.

Though to be honest, I guess that's pretty romantic, too.

Fran drives me home after the movie's over, after we're stuffed with pad see ew and curry and mango with coconut sauce. I wonder if this is a normal night for Fran, movies and dreams and family, what any girl who asked would get invited to, but for some reason, I don't think so. Maybe it's just wishful thinking, but this feels special and just for us.

"So what about you?" Fran asks, glancing over at me and then back to the road ahead. "Why do you like theater?"

"Oh," I say, caught off guard and feeling dumb. Have I ever spoken about *anything* as beautifully as Fran talked about movies today? "You don't have to ask."

"What do you mean, *I don't have to ask.* I want to know."

I shrug, even though her eyes are on the road. "It's this thing you build together, I guess. Not, like, *literally* build together—though, that too. It's that you all start with this completely empty stage, and then all the teams together figure out how to make it—well, something, you know? Lights and sets and costumes and that's all on top of the actors and the script and in musicals all the songs. It's like we're all making something pretend together and everyone just agrees to be in on it and commit to it like it's the realest thing ever, for people behind-the-scenes, people onstage, even people just watching. And it's always really stressful and someone's always in tears at some point and then it just ends up coming together. Like it's magic."

Fran parks her truck in her usual spot in the red zone at the end of my block. "Thanks for coming over."

"Thank *you*," I say. "I really hope you get to make the kind of movies you want to, Fran, but honestly I feel like anyone who'd try to stop you is an idiot."

She wraps an arm around my shoulders, pulls me close, kisses me, gentle and rough at the same time. "Thank you, Lydia."

"I should . . ." I slide over, open the passenger side door. "I had a really good time tonight."

"Me too."

I say good night and hop down from the truck. It's a short walk to Grace and Oscar's front door, but enough time to accept all the facts that flood my system in this, the first moment I've had alone for hours.

One: I promised my sister there would be no boys this summer, and while I've managed that just fine, one could make the argument that it was about falling for someone, kissing someone, dating someone, and while technically I'm upholding my promise, Penny would probably not see it that way.

Two: Fran Ford is not into relationships and seems determined not to be in one.

Three: By the end of the summer, I'll be an hour away.

The second and third items made the first one seem, well, doable— for the most part. This couldn't get out of hand. Maybe Penny wouldn't be thrilled if she knew, but how could my summer spin out of control if this was just temporary and fun?

But now there was a fourth fact that I could in no way deny.

Four: I was falling very, very hard for Fran Ford.

Chapter Fourteen

I feel so overwhelmed with my completely accidental feelings for Fran that I'm sure Penny will notice, but instead she wants to talk about the baseball game she just watched, and I let her discuss run production and on-base percentages and even do my best to actually pay attention.

Of course I should say something. That much is obvious. I'm not a genius like Penny, but I'm not completely stupid, and I know I probably still have some room for not being a terrible sister if I just lay it all out right now. After all, Fran's not my girlfriend, nothing is *serious*, and, unlike how everything else seemed this year, nothing's gone badly because of Fran. I have a job and new friends and I'm hanging out more with Penny than I ever have, even all those boy talks included.

But it's ... a lot. It's not just that Penny might see it as I broke the pledge. I'll have to come out to Penny, and she'll probably rattle off some annoying statistics about LGBTQ+ teens and the Kinsey scale. And, also, what if Penny says I have to stop seeing Fran for the rest of the summer? She might. And the summer is all Fran and I have anyway. Risking even a day of that—even for my sister—doesn't feel worth it.

~

Penny asks to reserve my whole Saturday, and I feel guilty that she asks in advance in a way that makes me feel like I haven't kept enough time reserved for her, period, in what's supposed to be our summer. I mean, if it is supposed to be our summer. Sometimes, believe it or not, I actually wish we'd clarified the rules more.

But we didn't, so there's Fran. Fran, who invited me over to watch Tom Hanks and Meg Ryan fall in love *twice*, who told me her dreams, who kissed me like it was an everyday occurrence, is again a girl I see almost every day at work for a few minutes and who hasn't texted me in days.

I can't even be mad, because Fran warned me! She hasn't promised me anything, but I think also there's a difference between not having a strictly defined relationship and just forgetting about me when I'm not convenient. Except I'm not even sure I can be mad about *that*, because she's busy and I'm busy too and why should I measure how much she likes me or respects me by how often she texts?

Obviously this is all stuff I'd discuss with Penny if I could. I know I could talk to Margaret and the rest of the group text, except that it's *Fran*, and they all have existing opinions of her, and also I don't want to admit that I'm no longer cool and casual about things and maybe I never was.

Initially I only agreed to a whole Saturday with Penny out of guilt, but now I'm glad to have some kind of all-day distraction ahead of me, glad to be on the train next to my sister where I can't stare at my phone willing the perfect message to come through. I can't be the girl who stays home to wait for that message anymore.

And not only because my sister is watching.

"I didn't bring my library stuff," I tell Penny. "You should have told me—"

"We're not going to the library," she says. "Though I do recommend keeping a notepad with you always."

"Of course you do," I say, though I feel rude and try to make it seem like a compliment.

"Are you OK?" Penny asks me, and I force myself to stop slouching and frowning, two things I didn't necessarily realize I was doing, but I'm definitely in bad mood mode.

"Sorry, I'm fine. Just not sure things are moving forward with the short film and I'm disappointed," I say, another true and *true* statement for Penny. "I hope you're not mad that my summer project might go nowhere."

She waves her hand. "Mine too."

"What? But you're doing all this baseball stuff with all your work people."

She scrunches up her face. "Yeah, I wanted to talk to you about that."

Please let Penny have a secret baseball boyfriend and then I can tell her about Fran and we'll be even!

"I just... I *like it,* Lydia," she says. "The statistics *are* interesting, but I'm barely thinking about them because there's so much about sports that's unpredictable and—I don't know. You'll laugh, but I think it's kind of beautiful. Yes, there are physics in a great pitch, but it's just incredible to watch, especially because people from the office are really nice about it all. I assumed there would be a ton of mansplaining, but there are people of multiple genders who watch games after work, and it's... it's *fun.*"

"You can like things just because they're fun and beautiful," I tell her.

"There are just so many risks in life," she says. "I thought I had it all figured out, or at least I was on the path to it. If everything I did had this proven and likely outcome, I'd have to succeed."

"I mean, you have—you are. You have straight As and everyone knows you can probably get into whatever college you want." I watch her for a moment, hardly understanding that Penny seems younger than me again. "But, like, I always thought you loved numbers and perfect outcomes and knowing all the facts of something. If you don't, then who cares if there's some guarantee that you'll become a fancy businesswoman? You should go like baseball and cute guys and—I don't know. Whatever else that isn't part of your whole MBA plan."

Penny sighs. "I don't know what else that would *be*. I'm not like you. Theater makes sense for you, and I see how much you love it. I don't have something like that."

"Well, maybe you have baseball," I say. "Or … libraries? Public transportation? Working in a fun office where people like to hang out after work, even if you're not super high-ranking or cutthroat? Being cutthroat sounds *terrible*."

Penny squeezes my hand. "You make it sound so not scary."

I squeeze back. "Penny, you're sixteen. You can decide way later if you want to be cutthroat and wear pantsuits and stuff. Right now you can just do stuff you enjoy. Especially since you're still going to get good grades and achieve shit. You do that in your sleep."

She looks like she has something to say to that, but then hops up. "This is our stop. Come on."

I follow her off the train into Downtown Los Angeles again, somehow one of my favorite places now. A few weeks ago I was overwhelmed by the noise and density of Grace and Oscar's neighborhood, and now that feels almost quaint compared to this part of the city. It's hard to believe soon we'll be giving this up and going back home where the closest thing there is to public transportation is a little train for kids that goes around our community park, and they really frown on teenagers riding it, especially if those teenagers are making out, not that I'd know from personal experience or anything.

Penny leads me to a complex that takes up a full block, and then up a couple flights of stairs where suddenly a whole little center is laid out. Pop-up restaurants, a little coffee shop, and—

"Three theaters?" I ask.

"Three theaters in one place," she says. "Don't get too excited, we're only going to one. I read reviews of the play that's running at the Mark Taper, and it's supposed to have an incredible set, and it seemed like something you'd like to see."

"Penny, this is..." I turn around to take in all of it, the theaters I'd heard about from classmates whose parents liked to drive into the city, from group road trips I hadn't been invited to. "This is so nice of you."

"I never meant to imply that you shouldn't pursue the education and career that you're interested in," she says. "I guess not everyone needs all of this information."

I nudge her. "I don't think even *you* need so much information sometimes. But this is amazing and I'm kind of overwhelmed, to be honest."

"There's a burger place we can go to for lunch," she says, pulling me by the arm.

"Let me guess, Yelp says it's the best option."

"No, one of my coworkers did. I'm being brave and trusting the opinion of one single person."

"You're going to think I'm kidding, but I'm actually very proud of you."

I treat to the burgers because Penny bought the theater tickets, and as we're waiting for our order, our phones both vibrate intensely, over and over and over. Normally that means there's some kind of terrifying local emergency, but I notice that this isn't happening to anyone else. It's just Penny and me.

"Oh god," she says, and laughs. "Mom and Dad docked somewhere today, didn't they? Greece?"

Penny's right. Mom and Dad are in Greece, and they must have been saving up messages for us, because it takes me over five minutes to scroll to the beginning of this chain. The photos are all pretty terrible because neither of our parents is any good at photography or even keeping their hands out of the frame at all times, but they look so happy. Mom and Dad are smiling in every single photo, and they look tan and way more relaxed than they normally do. I mean, normally they don't look relaxed at all. They're like Penny that way.

"Stop tapping the heart on every single one," Penny says. "You're blowing up my phone."

"You should be doing the same," I warn. "You know they love that shit."

Penny sighs heavily but begins doing the same, and soon we're laughing at this weird routine that we promptly abandon when our burgers and fries are ready. I text an explanation, and Dad responds right away. *Burgers always take priority! Glad you girls are having fun! Greece is so beautiful!!*

"The thing is, they're so happy," I say. "With their boring jobs and no friends and this being their first vacation together since—I don't know, before I was born?"

"What's your point?" Penny asks.

"I don't know, I'm just starting to feel like that happiness confused me somehow," I say. "I don't want that exact same kind of relationship, or not *just* that, you know? Not just the two of them doing the most prudent careers or whatever. It's still kind of weird to me that it's happened, but I like having Margaret and her friends in my life. And I also feel weird about *this*, but I still want to try to go to school for theater tech, even if I'm broke later, because that sounds less depressing to me than owning a house or whatever but having to do people's taxes."

"Obviously, of course," Penny says. "For you, that is. Not that I want to do anyone's taxes, either, but I understand why Mom and Dad chose it. And sometimes having or not having friends isn't a choice someone makes. It's how things work out."

I shrug, because Penny has a point. Up until a few weeks ago it all made sense to me, after all, and my new—and probably temporary—group of friends doesn't feel like a choice I made. They just happened. But I don't know how to explain that to Penny, since I barely understand it myself. I just know that it feels less strange with every passing day, and if it's in my power at all, I want a future filled with group texts and KBBQ nights out. That part—the part where I try—*is* up to me.

And, yeah, it's easy to think that now, of course, with my summer world where things are easy—well, most things—but it makes me more optimistic about the fall, about senior year, about finishing high school feeling slightly less like the only value I have is with REACT and being someone's girlfriend.

Not that I know what value I really have yet. But it can't be *none at all* if this summer so far has shown me anything.

Even if Fran still hasn't texted. I hate that I still notice that. It feels great to power down my phone once we're inside the small theater and forget about the world outside, even Mom and Dad and Greece.

Even group texts. Even non-girlfriends and whatever they're doing that's not texting you.

And that's what I love about theater anyway, how it's entirely its own world. I'd heard of productions at the Mark Taper Forum before, so I always pictured it as big and opulent, but it's a simple theater with fewer seats than our high school auditorium. Penny apologizes that our discount student tickets are way over to one side, but I love it, because once the show's started I can peer around the corner and watch actors enter from the wings and see the stage crew hustling around backstage. I like how the two things exist at once, the pretend world we're following onstage plus the things making it happen. I love following the story but also figuring out how they safely got actual water surrounding the set as a fictional flood encroaches.

After the curtain call, I'm worried Penny's about to start listing off flood safety facts or something, but she just smiles at me as we walk out of the theater.

"The reviews were right. I have no idea how they even built the set like that."

"Me either!" I smile at her, and I'm so happy that I don't even care when I turn on my phone that the dozens of new messages I have are all from my parents and my group text. I don't even notice how Fran's nowhere to be found, nope. I haven't thought of her in—no, seriously, I can't even trick myself with this one.

"Everything OK?" Penny asks. "There are a few dessert shops that aren't too far from here. Want to walk around a bit and get ice cream before we head back?"

"I'm great, because that sounds like the best plan in the world." I force myself to keep smiling, but then Penny *does* start listing off some flood statistics, and I can't stop laughing, and by the time we're eating soft-serve cones carefully so that they don't drip on our shoes, I realize that I do actually feel great again.

~~

I wake up on Sunday morning to an invite to breakfast tacos from the group text, and since I spent literally all of Saturday with Penny, I accept. I don't even feel guilty when I explain where I'm going when she sees me getting ready. OK, I feel a little guilty, especially after that discussion about friendship yesterday, but I say goodbye and walk over anyway. We somehow all arrive within a couple minutes of one another, and since it's not unreasonably early, the line's already down the block. Standing here with my new friends, though, I don't mind the wait. The wait's part of hanging out.

"So Lyds convinced me that I should definitely ask Lucas to the summer street fest," Margaret tells everyone, and I elbow her.

"I don't think I had to convince you too hard."

"Thank god we got a boy expert for the group," Ava says. "It's been pretty bleak."

"I don't like to think of myself as a boy expert," I say.

"Sorry, *person* expert," Margaret says.

"Hmmmph," Su Jin says. "I mean, you're in whatever scenario with Fran, who breaks hearts indiscriminately. That makes me feel like you might not be an expert with all genders."

"Harsh," Tara says, as Margaret shrieks. The hipster couple ahead of us in line shoots us looks for being loud and annoying, and I know we should care, but even in sort of getting insulted, I'm having way too much fun.

"Speaking of Fran," Su Jin starts.

"Wait, Ava, what are you wearing?" Tara interrupts.

Margaret reaches around me and pretends to make my glasses shoot off of my face in Ava's direction. "Wha-what?"

"Vintage Del Taco uniform shirt, I believe," Su Jin says.

"Oh, this?" Ava laughs, striking a pose. She's wearing it with a little bandana tied like a scarf, and I can't deny she looks great. "Yeah, fast food but make it fashion, right?"

"You are a constant gift," Margaret tells her, and squishes her into a hug. "I don't know what we're going to do when we're all in different cities, guys."

"I'm trying not to think about it," Tara says. "Especially since I'll still be here, and all of you will be spread out over the whole country."

"Lyds will be close," Margaret says, because Tara's going to USC, and Tara and I say, at the exact same time, "Well, *sort of.*"

"Actually," I say, as our group is first in line and Su Jin steps up to order first, "USC might be on my college list for next year. So I might have some questions for you."

"Yeah, just text, I'm happy to help," Tara says. "And once I'm on campus in September, you can drive down and I can show you around, too. It'd be cool if you ended up there next year. Are you thinking of their theater program?"

"Yeah, maybe," I say, holding my smile down as much as I can. "What about you?"

Tara shrugs, flipping her mane of hair out of her eyes. "Still figuring it out, public policy or urban studies or sociology, whatever hopefully lets me do some good for people in this city who need it."

"Our friends are all going to save the world," Margaret says. "While me and Lyds are getting arts degrees."

Ava holds her hands to her heart. "As if art doesn't save the world all the time."

"Also you've conveniently left me and my math degree out of this equation," Su Jin says, turning back to us, and we all laugh because no one can bring themselves to say that math can save the world at all.

I'm still smiling once we've all ordered and I'm following the rest of the group through the restaurant to find a table big enough for us. Of course it's just a simple offer from Tara, who I barely know, that she probably didn't think much of, but it feels like proof of something. The summer doesn't have to end with the literal summer.

"So, how's Fran stuff?" Su Jin asks me in kind of a pointed tone once we're all sitting down, and I remember that she got interrupted on this same topic before we noticed Ava's fast-food couture.

"It's fine," I say, instead of the truth, that sometimes she's all I can think of, that I thought we were getting somewhere together but I've barely heard from her in almost a week and so maybe we weren't headed to the same place, after all.

Tara and Su Jin exchange a look.

"What?" I ask, maybe not really wanting to know the answer.

"Yeah, what are you guys being all sneaky about?" Margaret asks. I'm relieved that whatever this is hasn't been discussed already among the whole group, minus me.

"I was at a party last night—"

"*We* were at a party last night," Su Jin says. "Since I was the only one who was willing to see that show downtown with Tara. We ended up at Lana Gilroy's party after, and Fran seemed to be there with some girl."

"It's fine," I say, even though maybe it's not? No, we haven't made any promises, so, technically, of course it's fine. No one's breaking any rules to anyone. I'm not falling for any boys, and Fran cleared her no-relationship rule with me from the start.

"I've been there," Tara says, and I'd wrap myself up in her understanding tone if it didn't mean admitting something I don't want to be true.

"I told you she's a player," Margaret says in a knowing tone.

"Yeah, yeah," I say, and I feel like I deserve an award because I just eat my breakfast tacos as they arrive and don't visibly freak out at all. I don't check my phone and I don't question anyone further. I just sit here and wonder if I actually understood the game at all.

And when I don't have that much fun, even after breakfast when we relocate to a cute pastry shop for fancy croissants, I feel like the biggest liar for a million reasons, not least of which is that if I were following the tenets of the no boy summer, my emotions wouldn't be so wrapped up in someone I fell for and I could actually appreciate this group of friends who hasn't let me down at all.

∿

Penny's out when I get back; she left a note that she's behind on podcasts and is taking a walk to catch up. I'm about to settle in for a midmorning nap when I notice a new text. *wyd family out*

"That's all I get?" I yell to myself, inside my head only, but I'm only so strong, because I type *Nothing, can you pick me up?* and before long I'm waiting outside again, like someone weak and desperate who never promised her sister an empowering summer. Boys have nothing to do with it; it's all about me and how much I can't hold on to reason or logic or my own ethics or whatever when there's someone I like on the horizon. More than on the horizon—in a pickup truck that's slowing down at the end of my block, that's waiting for me and me alone.

We didn't make any promises, I tell myself as I get in and slide over to join Fran. She said she wasn't for relationships and I told her I didn't want anything like that, either, I remind myself as we kiss before she pulls the truck back onto the street. Fran Ford hasn't violated anything. The rule-breaking and the morals-bending, that stuff is all me.

At Fran's, we don't hesitate. We don't talk. We're in her room right away, on her bed right away. And I keep reminding myself how good this is and how it's all I should really want and that the summer will be over before I know it and I'm getting all the good parts of it while I can.

"Are you OK?" Fran sits up a little. "You seem... somewhere else."

"I'm sorry," I say, and then my stupid heart warms because she's noticed even while it would be pretty easy not to. Fran's paying close attention to me.

"We can stop," she says. "Or do something else. Or—"

"This is... kind of embarrassing." I'm not as OK as I want to be, I'm realizing. I sent that text like I was fine, but even if Fran hasn't done anything wrong, I'm not fine. I'm in new territory because normally by this point, things have gone the way I've hoped they would. Even the boys that gave little speeches fell for me, wanted something more, weren't seen at parties kissing other girls. OK, no one said she was kissing other girls, but I'm not stupid.

"Don't be embarrassed," Fran says. "What's up? If you want to talk."

"So I know that we said this wasn't going to be anything—"

"I didn't say that," Fran says.

"That you don't do relationships or whatever," I say. "That you're just having fun for now."

"Ah. Sure."

"I guess... I guess maybe I'm not OK with it," I say, and add "anymore," even if I never was. Before I thought that's where we were both headed and Fran just needed a little direction. Now I'm the one who's lost her way. Or maybe I found it, this stupid annoying path I'm on where every fork in the road leads to Fran.

"Oh." Fran sighs and shrugs. "Lyds, you're... you're great but..."

"Oh," I say, because it seems impossible we're exactly where we started with Fran's little speech to me on the beach. It's not sex and it's not the time spent together and it's not confessing our dreams and what we love. But maybe all of these things together add up to something real and bigger between us. Regardless of what moved the needle for me, though, the needle's moved, and I hate that I'm the only one who thinks so. "I thought maybe since..." But listing it feels cheap, somehow. It's not like I completed a checklist and earned a girlfriend. Saying that I want more wasn't easy, but I knew the words. Why I feel that way is harder to verbalize.

"Not everyone needs a relationship," Fran says. "I'm eighteen, and it's not like I plan on getting married any time soon. There's nothing wrong with having fun."

"No, I get it," I say. "I'm not mad or think you're—I don't know. Betraying me somehow. It's just that I *like* you. I wish I could be cooler now, but I'd rather just be honest. I like you, and I wish you were my girlfriend."

Fran's still silent, and I can't tell if I've said too much. I can't believe how lost I feel when normally early relationship stuff is what I'm good at. I'd love to think that it's because she's not a boy, and I'm only used to boys, but the truth is that it just hasn't gone like this for me before. I've never had to say all of this out loud.

"I really appreciate how honest you're being," Fran finally says.

"But?"

She laughs. "But nothing. It's not like I've never had this conversation before, but . . . it's never been like this. It usually starts . . . pretty passive-aggressively. People get hurt even though I think I'm completely up front."

Fran's a player echoes again in my head.

"Well, then I'm glad I'm up front too," I say, and I think Fran catches my tone because she takes one of my hands and links her fingers through mine.

"That's not what I meant. It's not just that you're honest." She kisses me softly. "I like you too, Lydia."

"But?"

She shrugs. "But nothing! I feel like we've been having a good time."

"You can make things hard," I admit. "You kind of disappear and then you show up out of nowhere demanding my attention and—I don't know. I hate how excited I get when I see your name on my phone. I don't want it to be like that, where it's all up to you."

"It's not all up to me," she says, but I see a flash of recognition in her eyes. "Fine, you've got me there. I'm not great at other people, and that's not the only reason I don't have girlfriends, but—"

"It's not *not?*"

Fran grins. "A lot's felt out of my control the last year. The film club made me feel like shit, my friends all got into fancy schools I can't afford or probably even get into, and I'm worried I'm just gonna stagnate here in my childhood bedroom and take over my dad's business and not get to do any of the things I want to do."

"Those are, like, literally my exact fears," I tell her. "And it's even worse because I'd have to become a tax accountant."

She laughs. "Yeah, that is worse. But that's where I am. Worrying about someone else and her feelings and—I don't know. It sounds shitty when I say it like that, that my life's too hard to care about someone else. I care about you. I care about plenty of people."

"I'm not asking you to do anything you don't want to," I say, even though it sucks that she hasn't swooped me into an earth-shattering kiss by now. I wish she wanted this—wanted *me*, but I like her honesty, too. "I guess I just felt like … ugh, I don't even know what to say. If I were my sister, I'd have some logical reason for what I want with you, but that's not what I'm like. I like you. I love how you talk about movies and share them with me. I love how you seem to understand what I love about theater. I don't know why, logically, I wish I was your girlfriend and that you didn't disappear and reappear on your own schedule, but—"

"Do you think I care about *logic?*" Fran laughs and kisses me. "No offense to your terrible sister. Give me a chance, OK?"

"A chance at what?" I ask, hope blooming in my heart.

"A chance at this," she says. "Where you call me out on my bullshit and I call you my girlfriend and we see what it feels like."

"Yeah, I mean, I'll be back home before long," I say, trying not to explode into ecstatic smiles. The last thing I want to do is scare Fran off. "Right now it's just the summer."

"Your home's not so far," she says. "It's closer than that beach you made me take you to."

"I didn't have to twist your arm or anything," I say. "But I guess that's true. I just mean that I'm not trying to fast-forward ahead or claim you forever. It's just what I want now—if you want it too—and—"

"You don't have to keep explaining yourself," Fran says with a smile. "Though, seriously, I love your honesty. This feels like the most mature conversation I've ever had."

"I'm sorry to hear that," I say, and then we're both laughing and the air feels different, somehow. I realize that *this* is what I wanted from Fran—not some pledge forever, not the title of *girlfriend*—but an actual talk where I said what I actually felt. When she drives me back later, I think of how new I feel. I'm not the Lydia who threw everything at a new relationship, let myself get all absorbed in someone else like they were my only hope for a future. With Fran, my future still feels its own. I still feel like I'm *my own,* and it's because I'd never had that kind of talk before, never said all the hard complicated parts, never felt so honest and open.

And then I walk inside and see Penny and remember that I'm hardly some hero standing up for honesty. Maybe Fran will end up only being my girlfriend for the summer, but even that is pretty much the opposite of what I promised my sister.

CHAPTER FIFTEEN

Ever since Penny took me to the play downtown, I've known I have to do something nice for her in return. No, not that I <u>have to</u>, I <u>want to.</u> My sister had put together a day just because she thought I'd like it—and I loved it—and it sounds nice to do the same thing in return.

But it isn't just that. I kind of have to. I went through, like, an entire life arc, a bunch of relationship phases, and Penny knows nothing about it. And now that Fran and I have talked, now that we're trying out this new way of being together, things have changed. My phone buzzes more often with texts, and she tagged me in a photo when we went out late again for hot fudge sundaes and talked about film and theater. I know it's a gesture, like the increased texting, and I find it so cute it's hard not to talk about it. But I don't, because Penny can't know, because my friends—I'm positive—will not believe Fran's anything but *a player*, and so I try to stop smiling so much even though it's all I want to do. Even when I'm feeling massively guilty about Penny. Especially when I'm feeling massively guilty about Penny. My smile has its own ideas.

Penny is scarier to plan a surprise for than me. Penny has so many rules and regulations and logical policies about life. If I choose wrong, I expect a lecture or at least a recited list of facts I should have known. I spot a listing for some kind of women's empowerment podcast event, but it's expensive and also sounds terrible to me, so I tell myself it's

OK not to consider it. Then I overhear Penny and Oscar discussing something to do with baseball, and I realize this plan might be easier than originally anticipated.

I rarely see Oscar when Penny's not around, so I text him one morning when I have downtime at Grounds Control. From what Penny's told me, she works in a weird wing of her office building with old pieces of technology most of the company is happy to forget exists, so I know that Penny's likely not sitting next to him. *Can you help me figure out how to buy Dodgers tickets to take Penny to see a baseball game in person? Also is it really expensive? Also can you get there on the subway?*

"Hi, Fran," I hear Grace say, and I look up and try to make eye contact with her. But she's chatting with Grace without a look to me, and honestly I like this about her, how she gives her attention to whoever's in front of her, how she's so freaking *cool* but doesn't act the way so-called cool people do, withholding and aloof.

"Lydia, why don't you ring up Fran so Margaret and I can get started on all of these drinks," Grace says, and while I like the extra moment and eye contact this gives me with Fran—*my girlfriend*—I hate that I'm still slow enough at the espresso machine for Grace to make this switch.

"Oh, hey," Fran says when I take Grace's spot.

"Oh, hey, yourself," I say, smiling through my beverage speed concerns. All my concerns, really. I didn't know I could be so happy and concerned at the same time, but that's my whole life now. "Big BG day?"

"Huge," she says, sweeping her hair out of her face. It's one of her most frequent gestures, but I do feel a little literally weak in the knees whenever she does it. The way her forearm crosses her face, the way her fingertips drag through her hair. "Busy day here?"

"Not too bad. I just wish I was faster at everything."

"What are you talking about?" Grace appears next to me, grabbing something out of the cabinet under the iPad register system. "Fran, I'm sure you can tell that Lydia's doing great."

"Yeah, color me unsurprised," Fran says with a grin.

"I still feel new and slow," I say, though I'm on high alert, Grace and Fran and me all standing right here. I don't want Grace to have any idea of what's going on, but also I don't want Fran to know that I don't want Grace to have any idea of what's going on. I'd practically *begged* Fran for this, commitment-for-now and better communication and openness, and also I'm doing my best to make sure that no one else finds out.

"You're doing a great job," Grace says gently before rejoining Margaret at the espresso machine. I feel my face flush as I finish ringing up Fran, and my phone buzzes when I'm helping the next customer. By the time I get a chance to look at it, I have messages from Oscar and Fran, but of course I look at Fran's first because, well, obviously, and also she's standing right here.

Are you free tonight? Can I take you out? I realize we haven't gone on an actual date yet. I feel like you're owed an actual date.

I glance up at her and smile before turning back to my phone. But then the door chimes again, and by the time I'm free, Fran's got her drinks and is heading out.

I feel like the McDonald's drive-thru counts as an actual date??

Fran turns around as she's almost out the door and shakes her head. "Absolutely not, Lydia."

I laugh as she turns back around and leaves, my face warm and my heart pounding like crazy and also my nerves reminding me I'm not doing a very good job acting like there's nothing here. I manage not to make eye contact with Grace for a while, as if that's going to hide anything.

I wait until after work, when Margaret and I are making one of our usual post-shift pizza runs, to check Oscar's response, and I feel her watching me as I read it.

"So what's up with Fran?" she asks, and I don't have to look at her to hear the smirk in her words.

"This is from Oscar," I say with probably more smugness than I deserve to use. As if I wouldn't be reading a message from Fran if one was awaiting me. As if I'm some completely upstanding girl who isn't hiding anything from anyone. "He's helping me plan taking Penny to a baseball game."

Margaret wrinkles her nose. "I thought your sister only liked numbers and blonde white women who make speeches."

"I mean, those are two of her main interests, sure." I sigh. "No, Penny's cooler than that, really. She could probably grow up to be one of those blonde white women giving speeches if she sets her mind to it. She's obviously most of the way there already. We're just—we're different."

Margaret snorts a little as she holds open the door of Town Pizza for me. "Yeah, obviously."

I should do more to defend Penny, I know, but it's still so new that if anyone even potentially thinks of me as the cooler sister it's stupid to fight it too much. And it wasn't that long ago when the truth was that I resented Penny. At the time I would have denied it, but from the distance of this summer, for some reason I no longer can unsee those feelings in my heart. I resented her for knowing what she wanted, for being prettier, for never questioning if she deserved a future, for being more responsible—whatever that even meant. We all knew she was and I wasn't.

But after this summer, I'm no longer sure about any of it. Penny had locked on to ideas about her future, but they seem based in avoiding risks and not going after what she actually wants. Obviously, she *is* responsible, but now that I have a job I'm—hopefully—at least slowly getting better at, the difference between us seems less striking. And I can't explain it, because I look exactly the same as I did when I arrived in LA, but I don't feel so much less pretty than Penny now. Or maybe prettiness just matters less, now? There's something about being included in Margaret's group, seeing photos of all of us, where I just look like another girl in the crowd. I *am* just another girl in the crowd, and it doesn't matter at all that I'm not blonde or thin like Penny. We're all just girls in the crowd, and that's OK.

But I don't know how to say even part of that to Margaret. *Oh, back home I didn't really have any friends and I really focused on boys and I thought I had no future and for some reason there's something about LA that makes me feel different and probably even that is stupid and I should have figured things out sooner but I'm just glad I did at all?*

"When are you going back to your suburban life?" Margaret asks once we've ordered and are sharing our usual booth in the back corner. "Like when school starts?"

"Before then," I say, that fact fully dawning on me, that I'm not really here for the whole summer, I'm here until the first week of August, and it's already July. Almost everything I've been thinking about seems to reverse in my head, like every thought is colliding. Back home, will it all be the same again? Resenting Penny, not having friends, getting obsessed about boys even if Fran—I mean, who truly even knows about Fran and me once I'm an hour away.

"You look terrified." Margaret laughs. "It's not *that* bad, right?"

"No, completely not."

"And you must miss your friends up there," she says. It's a casual thing to say, of course, unless you're saying it to me, a girl who somehow managed not to have friends for a long time. Not that I plan to bring that up.

"Oh, yeah, of course, thank god for phones and everything," I say. And it's kind of true, because I do comment on other REACT members' photos, and them on mine, and we're already on the main group chat speculating on what show Mr. Landiss will announce. Since I'll be a senior, I should get to take more of a lead in planning and design this year, and even though nothing at school has changed, this summer has made this all sound more possible. Maybe I'll never be the coolest member of REACT—no, there's no *maybe* about it. I won't be! But I know I can still contribute. And no matter how the year turns out, no matter what actually *happens*, I'm realizing I can try for the dream schools and dream future I want, even if I'm the least likely to get all of it. It doesn't mean I have to give up before even starting.

"I legit don't know what I'm going to do without my friends around every day," Margaret says. "We'll be spread out over the entire country, and I know we'll see each other for holidays and summers and whatever, but it won't be the same. And you hear adults talking all the time about how they made all their best friends in college, and so I'm like, what about all of *this*? Does it just not count?"

"If it makes you feel better, I don't think my parents have any friends from college, either."

Margaret cracks up at that. "Thanks, Lyds, tons."

"I can't believe you worry about stuff like this," I admit.

"What do you mean? Oh, because you've been away from your friends all summer and you're doing fine?"

"No, because you're just—you have so many friends. Like, these really great solid friendships with people that go back years and years. I just feel like if I were you I'd assume that wherever I showed up it would be the same."

"No, it feels completely different. Who knows what this year's going to be like," she says. "I've been in school with the same people for forever. What about you?"

"What *about* me?" I ask as the cashier calls out that our pizza's ready at the counter. I hop up to grab the slices for us and slide back in across from Margaret.

Margaret shakes red pepper flakes on her slice. "You're the one who showed up here and gets along with everyone and has whatever going on with Fran Ford."

"That really makes me sound cooler than I am. Look at me! I'm mainly a disaster. All my shirts have theater production logos on them! I don't know anymore if my boots are cool or not! Even when my hair is up it somehow gets frizzy, which doesn't even make sense to me, I didn't think I was giving it room to . . . you know, frizz."

Margaret laughs, then stops herself. "Wait, are you serious? Lyds, you're supercute and so are your boots. You know that, right? But also if you want to shop for shoes and product, I don't ever *not* want to do that."

I don't understand this version of me that Margaret seems to see. But even if it seems composed of half-truths and hidden-other-truths,

I don't mind it. And *obviously* I want cute shoes besides the one pair I wear every single day and whatever I'm supposed to put in my hair that I don't know about. All this mysterious knowledge I've never had, maybe it turns out I could have just asked this whole time. Not that anyone's ever made me feel as welcome as Margaret, but still.

At Grace and Oscar's that evening, everyone's in for the night, so Grace and Oscar cook pasta and assemble a salad, and we sit around their kitchen table all four of us together. It's good timing because Oscar and I worked out a whole plan—or I guess technically Oscar worked it out and I answered a few key questions and acted very enthusiastic over text.

"So Lydia had a really good idea," he says, as we're all on second helpings of cacio e pepe. "Pen, I know you've been going to the Greyhound to watch games with a bunch of our colleagues, so Lydia thought it'd be fun for us all to go see a game together."

"At the Greyhound?" Penny asks.

"No, an actual game wherever they play the actual game," I say, which makes Oscar laugh. "This is why Oscar had to help me plan— I'm a sports idiot."

It had been Oscar's idea to make it the four of us, but he also offered to treat Penny and me, plus we'd all go together in his car, so it did seem like the best solution. And it was sweet that he was giving me credit; hopefully Penny understood I was doing all of this for her, even though I'd gotten help. My next Saturday was all for her, girlfriend or not, friend group or not, deep apathetic feelings toward all sports or not.

"How'd *I* get roped into this?" Grace asks me after dinner, while Oscar and Penny sit at the table and discuss some office thing and I'm helping Grace load the dishwasher. "Sports? Who do you think I am?"

I laugh, passing her a handful of rinsed-off cutlery. "Trust me, I know. But Penny's been so cool and took me to that amazing play, even though she's pretty neutral on theater. So I owe her."

Grace smiles. "You're a good sister."

I'm not sure that's true, especially when I finally have a moment alone and see that Fran's proposing next Saturday as our actual date night. Obviously I tell her it'll have to be another night, but would a good sister feel *disappointed* about that?

"Thanks," Penny says, walking into the room. I worry she's being sarcastic, but Penny's not really capable of sarcasm. "I'm a little embarrassed that I've been enjoying baseball so much, but I'm really looking forward to going to a game in person."

"Why embarrassed?" I ask. "Because sports are for dumb people, not geniuses?"

Penny waves her hand at me. "Obviously, no. It's just that I don't have a real *reason* for it. I don't think it's that I have some future in anything to do with baseball or sports management, though I guess it sounds a little fun. Like I've told you, I just *like it*."

"Like I've told *you*, you can just do stuff you like. For no reason. Or, like, that *is* the reason. Don't make it all hard on yourself, like you have to earn what you do or what you like. Just like it!"

"Sure, but now I've pulled all of you into it."

"Oscar didn't have to be pulled too hard," I said. "And Grace and I can hang out and talk while you guys recite statistics or whatever."

"Dodger Stadium is supposed to have very good snacks," Penny says.

"OK, that part does sound exciting. Also I want you to have fun."

She flops down on the bed next to me. It's so rare to see Penny flop that I kind of do a double take, and I hope I don't make her feel weird. Who even am I? Worrying about Penny's feelings?

"Everything you say makes me doubt what I already thought," she says.

"Yeah, that's how I feel about everything you say, too," I reply, but maybe that was too mean for this moment. I'm not completely sure what this moment even is, these conversations that start normally and end up somewhere new for the two of us.

"Hmmm" is all Penny says.

"Want to go take a walk and get ice cream or something? A hipster donut?"

"Ice cream," she says, hopping back up. "I know you like those donuts, but I tried to look up all the bands that those names referenced and I ended up in a three-hour Wikipedia rabbit hole."

"A *donut hole*," I say, and she actually laughs. I feel pretty triumphant.

"When the summer's over," she says once we're outside and on our way to Scoops, "I hope we can still figure this out."

"Figure what out?" I ask, even though I feel what she's getting at.

"It's nice hanging out," she says, "I hope that if you have a boyfriend—when you have a boyfriend—that you'll still hang out with me sometimes."

"I hope that when you have a boyfriend and you're managing the Rancho El Aderezo Fighting Rabbits baseball team and doing Model UN that you'll still hang out with me."

"Hmmm," Penny says, a gleam in her eye and a raised eyebrow.

"I mean, I was kidding, but only a little."

Chapter Sixteen

I'm still learning how to be someone with friends—real friends you text about more than just rehearsal and lighting grids—but I know enough to know what I don't know. And that's why even though I'm always the first person to tell my new friends that what you wear doesn't matter, I still send out a text to Margaret asking what I should wear on this actually official date with Fran tonight. There's no official uniform for making someone fall for you; they should fall for the person you actually are. At least the best version of that. But Fran's already fallen, so I just want to look really cute. And everyone else might judge me if I confess that Fran and I are official now, but I know I don't have to explain any of that to Margaret. I can tell she roots for us already.

"Ooh, so this is Grace's house!" She eyes the front room as she walks in. I'd expected we'd just do this over text or, at most, FaceTime, but she offered to come over right away, and since Oscar and Penny are still at work and Grace is still at Grounds Control, I agreed.

"So cute, of course," Margaret continues. "What else would I expect from Grace?"

"She's not home, so you can be as weird as you want about it," I say, and she cracks up.

"Seriously, I have like a friend crush on your aunt. If she was my age I'd demand we become besties and hang out on a very regular basis. Where's your room?"

"It's not really my room." I lead her down the hallway. "I mean, I'm only here for a few more weeks, and I'm sharing it with Penny anyway."

"Ahhh, the elusive Penny. Is she here?"

"She's still at work. She keeps, like, grown-up hours."

Margaret surveys the room. "Let me guess which half is hers." She picks up a stack of books and shrieks. "The top one is actually *Lean In*. Lyds, I am dying."

"Yeah, well, she's probably going to be president someday so maybe I shouldn't make fun of her," I say.

"Ooh, you'd be First Sister. Is that a thing?" Margaret dumps out a giant pink bag onto the dresser. "So I just brought a ton of stuff since I don't really know what'll work on your coloring. Do you want me to braid your hair or do something else cute with it?"

"Is my hair too flyaway to do a braid crown?" I ask.

"No way, it'll look supercute, and I can tell you're using that hair gloss I forced you to get. Sit down on the bed and hand me that kinda square brush."

I do as I'm told and feel myself tense a little when Margaret starts brushing and separating out my hair. It's just such new territory. I was positive I'd make it my entire life without being part of such a stereotypical friend activity, but here I am, literally having my hair braided.

"Can I ask you something?" Margaret's close to my head with a look of intense concentration. "I'm afraid it's going to come out bad but you hopefully will know what I mean."

"How could I not say yes to that?"

She grins. "So you've had, like, a lot of boyfriends, right?"

I nod as best I can with my hair being pulled in a few directions.

"So I know it's not like an actual *real* date with Lucas, but it's not *nothing*, and I'm hoping maybe we can go out at least once for real before college, and..." She shrugs. "I can't stop worrying about things, like that he won't think I'm pretty enough to go out with, or that he doesn't think my body is, like, *hot* or whatever, or that he'll think all my jokes are dumb. And you're, like, just *good* with that stuff."

"Everyone's body is hot," I say, because I think it's true. I've crushed on people of all shapes and sizes, had people crush on me right back. It was almost like I never had a chance to worry about if my body wasn't the right type—too big or curvy in the wrong ways or whatever else society tells me I *should* worry about—because instead there were boys who wanted to kiss me, and so none of that stuff seemed to be a factor. "Also my jokes are much dumber."

"Hmmm, fair," she says with a giggle. "Seriously. Don't you ever worry about what boys—what *people* think about your body or whatever? *Not that you should*," she adds in a rushed panicked tone. "I mean, you're the one who's taming Fran Ford!"

"She's not a wild animal," I say. "And...I don't know. My mom has all these magazines lying around with advice columns like, *I can't get the man of my dreams! Should I lose weight?* but I've never worried about it. Boys have always..."

Margaret half watches me, half keeps an eye on my hair as she works.

"I guess I've never felt like I had to look differently to get someone," I say. "You just sort of know when you have chemistry, and it's like, why deny it? It's fun to give in. It's fun to like someone and have them like you back. I try not to make it more complicated than that until it actually is."

"Ugh, so mature, and you're still in high school. I'm a disaster."

"You're the furthest thing from a disaster," I say as the front door opens. "It's probably Grace or Oscar, so you have a moment to prepare to not be too weird."

"Look, there's only so much I can do, Lyds."

But it's Penny who walks into the room. "Oh, hi."

"Oh, hi," I say in return, trying to project *calm and not at all worried* though this is potentially a very bad combo. "This is Margaret. She works at Grounds Control with me."

Penny nods. "Hi."

"Hi, Penny! I'd shake your hand but mine are full of your sister's hair."

"*Ew*," I say, and Margaret and I burst into laughter. Penny does not.

"What are you guys doing?" Penny asks.

I can't give Margaret a look, because she's standing behind me, but I am good at talking quickly. "I'm just going out tonight to celebrate the short film I'm working on, and since I'm bad at hair, Margaret's making me look fancy."

"Fancy as *heck*," Margaret says.

Penny's eyes are narrow. "Who are you going with?"

"Fran," I say. "Who else?"

"OK, look in the mirror," Margaret tells me, and I can't believe it when I do. My hair looks sleek, neatly tucked into a perfect little crown. My space buns have looked better since I took Margaret's product recommendation, but this is far beyond.

"Can you come over every day and do this?" I ask her, and she laughs.

"You wish, Lyds. Here, try this lip gloss. But hold still, I'm going to use this blush stick on your face."

"I'm not sure I can do all that at once," I say, and so I let her go first and then dab on the gloss. "Holy shit, I look like an Instagram girl. Like an actual cool girl."

"You *are* an actual cool girl, dork."

"You know that's a lie," I say.

"Your phone's lighting up," Penny says, glancing over at it lying on the nightstand between the beds. Penny's books take up most of it, so there's really just space for my giant phone and none of my other things. "Someone named Phil is texting a lot."

Margaret cracks up. "I can't believe you put that in your phone."

"I know, I guess I should change it, but…" I shrug. "It's too good."

"Who's Phil? Phil who's picking you up soon?" Penny holds out the phone in my direction, and I feel my heart thudding in my chest. She's clearly reading some of the texts. And what all did Fran message?

"It's Fran," I say. The messages are all, luckily, entirely about when she'll be here to pick me up and not cute at all. "BG Phil is just what I call her because of this dumb thing that happened at work on my first day."

"Oh my god." Margaret is cackling. "I was teaching Lyds how to call drinks at the bar, and I was like, for example, if it's a double latte for Phil, you'd say, *double latte for Phil!* and Lydia just *yells that* even though it was a hypothetical and it was actually a latte for Fran."

I can tell it doesn't sound that funny now, even though Margaret and I are still laughing.

Penny glances between Margaret and me. "So Phil's not a guy?"

"Didn't you just hear us?" I hear the lack of patience in my voice and I hate it. Penny and I have come so far this summer, but right now I just need this to stop. There are too many really dangerous possibilities lurking in this interaction. "Phil's just a dumb joke. Phil's a girl. Phil's *Fran*."

Margaret glances back and forth between Penny and me. "I should go."

"I'll walk you out. Fran'll be here soon anyway. See you later, Pen."

Margaret waves to her. "It was so nice to meet you, Penny!"

"You too," Penny says. "See you later, Lydia."

Margaret and I walk outside, to the end of the block where I always meet Fran.

"Your sister ... lived up to my expectations," Margaret says. "And she's so pretty!"

"Yeah," I say. "She's good at everything. Including being pretty."

"You're good at it too," Margaret says, and even though I don't believe her, it's still nice to hear. "You look supercute and Fran will swoon. Text me later!"

Fran pulls up, and I say goodbye to Margaret before hopping inside. I can't believe I'm used to the height of this thing. I guess there are a lot of things I can't believe I'm used to.

"Whoa," Fran says as I slide in next to her. "Lydia, you look gorgeous."

"You do too," I say, because Fran's in a blue patterned button-down and nice pants, not jeans for once. I don't know what I really expected, but I guess there's part of me that was worried I had to talk Fran into this, that she agreed to a relationship against her own instincts. But here she is, all cleaned up and in date mode for me.

"I planned something," she says, "but I'm hoping it won't be cheesy and you won't think I'm—I don't know. I haven't planned a date before."

"So far, so good," I say.

"It's been two minutes," Fran says, and we both laugh. There's this nibbling darkness in me, though, despite Fran's nice outfit and date plans and my spot in this truck right next to her. Something about the few minutes when it was Penny and Margaret in the same room with me still doesn't feel right, and even though I don't actually know what I would have done differently, I clearly should have done something differently. Sure, I had to make something up to explain why my hair was extra fancy and my outfit didn't involve a logo T, but it was like every exchange I had with Margaret highlighted all the ways Penny wasn't included in my summer. The two of us had plenty of things going on—her job and her coworkers and my job and my new friends—that didn't include the other, but the conversation reminded me of the way groups of friends had always made me feel before, except it was me doing the excluding to Penny. It was me not bothering to loop her in, to make sure the private jokes and dumb references didn't feel so alienating.

"You OK?" Fran asked. "You look...serious."

I decide I can at least make one lie less...untrue. "Can I ask you about the short film you want to make?"

She laughed. "God, now I know why you thought it was so weird to get a question about movies out of nowhere. It *is* weird."

"I'm not really asking about movies," I say. "I'm asking about you."

"Yeah, and I was asking about you, too," she says with a soft smile. "Do we have to talk about it?"

"No, we don't *have* to, but I just—I'm interested. And also I feel like people made you feel bad about the stuff you like and care about and I just wanted to make sure you knew I wasn't going to be like that."

"I already knew you weren't going to be like that," she says, and I feel my face warm with—I don't know. I really always do like people, even if I fall for them fast, even if I'm always fast-forwarding to the happily ever after before seeing if the now works. But I've had to stop and reevaluate so many times with Fran, and I feel so in the present with her. And it's right here in the present that she trusts me, that she knows I'm trustworthy to share her feelings and goals and dreams with.

"There's this movie theater kind of mid-city," Fran says. "They do double features of—well, not just classic movies. Iconic movies. Cult favorites. Not just the stuff the assholes in my school's film club are into, though that stuff, too. Anyway, they're doing classic movie musicals tonight and tomorrow, which is why I wanted to take you out this weekend. Is that OK? We'll be out late, and we'll have to eat movie theater hot dogs for dinner instead of—well, you know. Actual food."

"What are you talking about, I love hot dogs for dinner," I say, which makes her laugh. "I'm serious, I do. I feel like you don't understand what dinner's like in my house. I don't have cool parents like yours. They're always shouting about quarterly tax returns and LLCs and it's kind of stressful."

"My parents aren't that cool," Fran says, but I hear the lie in her voice.

"You can accept that your parents are cool, you know. Nothing bad will happen."

Fran laughs. "It's been a weird year. I feel like as soon as all this adult shit was on the horizon, I saw them differently. They've both always been so chill about everything and suddenly they had these goals and milestones for me, and it was like, who the hell *are* you guys?"

"Trust me, it sounds nice. My parents are just leaving it all up to us and it feels—I don't know." I think of the flurry of texts and photos the other weekend, and it's hardly that I've never felt loved or cared about. It's the opposite of that, really. Penny and I are really lucky. "I feel like they leave Penny alone because they know she'll achieve all her goals without any help, and they leave me alone because they don't even *understand* my goals, but lately I've realized maybe we've both needed more than that."

"Mine were always pretty laid-back until I quit the film club and didn't apply for any of the schools on my list, and then it was like . . . these new parents showed up who'd never even heard the word *chill* before." Fran sighs, shoving her hair out of her face. Her eyes are on the road, straight ahead. "And to be fair, some of it now feels stupid, but . . ."

"But people made you feel *shitty* about what mattered to you," I say. "I've felt that way for a long time, actually, but lately—" I cut myself off because a lot seems to be flooding out, and my plans for Fran involve staying right here in the now. It's so easy to say too much, to go too far.

"Lately?" Fran asks softly.

"Well. This is probably not at all true for stupid film bros, but a lot of what I felt coming from Penny and whoever else wasn't meant the way I was taking it. Like, they don't actually get what's important to me but . . . they don't want it *not* to be important to me, either."

Fran nods. "Yeah. That's definitely not true for film bros. But I know what you mean. Sometimes—do you feel how hard it is? How it's hard enough *making stuff*, but then it's harder because people are ready to say girls shouldn't, or the only art that matters is this one kind, or if it's about someone just like me it's not relatable? I know it's when I'm supposed to rise up and work harder but it just makes me feel shitty."

"Yeah, same. Penny'll cite these statistics and she's just trying to give me interesting information but all I feel when I hear it is *give up now.*" I rest my fingertips on Fran's forearm. "I'm working on not reacting that way, though."

She pulls up to a red light and turns just slightly to kiss my cheek. "I think I'm working on it, too. But I needed that reminder."

There's a line down the block at the theater, and instead of being annoyed we have to wait, I feel an excitement tingle in my stomach that all these people are here to see two old movie musicals, when there are probably one million ostensibly cooler things to do on a Friday night in Los Angeles. There are people of all ages, genders, colors, and I love being part of this crowd, holding Fran's hand, debating best movie snacks and seat locations. We compromise: I let her choose seats closer than I normally like, and she buys me a big box of Sno-Caps even though she says the white balls on them make her mouth feel weird. Fran hasn't seen either movie before, so she raves to me about *Singin' in the Rain* while we're waiting for *Meet Me in St. Louis* to start, and then she raves about that one when we're walking to her truck in the hushed nighttime after.

No one's texted me—other than the group text, active as always—so it feels fine to agree when Fran asks if I want to stop off for late-night diner food on the way back. We grab a booth in the back of the restaurant and decide to split a grilled cheese and fries, perfect diner food.

"When I was little," Fran says, taking a sip of her Dr Pepper while we're waiting for our food to arrive, "I had these imaginary friends.

Well, not exactly *imaginary*—they were these stuffed animals, but to me they had these really specific personalities, and whenever I was nervous or scared about anything, I went to them for advice."

"Fran, that's *so cute.*"

She rolls her eyes, but I can tell she agrees. "Anyway, I started thinking, you know, what if they weren't imaginary? Like that they were still who I was going to for advice and pep talks and all of that. Especially a few years back, when I was figuring out coming out and girls and all of that."

I realize what she's telling me. "Your script?"

She nods. "Yeah. It's kind of cheesy, but—I don't know. I like the symbolism of it, whoever's supported you since you were a kid likes the person you're growing into. Just wants you to succeed, to kiss that cute girl, to tell your mom you want to stop going to her hair stylist and let someone cut your hair short like this. All the shit I was worried about when I was younger and understanding who I was."

"It's so weird to imagine you nervous about kissing a girl," I say.

"Yeah, yeah," she says with a grin. "Clearly my imaginary friends gave good advice."

"Were you scared to tell your parents?" I ask.

She watches me for a moment. "Your parents don't know?"

I shake my head. "No one knows. Well, Margaret and my other friends do. But that's mainly because I don't think me and you are very subtle."

Fran grins. "Nah, I'm not known for that. Yeah, I was scared. My parents are—yes, fine, cool as hell. But my dad's a boring white guy from Iowa, and even though my mom looks like—well, my brother and I say she looks like an art teacher, or like a yoga teacher who has a day job—she grew up Catholic, her parents are still really Catholic, and I know sometimes it's hard to let go of stuff, even if—like her—you don't completely believe all of it anymore."

"But...I mean, I guess it went OK?" I ask.

"It went great, yeah. They were so cool about it, just thanked me for telling them and didn't act like it was a huge deal, and then later I overheard them talking and *clearly they were onto me* and hadn't wanted to make me feel weird about it and—I don't know. It was exactly what I needed. I'm lucky."

Our waitress drops off our sandwich and huge plate of fries. Fran and I pull the two sandwich halves apart, the bright orange cheese stretching between. Right now, living in this moment, nothing seems scary at all.

"I'll help you with the movie," I say. "Not that you need my—anyway, you said something about figuring out lighting and a set, and that's the stuff I'm good at. Well, I'm good at it for theater, and I've done some reading, and—"

"You really want to help?" she asks.

"I mean, if you want me to. I think it'd be fun to learn something new, and—it sounds fun to work together. I've never dated someone before sort of interested in the same stuff as me. A guy in REACT—that's our theater tech club—but it was sophomore year, we weren't, like, *creating* together or anything."

Fran grins, popping the last corner of her sandwich half into her mouth.

"What?"

"This might sound weird, but—I like that you have a history. The things people I've hooked up with have said. *Oh, Fran, you're such a player.*"

I try to look innocent and like I've never heard that before.

"Whatever you're doing with your face, stop," she says, and we both laugh. "I don't know. Like I'm this fucking *novelty* for having fun. For thinking a lot of people are worth getting to know."

"Literally, all of pop culture is like, love and sex are the best things, and then if you're like, *yes, I agree,* you're a slut or a player or whatever," I say. "Like you said, as if thinking a lot of people are worth knowing is . . . *dirty* or something."

Fran nods emphatically. "Especially when you're upfront. You still get treated like you're doing something wrong."

"I hope I didn't—"

She holds up her hand. "Lydia. The thing I like most about you is how open and honest you are about everything. It's like it's not even in your nature to think of hiding something."

When I get back a little later I think of that sentence over and over while hoping Penny doesn't wake up and ask me why I'm home so late.

Chapter Seventeen

The truth is that I was sort of dreading the Dodgers game ever since planning it with Oscar. Even though I knew it would make Penny happy, the thought of sitting in hard plastic seats for however many hours baseball games last sounded kind of terrible, especially since I knew I owed it to my sister to pay attention and not just scroll Instagram and TikTok the whole time.

I knew I hadn't imagined how weird yesterday evening had been, because today Penny's been quieter, and even though I asked if she wanted to take a hike or just a long neighborhood walk before the game, she said she had to catch up on podcasts and headed out alone. Yes, she's done that before, but it hasn't felt quite so pointed, and instead of taking advantage of a Saturday with nothing owed to Penny until later, I walk to Grounds Control for a free pastry and latte and just head back to Grace and Oscar's alone.

Everyone else is out, so I settle at the kitchen table with my breakfast and my phone. Fran's tagged me again, a photo from last night that I didn't know she was taking, when I was examining my menu at the diner, fluorescent lighting bouncing off my glasses, my eyes wide with the possibility of diner food and our conversation. I can't stop looking at it, because there's something different in me that wasn't apparent in the mirror. Maybe it was Margaret's hair and makeup skills, or maybe it was Fran's filmmaking talent behind a camera—even an iPhone camera—or even Fran's feelings. But I don't look like a girl to be ignored, who has little to look forward to. I look like a girl with opinions and plans.

Fran texts not long after I tap the heart on the photo, making sure I'm not in trouble for staying out so late and expressing her sympathy I'll be trapped at a sporting event for much of today. I tell myself not to wish things were different, that it's good to do what Penny wants, especially after yesterday's awkwardness. The old Lydia would have done everything in her power for more time with Fran. Even if I hadn't felt guilty about Penny and breaking our pledge, I'm understanding now why it's not a great idea to live that way.

Penny lets herself in, and I set my phone down and pretend that I wasn't texting.

"Hey," I say. "I still have half a muffin, if you want it."

Penny eyes it suspiciously but sits down next to me and tears off half of the half. "Does Grace bake the muffins?"

"No, that hot guy drops them off during the week. I don't know who drops them off on the weekend. Probably someone less hot is my guess, though I think it's a family business. So maybe all the relatives are hot."

I can tell Penny doesn't want to smile, but she does.

"Are you excited about today?" I ask. "Maybe all your favorite baseball guys will hit home runs. That's good, right?"

Penny laughs. "Yes, Lydia, that'd be great. It's cute how hard you're trying to say something so obvious."

"That's me, cute and obvious," I say.

"I *am* looking forward to it," she says. "Thanks for arranging it. Did you have fun last night? Did you work on the film?"

"It's more like the planning stages right now," I say, which is true, sort of. Was Fran going to let me actually help her? I'm not sure Fran feels comfortable sharing her script with anyone, and, honestly, I get that. It's vulnerable telling people the things you hoped for, the places you see yourself someday. I know that sharing your work is something beyond even that, and I don't want to push.

"I've heard that films can take a long time to shoot," Penny says. "Will you have time while we're still here?"

"Maybe not, but hopefully—" I cut myself off because the reality of the calendar isn't my favorite thing to think about. Yes, Fran has her truck, and I share a car with Penny, but it's an hour drive between us, and things won't be so easy once Mom and Dad are home. Living in the now has felt so mature, so healthy, but maybe I've been protecting myself, too. If I don't think too hard about the coming months, none of the logistics matter.

"What?" Penny asks.

"I don't know. You're right, it could take a while, and I won't always be able to drive down."

"We can make it work with the car," Penny says. "I know that the film is a big deal to you, and it could be something that adds to your college applications and essays."

"Yeah, but you're the one who's actually guaranteed to get into a good school and all of that. I don't want to sacrifice anything of yours for my stupid dreams."

Penny stares at me. "Lydia."

I wonder if I've somehow given something away. I even glance down at my phone screen to make sure Fran hasn't texted something potentially incriminating. "What?"

"You know that your dreams aren't stupid. Negative self-talk can be so defeating. I'm going to send you a link to a—"

I mean to just roll my eyes, but I accidentally let out an *ugghhh*.

"I know you think you hate things like this, but just watch it, all right?" Penny takes the last bite of muffin and stands up. "I'm going to find you the link and then take a shower. You stay here and watch the video."

"I don't feel like advice from intense blonde ladies is applicable to me," I say.

"Untrue, you listen to me all the time," she says before leaving the room, and I'm so happily surprised at Penny's sense of humor about all of this that I wait until I hear the shower running and then click on the video. I mean, I can't give her *too* much satisfaction, but this video isn't from a fancy TED Talk, it's just a woman talking to the camera without fancy lighting. Also, she's not blonde. She has dark olive skin and dark brown curly hair, she's wearing glasses, and she's not thin. I had no idea Penny listened to people who weren't just like her, and not only am I determined to pay attention to the video, but I'm immediately less annoyed at my sister.

By the time Penny's back in our room, I'm on, like, my sixth video from this woman because I just kept letting them autoplay. Part of me feels new and alive, all this positivity and *you can do it, yes, even girls like you* coursing through my veins. But part of me has never been so confused, because if this is the kind of stuff my sister is ingesting on a regular basis, why is she so nervous about numbers and research and proving which life paths will be low-risk and high-reward? I've only been watching this stuff for about a half an hour and I already feel like I can go achieve anything I put my mind to.

"Penny," I say, feeling wise, "what would you do if you knew you would not fail?"

She stares at me. "Have you been shopping for inspirational embroidered pillows or something?"

"Wait, is that a saying already?"

Penny's laughing so hard she can't even answer. I google it and find out I'm only the millionth person to ask this question, and also that there *are* a lot of embroidered pillows featuring it. I threaten to order the ugliest one I find for Penny, and she grabs my phone from me.

"Don't you dare—oh, never mind. It's *three hundred and twenty dollars* because of the custom beadwork. I doubt you'll feel confident sneaking that onto the emergency card."

"Penny, don't disparage custom beadwork."

My phone buzzes in her hand, and I see something flash behind her eyes. "Phil's texting you."

"I told you, it's Fran," I say, while trying to figure out a super casual way to quickly snatch my phone away from her and check the message.

"Would you tell me if it wasn't?" she asks, her tone all business.

"I mean, Margaret told you the story," I say with a shrug. "And it's just become this dumb joke. And, yes, if I were actually texting some guy named Phil, I would tell you."

"Instead it's just a girl named Fran," Penny says, and I shrug again.

"I like the name Fran. It's cool when other people have grandma names, too," I say.

Penny still looks serious.

"Are we expected to continue that tradition?" I ask. "Grandma names for our future children?"

"Oh, wow, I hope not, poor Susan and Karen," she says, with the tiniest smile, and I decide I can check Fran's message later. Staying right here in this moment with my sister is the most important thing I can do.

~

Grace drives us to Dodger Stadium later, and I don't know what I was expecting, but it's tucked into hills, near a park, almost like a secret. My dread-levels drop almost immediately. I love that LA keeps surprising me.

"You're a good sister," Grace tells me as the four of us make our way across the parking lot toward the giant stadium. "Hope and I never did things like this for each other."

"It's like a special summer, you know that," I say. "Also Penny took me to the coolest play downtown, I've got to repay her somehow. And thank god Oscar got involved so I didn't actually have to figure out any of the logistics."

Grace grins at me. "He's so good at that. That's always my relationship advice. Find yourself someone who's good with all the small details."

"Romantic!"

"Romance is so easy," Grace says. "Building a life with someone is about all the unromantic stuff, too. But you're seventeen and don't need to worry about any of that yet. Small details can come later. Just don't forget."

Oscar hands out our tickets and directs us toward the right entrance, and I make eye contact with Grace, who smirks. I laugh and shrug, because it *is* nice that he's handling this, that we don't have to think about it, and that he and Penny coordinate a snack run so that Grace and I can relax in our seats in the bright sunshine. It's one aspect I hadn't even considered, that so much of today might just be hanging out with Grace, away from Grounds Control, and my mood lifts further.

"How's everything?" Grace asks me.

"What's everything?"

She laughed. "Why the suspicion? Your parents put me in charge of you for most of the summer. Shouldn't I check in?"

"Do you check in with Penny?" I ask.

"I overheard Penny advising Oscar on some long-term investment strategies," she says. "I feel like she should check in with me."

I laugh. "Yeah, welcome to the club."

"Seriously," Grace says, her tone soft in the huge stadium echoing with noise. "You know that I'm here for you, right, Lyds?"

I do love that Margaret's nickname for me has taken on a life of its own.

"I'm fine," I say, because I am and also because I'm nervous at anything Grace could be getting at. Sure, there's Fran, and the fact that Grace is the only person at Grounds Control who knows about my pledge to Penny. But I also wonder if Grace worries about me and Margaret, me and a group of friends. Surely—even though I've somehow fooled four cool girls into thinking I'm also cool enough to be included in their circle—Grace sees that I don't fully belong.

"I'm really glad to hear that," Grace says though, with a smile I think is genuine, and I try to relax again.

Penny and Oscar make their way down the row of seats toward us, arms loaded with food and beverage trays. I'm grateful to see this bounty of snacks and also for how happy my sister looks.

"Grace," Penny says, "do you know that Lydia thought she made up the phrase *What would you do if you knew you would not fail?* today?"

OK, maybe I could take her a little less happy.

Grace laughs. "Wow, Lyds, maybe tomorrow you can come up with *live, laugh, love!*"

"I hate you both," I say, while Penny and Oscar pass out sodas, hot dogs, and giant overflowing containers of garlic fries. It's immediately impossible to hate anyone. Plus, I quickly realize, it's fun, sitting outside in the bright sunshine with my family, getting caught up in the noise and energy of the crowd. There's a laid-back quality, too, where it's OK that Oscar and Penny are leaning forward, intent on all of the action on the baseball field, while Grace and I mostly pay attention but also both scroll Instagram and chat, too. In a lot of ways, it's the perfect late afternoon, and I feel silly for dreading it even a little. I should have realized how every part of the summer that's been great has been completely unexpected, and so it should be no surprise that I like this, too.

"So are you still enjoying the job?" Grace asks me, a few innings into the game. The Dodgers are behind, but Oscar keeps saying, *they've still got lots of time to pull ahead.* "It's been great having you at the shop. Margaret and I are already pretty despondent that you'll be gone before long, and then of course she'll be off a few weeks after that. I'll need a whole new morning crew."

"Yeah, I love it. Sometimes I wish I could stay." It's safe to admit because it's not really possible, and we both know that.

"Me too, obviously. But I always manage to find good people. And maybe you can come back next summer, if you want."

"Seriously? That'd be amazing." I let myself think of it, even though I've been careful lately not to get ahead of myself. My new friends, back from college. Fran, still my girlfriend, working with me on our next project. It's not real, but maybe it could be.

"We got you something," Penny says to me. "Now that my hands aren't greasy with garlic fries anymore, I can show you."

"This is supposed to be your day," I say, but I smile as Penny takes out a blue baseball cap from a bag and shoves it on my head. "You have to warn a person before you do that, give them a chance to prepare for having hat-hair."

"Hat-hair takes longer than one second to set in," she says with authority, and I laugh, because of course Penny's an expert on this, too. "What?"

"Thank you for my hat, it's very cute. Did you get one, too?"

She grins and takes a matching one out of her bag and carefully loops her ponytail through the back as she puts it on. We haven't worn anything matching since we were really little, but I don't mind it. I even take a selfie of us and post it to my Instagram and realize that I've done this a lot this summer. There's proof that something is different between us now, and I like seeing it captured here, our smiling faces with pieces of Los Angeles in the background. And even though Penny seems more caught up in the moment, her eyes mostly locked on the field below us, she pulls her phone from her bag to like the photo and comment with a string of baseball- and snack-related emojis. Our team loses the game, but it doesn't matter to me because it feels like I'm winning at something bigger. But Oscar and Penny are pretty disappointed, so I decide not to bring up my exciting personal wins and just let them complain about the manager's bad decisions our whole drive back.

Chapter Eighteen

I'm not sure I've fully fixed things with Penny since accidentally making it weird with Margaret.

Penny's eyes have stopped flashing with suspicion, but something doesn't feel quite right. I wish I could just throw myself at maintaining our bond again, nothing but Grounds Control and Penny activities, but—well, technically, I guess I *could* do that. I just don't want to. I want my friends, and obviously I want Fran, too. The summer will be over so soon, and then it'll be easier to be a good sister. Sure, Penny and I will both be busy with our various extracurriculars—well, *she'll* be busy with various extracurriculars, and REACT takes up plenty of my time on its own—but those things can be planned around less awkwardly. Rehearsals and Model UN meetings and debate preps are allowable get-out-of-sister-time excuses. Friends during this particular summer feel—I don't know. *An affront* is a really dramatic way to put it. But whenever I hang out with them when I could be with Penny, part of me feels like a jerk.

And, of course, when I'm with Fran, it's even worse. Except that it also isn't, because—well, Fran's *incredible.* And so even though I should save as many of my evenings for Penny as possible, when Fran and I are both free, it's really hard not to make plans to walk to the end of the block and hop into her truck.

Just like at my home—the one all the way out in the suburbs, that is—we have a lot of freedom at Fran's. My parents' work hours have always kept them busy enough that my boyfriends and I have had plenty of time to ourselves over the years. Fran's parents are around more, but it always seems OK that I'm there—though of course we wait until they're gone or sound asleep to close her door.

Tonight, almost two full weeks since our first official date, I finally get up the nerve to stop hinting around something and just say it. Fran and I have been watching movies all afternoon on the small TV in her room, since her brother and his friends have commandeered the living room for video games, and the air in here feels hazy with art and dreams (which is much better than what their living room currently feels hazy with).

"Can I read your script?" I ask. "For the short film?"

Fran makes a face, and I laugh.

"Sorry," I say. "I support you and I'm not pressuring you. But I meant all the stuff I said. I'd really be happy to help with whatever you need. And after seeing all these movies by female directors and screenwriters, it just makes me—I don't know. I want you to get to do this. If this is a step toward being a director, is it one we can do together?"

Fran studies me silently. "*We?*"

"Oh shit—was it weird I said *we?*"

She shakes her head and smiles. "No. I'm kind of—you make me nervous, Lydia, because you give me all this hope again that—I don't know. You have to understand that if you'd met me even a year ago, I was so ready. I wrote constantly, had all this stuff I was excited about. And then senior year hit, and all the feedback I got—or, I admit, the feedback I heard the loudest—made me feel like I'd never get anywhere being myself. And since I didn't want to be anyone else, I had to figure out some new plan. So here I am without my own plan, interning on someone else's project—which is fine, that's how you get started, but it felt different knowing I wouldn't be the director someday. And now—I don't know. Now I feel like I can. Or at least that I'm not an idiot to try."

"It's hard to explain, but my whole summer's felt that way, too," I say.

"Yeah?" Fran leans over and kisses me, her hands clasping my face as her lips overlap mine. When we were new to each other, it all felt so frantic and big. It's nice to be here, sitting across from her on the floor of her bedroom, kissing gently like there'll be plenty more time later for us. I know that there's no guarantee, but that doesn't seem to matter. After all, there was never a guarantee. Tate lives a five-minute drive from me, and he still found a way to unexpectedly break my heart. Not that Tate feels like a five-minute heartbreak away anymore. Somehow I've almost forgotten he exists.

"OK," Fran says, and leans past me for something. Suddenly she's plunking down her MacBook on my lap. "You can read it, but let's not get ahead of ourselves. Maybe I'm just going to spend my life working on other people's projects, and as long as it pays enough that I can eventually move out of this house, that's good enough for me."

"I promise," I say, though almost as soon as I start reading, I'm imagining it. The script is just like Fran had described, a girl talking to her imaginary friends—though I guess they're not so imaginary in this world, the world Fran's created with her words. They give the girl advice about school, about kissing, about dealing with parents. It's the kind of thing that could be really cheesy, but it shines with this sweetness and still feels *real*—even though two of the characters are stuffed animals.

I realize I'm actually picturing it in Margaret's bedroom, with her fairy lights and tulle, how sweet and fairy-tale it already looks. I wonder if we could film there; would that be weird? And will Fran be in it? She's never mentioned anything but being behind the camera, but I think of the lines of her face, the little tilt at the end of her nose, her lips that always look freshly kissed even when she's running beverage errands or watching me read her script. Though I guess technically right now she *is* pretty freshly kissed.

"We could totally make this," I say.

"There you go with that *we* again," she says, but she smiles. "What if we do make this, and it gets me laughed out of all the film programs I was too afraid to apply to last year?"

"I mean, that would suck," I say, and we both laugh. "But it's not just about that, right? Like, I don't work so hard on the shows at my school because we're guaranteed a Jimmy Award—"

"What," Fran asks, "is a Jimmy Award?"

"They're the high school musical theater awards," I say. "And, no, we've never won. Our teacher's really thirsty for one, though. Anyway, my point is that you can just want to make something for the point of making it. And because even if film bros don't get it, people will get it. My parents will be back soon and I'm going to have to talk to them at some point and—I don't know. This probably sounds silly but I really did feel less alone reading this. It would probably do that for other people, too."

Fran watches me for a few moments. "How do you always say the right thing?"

"You're the first person who's ever asked me that."

We plan for the rest of the evening. Well, we plan for hours, and then her parents go to bed and we're able to close Fran's door and focus on other things. By the time I'm back at Grace and Oscar's—

too late, I know—my head's flooded with so many thoughts that all I can hope is for Penny to already be fast asleep and not waiting with any questions. But as I walk to our room, I see the bright slit of light glowing underneath the closed door.

"Hey," Penny says, looking up when I walk into the room. "Late night on your movie?"

At least I don't have to lie. Not completely, at least.

"Yes," I say. "We got so much mapped out, though! I mean, theoretically. It's not really my project, so I get excited about stuff but then I'm like, calm down, this is someone else's thing, let them make a decision first."

Penny watches me, not completely differently from how Fran watched me earlier. Like I'm saying a thousand things at once and catch-up time is required, maybe.

"It sounds fun," Penny says. "Maybe I should have chosen a summer project that has group participation."

"Group participation *is* fun," I say, doing my best not to smile and give it all away. "But you watch baseball with other people! And it's like America's national pastime, right? You're never really alone."

Penny smiles at that. "Sure. I might go to another game with some people from work. I think everyone'll be more into it than you and Grace testing out Instagram filters the whole time."

"It wasn't *the whole time*," I say, but I know since Penny's still smiling that it's OK. "Also some of the filters were baseball-related."

"Yeah, I saw all your stories later," she says, sounding exhausted, but I remember that it's midnight and so maybe that's OK. Somehow I've made it through interacting with my sister after hours spent with Fran feeling like new worlds were constantly opening up for us. For *me*.

"We're still doing whatever you're planning tomorrow, right?" I grab my pajamas and wait for Penny's answer before heading to the bathroom.

"Why wouldn't we?" she asks, and I hate that there's a note of—I don't know. It would all be easier if I didn't have new friends, if I didn't have Fran, if I didn't care so much already about this movie we might make together. Sometimes I genuinely wish I'd fallen for something like baseball instead, something big and impersonal and lie-proof.

There are moments—like this one—when I think the easiest thing to do is just *say* all of that. But the summer is already careening to an end—or at least, this part of the summer is. Los Angeles and Fran and my friends. Soon every night won't feel this way, maybe not the good parts like getting dropped off by Fran mere moments ago, but not the bad ones, either, not feeling like I'm constantly letting my sister down. I just have to get through the now. The rest I can figure out later.

$\sim$

Penny's gotten permission to use Grace's car on Saturday, but our first stop is a walk to Grounds Control for coffee and pastries. I can't believe that Grace was right, but the half-mile no longer feels like much of anything; it's part of my daily routine and so even on the weekends I like starting my day with it.

It's seriously weird to feel like such a different person and also completely the same. I wonder if that's what growing up is, and I want to ask Penny, but even the less-judgmental easier-going baseball-loving summer version of my sister might have a field day with that one, so I let it go.

"Be sure to bring your notepad today," Penny says on our way back. I'm in the middle of learning that a delicate pear and gorgonzola tart is tricky to eat walking down a sidewalk. "And, no, we're not going to the library."

"I figured we didn't need to borrow a car for the library. Though depending on—I don't know. If the movie ends up *happening* happening, I'll definitely need to research a few more things."

"Why wouldn't it happen?" Penny asks. "You've been working on it so much. I figured it already was in-progress."

"There's a lot of planning beforehand," I say. "And Fran's—I don't know. Some film guys were jerks to her and it's like—I mean, I didn't know her last year! But I feel like they zapped her self-esteem somehow and it sucks."

Penny wrinkles her brow. "That does suck. I have a really good lecture I saved—"

"Of *course* you do," I say.

"Fine, be rude, but it's a documented thing that happens to non-male artists all the time, and I just thought it might be helpful for your friend."

"Sorry," I say. "Send it to me and I'll share it with her. I just feel like you have videos for every occasion."

"Well, there are a lot of occasions," she says as we arrive back at Grace and Oscar's. I get my notepad and follow her out back to Grace's car. By this point, she's already sent me the video, and because Penny's driving—she's become the default big sister, after all—I send it to Fran as soon as I'm in the car with a shrug emoji and an explanation about my sister's motivational video habits.

"I actually liked that video you sent the other week," I admit to Penny as she navigates across town. It's funny how small it seems in a car.

Blocks zip by so quickly. "The one about stopping negative self-talk? I didn't know you listened to people like that."

"What do you mean, people like that?"

"Like, not blonde and thin and—I don't know. Not just like you."

"I listen to a lot of people who aren't like me," she says. "And also there are plenty of people who might seem like me on the surface but we don't have anything in common. Do you think my main traits are *blonde and thin?*"

I shrug. "No, obviously not." But the truth is that I don't *not* think that, and it sounds terrible. Penny is so many things: funny and smart and really driven and way more sensitive than I'd ever realized.

"I know you think it's silly that I rely on research and other people's speeches, but it helps me," Penny says, as she maneuvers the car onto the freeway. I'm kind of enjoying that I have no idea where she's taking us. "Life is...well, there's so much to figure out. If someone's already done the work and figured out solutions, I want to hear those. If there's a guarantee built in somehow, that's what I want. I know that doesn't make sense to you, but—"

"No, honestly, it does," I say. "I've realized that this summer, actually. It's why I've always fallen apart or whatever over boys. Because I was trying to guarantee something with them."

"A happily ever after?" she asks.

"*Exactly.* But trying to jump to the end at the beginning just actually made things worse. Because I wasn't, like, losing my boyfriend. I was losing the freaking love of my life. Like *Tate Shepard* was gonna be the love of my life. He can't even take a good photo."

Penny bursts out laughing. "He's cute, though. You could have done worse."

"I could have done way worse for sure. Anyway, though, this summer was a good idea. It made me stop and think about everything in a different way, I guess."

"Yeah, boys were never rational," Penny says. "Or I guess that I should say that I was never rational about boys."

"Do you have to be rational about everything?"

Penny shoots me a brief look before looking back to the freeway ahead. "Didn't you just say that this is why you've always fallen apart over boys? The irrationality of all of it?"

"No, that definitely doesn't sound like me. I said that you can't force a guarantee. Life doesn't give you any guarantees; that's the thing I'm understanding more and more. But boys—crushes, relationships, whatever, lots of that stuff isn't rational, right? You look at someone and you just have these *feelings*."

"Yes, and I hate that," Penny says, which makes me laugh.

"Sure, but it's fun, too, right? I think as long as I don't try to fast-forward to the ending, I'll be fine."

"I just hate risk," she says. "I feel like Mom and Dad figured that much out. They met each other, got married, got degrees that have a high rate of return compared to cost spent, and they built a business for themselves that pays for a house and whatever we need. I figure if I calculate something similar, I can manage a higher income, and—"

"Yeah, and if that's what you want, you totally should," I say. "Mom and Dad are *so freaking happy* doing people's taxes in the suburbs. But it feels like this summer you've found other things you like too, and maybe you should just—"

"Maybe you'll be happy eating ramen noodles and just getting by, but I don't want that for myself, Lydia."

"Excuse me, *ramen noodles are delicious*," I say. "If I get to eat ramen noodles and design musicals or whatever, I'll be so freaking happy. It's totally fine if you want to get rich and eat fancy salads all the time—"

"*Fancy salads?*"

"—but I still think you should try to also do something that makes you happy. Like you said, Mom and Dad have boring lives—"

"I didn't actually say that."

"—but they *are* happy. That's all I'm saying. Don't pick the best-paying career just for that reason. Also you *love* fancy salads, don't act like you've never heard of them before."

We end up in the suburbs, but only halfway back to our town, and I figure out what's happening while Penny's still driving us to our destination.

"Are you taking me to CalArts?" I ask.

"I am. I know it's probably not your top choice, since you wouldn't be in a proper city, but—"

"No, I'm so excited! The tech program's supposed to be really good, and I'm not completely sure I want to go *away* away to school, you know? It would be a really good compromise, maybe."

Penny parks near the campus, and we wander around. The buildings look modern and sleek, not suburban at all, and I try to imagine myself here next fall. Yes, I'm getting better at not fast-forwarding to endings, but I like this guess at my future. The kids wandering the campus seem cool and artsy, but not any much more than, like, Ava or Tara. If the school wants me, I realized, I could totally do this.

"We can sign up later for an official campus tour," Penny says. "I thought for now it would just be fun to do it at our own pace."

"Totally. Thank you so much. You're actually really thoughtful, Pen."

She waves her hand at me. "Thanks for that *actually.*"

"Oh, come on, you know what I mean. You've said a lot of really hurtful things about theater and the arts and degrees to me. And I know you didn't mean them the way they sounded—or the way I took them, at least—but your words do have effects on others. You can't just throw them out all carelessly."

"I know this isn't the appropriate reaction," Penny says, "but hearing you call me *careless* is kind of exciting. I never manage to be careless except with boys."

"You've never seemed that careless to me," I say.

"It doesn't feel that way." Penny sighs loudly and adjusts her sunglasses in the bright sunshine. I, as always, without prescription sunglasses, just have to squint. "Lydia, I have to tell you something."

"You do?" I ask.

"Miguel texted me yesterday," she says, and my head snaps to stare at her almost on its own. "I know, I should have told you sooner, but—"

"I don't think we made any specific rules about that. The rule was really just *no boys,* and then you added that we should have projects."

After all, if Penny starts tightening the rules, examining all those loopholes, texting with Miguel is going to look like a very small deal, all things considered.

"No, but I still felt that anything in that general . . . area should probably be discussed," she says. "Even after the summer's over, I want things to be different. We can't just sit around and debate what boys actually mean in their oblique text messages. We have to stay on task for our goals and not fall apart."

"Yeah, obviously. So what did Miguel want?"

Penny had gone out with a guy named Drew for most of her soph-omore year. He was practically as high-achieving as she was, so they seemed like a very well-matched couple. I was convinced she'd found her soul mate—and more than a little jealous she'd done so before I had—but then she began volunteering with a guy from a nearby high school, and suddenly sweet and successful Drew was kind of an asshole about it. I believed Penny that nothing ever happened with Miguel, but Drew didn't.

"It was a sweet text," Penny says. "He says he wanted to check in and see how I was, and if I planned to do more work with Feeding Communities next year."

"What did you say?"

"Well, I *do* plan on volunteering once I'm back home, so I said yes. And I kind of left it at that because..." Penny shrugs as we continue walking through the campus. It hits me that if I'm here in a year, my sister won't be, and I'll be figuring things out on my own. Suddenly that seems almost terrifying. "It's the summer, there are no boys, and I don't think... lining boys up on the horizon is taking the rules, as you call them, very seriously."

"But you like him?" I ask.

"I might. It would be nice to find out, now that Drew's not my boyfriend and I don't feel so pressured about all of it. Nothing ever happened with Miguel, but it still wouldn't have been right to jump into something with him once Drew and I broke up. Not just because of this summer, but because I needed time away from all of it. Anyway, the short answer is that, yes, I think I like him, but I'm not dealing with any of it until the summer's over and I can think clearly about all of it."

"Wait, so this whole thing was just so you could get a break between Drew and Miguel?" I ask, but I smile so she knows I'm not accusing her of anything. "And then *I* get dragged into it?"

"Lydia, seriously, you had flipped out about Tate. It felt best for both of us." She slips her arm through mine; we were again acting like girls we weren't. Except maybe now we were. *Are.* Maybe the summer really is doing its job and we're changing in good ways. "I wanted to tell you about the texts yesterday, but you got home so late. So I'm telling you now, and that I really am pausing all of it—including obsessing over it—until later. And hopefully I don't obsess at all."

"I bet that you won't," I say. "Thanks for telling me. I don't actually think you owed it to me or anything, but I'm glad you did. Especially since—I mean, it's been nice talking about things other than boys this summer. I just learned about the Bechdel Test from Fran. Do you know about this thing?"

Penny laughs. "Yes, Lydia, you didn't invent knowing about the Bechdel Test. It's about films having at least two female characters in them who have a conversation about something other than a man."

"It made me feel like maybe *we* hadn't passed the Bechdel Test since we were, like, eleven. And maybe not even then."

"Definitely not then, you never stopped talking about Justin Bieber," Penny says, and I cringe at the memory. "Fran sounds great. I'd like to meet her sometime, maybe."

My heart pounds. "Oh, sure, yeah, if the timing works out or whatever."

Penny gestures behind us, and I'm relieved she didn't clock my severe momentary weirdness. "Want to head back? I thought we could check out the USC campus too, and we can get lunch on the way."

"Oh my god, thank you," I say. "This was so nice of you, Penny."

"Lydia, you have to stop sounding so surprised when you say things like that."

Chapter Nineteen

Shockingly, I think it's the video Penny told me to send to Fran that does it. Because by that night, we're texting real actual plans for the film, and Fran even lets me ask Margaret permission to film in her room for two days, plus a few days' access beforehand for testing out lighting and everything.

None of my new friends, of course, know that Fran and I are serious now—girlfriends and whatever that holds for the future—but it's still easier than hiding all of it entirely from Penny. It's different with them, saying some of it but not all of it, though I guess I say some of it to Penny, too, the parts about filmmaking and sexism and scheduling. I imagine someone saying that the easiest thing in the world would be to just *tell the truth*, but it's not as if *the truth* is some kind of fixed and set thing that's easy to understand. I feel like I'm still understanding what this is every day. There's no quick short answer for anyone else.

But the group text doesn't explode into the usual *Fran's a player*. Everyone just offers to help with the shoot, even Tara, once heartbroken by Fran the player, and the project becomes more real. I really was always interested in working on the film, but it's also been a convenient excuse for my absence and my focus on Fran, at least as far as Penny's concerned. But now it's dates on my calendar, and something only discussed will soon be a tangible thing.

Fran's been lucky enough lately to time some of her breaks from her internship with my hours at Grounds Control, so a couple weeks out from our planned shoot, she joins me there, and we ask Margaret to sit with us to discuss shooting in her room. Fran hasn't been over yet, but Margaret's already shared tons of photos so Fran seems comfortable with it. I mean, she's agreed to shoot there. I'm not used to being the one calling the shots; REACT is such a team effort, and Mr. Landiss is the one with the final say. But I've said Margaret's room is the perfect setting, and we're just going with my opinion.

"So are you going to be in it too, Fran?" Margaret asks. "And do you guys want to go get pizza or something? I'm starving."

"I have to be back on set soon," Fran says. "And, no, I don't want to be in front of the camera. I should probably have thought of this already."

"There's probably tons of people from school who'd do it," Margaret says like this is no big deal. I see Fran's shoulders relax a little, and I'm grateful that it's going so well with Margaret. I don't fully understand the social dynamics here. Obviously Fran was in the same class as all of my new friends and even, once upon a time, dated Tara, but beyond that I have no idea. Was everyone friendly? Was Fran the enemy after things with Tara ended? Is it weird everyone's been brought back together through me of all people?

All I know is right now, Margaret and Fran are enthusiastically discussing other kids from their school, and land on a couple of people they think are worth asking, and so things seem OK. I think things *are* OK.

"I really have to get back to set now," Fran says. "Thanks for your help, Margaret. Lydia, I'll text you later."

Margaret nudges me as Fran heads off. "I feel like this has gotten—well, not *serious*, it's Fran, after all, but—"

"It's serious enough," I say, which is true though not the whole truth. It's not that I think Margaret would handle it badly, but I can't imagine the rest of the group would. And even Margaret would probably think she knows better about who Fran is and what she is and isn't capable of. But for now, Margaret just squeals a little, and I let myself enjoy her excitement at face value.

"It's fun helping with Fran's project," Margaret says as we head down the block for pizza. "I've done clubs in school and group projects and whatever else, but I love that you guys are just *making a movie on your own*."

"Well, Fran's making a movie," I say. "I'm just helping, it's all her vision and story. It's why I like the parts I do—I mean the parts I've always liked to do in theater. This is my first time working on a short film. But it's, like, someone else has this whole vision, and my job is to make that happen."

"Doesn't it become your vision too, then?" Margaret asks as she holds open the door to Town Pizza for me. "It's clearly not just Fran's thing."

"Maybe. In theater I stop thinking of it as anyone's, it's just this thing everyone is building together. It'll be a smaller group on this than doing a show at my school, but I still think it'll feel that way. In some ways, it already does."

"*In some ways,* like making out with the director," Margaret says, laughing, and I pretend to look a little offended. And of course a huge reason I'm doing this is because Fran's Fran. But I also know what

Margaret meant when she said that it's fun helping and just doing our own thing, outside of school or extracurriculars. That's a first for me, too.

"I'm completely good about where Fran and I are and everything," I say while we're peering into the case to figure out what pizza we want, even though both of us almost always get one slice of cheese and one slice of pepperoni. "But did she hook up with any of those people who might be in the movie? Just for my own knowledge or whatever."

Margaret practically snorts. "Lyds, even though I am well aware that Fran has, you know, *exploits*, I haven't been tracking them or anything. They weren't involved in anything dramatic, though, I can tell you that."

"Was it dramatic with Tara?"

The cashier takes our order, and we grab our usual booth. It's going to be hard going home in a few weeks and losing all my new regular things. But, of course, Margaret and friends will all be off to college soon anyway. There's no way to save this summer for later.

"It was *a little* dramatic with Tara," Margaret tells me, resting her elbows on the table and holding her chin in her hands. "Sophomore year, like, none of us had dated that much, so it felt like a big deal, even though Fran's however she is, and it felt really shocking when it just ended and Tara felt so cast aside. But I feel like now she gets that it just happens that way sometimes. I don't think Fran was trying to be an asshole or anything."

"I hope I haven't made things weird."

Margaret grins. "I mean, a little, and I love it."

〜

Penny asks me to meet her and her coworkers to watch baseball and eat wings after work that evening, and even though I can think of at least twenty-five things I'd rather do, I agree and make the walk over to the Greyhound. For a split second I think about asking Margaret along, because I'd have more fun, but things had gone so weirdly the one time they'd interacted, and I'd hate a repeat performance.

Penny and her team have beaten me there, but Penny's saved me a seat next to her and across from Oscar, so joining everyone doesn't feel too awkward. I feel bad for Penny immediately, though, because my summer coworker is Margaret, genuinely the coolest person I've ever known, and hers are a bunch of middle-aged people. But I notice that everyone includes her in their conversations, and I'm glad that my sister fits into this world, even if the one she's going to grow up to join will likely be higher-stakes and more exciting. This summer feels like the first glimpse of the lives we'll lead later on, after college, after it's no longer unusual to make all of our own choices. Making friends doesn't feel terrifying, and I'm determined to find a way to find a career that's mine and not Mom and Dad's.

But besides Penny's new thing with baseball, I have no idea if the summer has been working the same way for her. For the first time, sitting here quietly while people discuss annoying clients and the way some baseball player has been pitching lately, I could see Penny's future too, and she was going to be happy in it, I was sure.

Conversation turns away from work and baseball to the upcoming local street festival, and I remember that even though I am at worst a fashion disaster and at best a fashion nothing, Margaret's demanded I come over to help her select an outfit to best win over Lucas, a boy I have never met. I'm obviously honored by this task, so I'm glad that it doesn't really matter what you wear in front of your crush, because I'd hate to screw this up for Margaret.

"Have you heard about this?" Penny asks me. "It should be a fun chance to interact with the local community. I should be able to take off from work a little early if you'd like to go."

Normally I'd take a moment to mock that *interact with the local community* bit, but I hate what I'm about to do. "Sorry, I already made plans with—"

"It's fine," Penny says, her voice tight.

"I didn't even know it was some big thing," I say. "Margaret's got this—"

I cut myself off, because *obviously* our no boy summer is just for the two of us, but is it weird that I'm helping a friend with boy advice? Should that be off-limits, too? Next time I undertake any kind of pledge with my sister, I'm ironing out the rules more ahead of time.

"It's fine," Penny says again.

Actually, if I knew then what I know now, I would have somehow set the whole summer up differently from the beginning. I wouldn't have painted Penny as such a villain to my friends, even though for a long time, as far as my dreams were concerned, she kind of *was* a villain. But now I know it was unintentional, and now I know I can just *ask her* when she sounds like a jerk because it turns out my sister is never a jerk intentionally. Especially not to me.

But I can't go back, especially because everything is almost over anyway, and also because there's the matter of Fran, a person Penny thinks is just a filmmaker and not a girl I'm also sleeping with and— somehow I think this part's worse—really freaking smitten with. I've never said the word *smitten* out loud, maybe never even thought it before. And here I am, smitten, and my sister thinks I just care about movies and feminism.

Later, when we're all home after the game is over, Oscar intercepts me when I'm in the kitchen to get a glass of water.

"Look, I know it's none of my business, and Grace likes to tell me guys can't understand anything about sisters, but can't you just take Penny to the street fair with all of your friends? She looked really—"

"I know," I say, feeling shaky and warm. It's one thing to know you could have handled something better, it's another when it's that obvious to someone else. "It's just complicated. You know, my friends are just—I mean, I love her, but Penny can be—"

"I can be what?" Penny asks, somehow suddenly in the room with me though moments ago she seemed settled in with her laptop and headphones.

"Nothing, sorry, can I just do a thing with my friends and have it not be a big deal?" I ask, my voice snippier than I intend, and it's so embarrassing that I sound like a jerk over a stupid street fair where our main goals are to eat tacos and ice cream and make sure a boy hangs out with Margaret.

"Yeah, of course," Oscar says, kind of backing away from me, while Penny leaves the room without a word.

"Sorry," I say to Oscar.

"No, maybe I shouldn't have said anything. I'm sorry, too."

"I thought you were also the dirtbag sibling and you understood," I say, and he cracks up.

"I said I was *literally not a rocket scientist,* but thanks for interpreting that as *dirtbag.*" He grins, leaning back against the kitchen counter. "Look, yeah, my brother was valedictorian and I was...we'll just say *not.* So I get it. But also you're the one with all the friends and all your stuff going on. Just because you're not going to be valedictorian doesn't mean you're a dirtbag."

Grace lets herself into the house and laughs. "Glad I caught the tail end of that. How was the thing at the Greyhound, Lyds?"

I shrug, not wanting to cry in front of either of them. "I'm a terrible sister but fine other than that."

"I doubt that's true," Grace says.

"Well..." Oscar starts, which somehow makes me laugh. "How was your day, Gracie?"

I leave them to their couple time and slink into our room. "Penny, I'm sorry if I seem like a jerk."

"You don't seem like a jerk," she says flatly. "And, obviously, I'm aware that I'm not cool or fun enough for your friends—"

"Pen, no," I say, even though I hate that it's not completely untrue. "You know that this is weird for me, right?"

She just watches me, one eyebrow raised.

"I don't have friends like this back home," I say, even though she should already be aware of this. "I never...fit in with people. Especially groups of girls. They always make me nervous, like they'll spot that I'm—I don't know. Not cool or not right somehow. I don't even know what I'm not. I've always just felt like I'm *not* and that everyone can tell."

Penny still doesn't say anything. But as long as her giant headphones stay off, I figure I should keep going.

"I don't know why it's different here," I say, sitting down on my bed. "I guess because Margaret's made it really easy. Almost like I didn't have a choice in it, we were just going to be friends because we got along, and it's been—mostly it's been easy. And when it wasn't, I felt like, what did I have to lose, and so I just *told her*. And—I don't know,

Pen, I still feel like it's too good to be true some days, and I'm not upsetting the balance if I can help it, especially considering before long we'll be back home and school will be starting and it won't be like this anymore."

"What do you mean?" Penny asks. "You have *lots* of friends. REACT and all of that."

"Yeah, but it's not like this. I'm not on group texts that talk about anything other than what we think Mr. Landiss will pick for the fall musical."

"It doesn't seem like that," Penny says.

"Well, it *is* like that," I say. "And—look, part of me thinks it's not other people, it's me. Like I've been so nervous feeling different or less cool than people that I never... This summer really has been different, but I do want to see what next year's like, actually. Not to say I haven't imagined every way I don't fit in, but I'm also going to try not dwelling on it."

This whole mostly-one-sided conversation has been way more honesty from me than I'd planned on, but it's hard to tell if Penny's moved by it. She's a tough crowd.

"Anyway, I didn't mean to be a jerk."

"I know." Penny goes to slip her headphones back on, and for some reason I feel like if she does that, this hasn't actually gotten any better, no matter how much I've revealed. At some point, I realize, opening up to Penny hasn't felt at all like giving her ammo for future lectures. It just feels like talking. Maybe I can take a chance and say more. If not now, when?

"Also Margaret has a crush on this guy and I'm giving her advice or whatever and I wasn't sure I should say anything to you about it considering," I say all in one rushed breath.

"Why not?" Penny asks, frowning. She lets go of the headphones, though, so I already feel victorious. "Is it a guy I know?"

"I mean, doubtful, it's some guy from her school here. I just mean that we're supposed to be taking the summer off from boys, so is it bad I'm talking about one to my friend? She's super obsessed with him and nervous about it because she hasn't had a ton of boy experience. I didn't want you to think I wasn't taking the rules seriously."

Penny actually laughs. "It's not like we can make boys disappear from the world. Why would I mind?"

"I don't know, don't your videos all talk about positive habit-forming and all of that? Maybe talking about Lucas is keeping my boy habit going."

Penny laughs harder. "Lydia, I know you've been taking it seriously. Now it seems so silly that at the beginning of the summer I was suspicious of that pastry delivery guy you mentioned. You've barely even mentioned him again."

"I mean, Ben is still very cute," I say. "Margaret and I look at his Instagram sometimes. His friends are also all cute."

"Wait, let me see," Penny says, and I hop over to her bed to pull up his account. "Oh *wow.* I can't believe you've stopped talking about him."

"He's, like, twenty-one and he has a girlfriend and also it's *so early* when I see him, Pen, people look less attractive when you're struggling to stay awake."

"I'm not entirely sure that's true," she says with a smile. "Thanks for telling me all of that. Not that you had to. I'm not trying to put any pressure on you or—"

"No, dude, I'm just still learning how to have friends and function in a group of them and I get stupid about things."

"Did you just call me *dude?*" she asks, and we both crack up. Moments later, there's a knock on the door, and we both call out to come in.

"You two sound OK in here," Grace says, leaning inside the doorway. "Oscar was worried there was sister drama afoot."

"We're drama-free," I say, whether or not that's true, and hope that Penny doesn't contradict me.

"It's nice that Oscar worries about things," Penny says. "You can tell that everyone in the office thinks he's really nice."

Grace smiles and sits next to us on Penny's bed. "Wait, I didn't think about the fact that you get Oscar office gossip. What else do they say about him?"

Penny smiles. "I think since everyone knows that we're basically related that they don't gossip rudely about him in front of me. But I do think everyone thinks he runs late to meetings but is good at selecting restaurants for group lunch orders."

Grace laughs. "Ah, that's my guy. Bad at punctuality, great at food."

"How did you guys meet?" I ask, and Penny perks up.

"Yes, I've never heard this story," she says.

"I can't believe I haven't told you," Grace says. "It's a good one. We actually went to college together, over at Loyola Marymount, but we were sort of—you know, peripheral to each other's groups of friends. And then, years later, he came into The Roast Of, the coffee shop I worked at before Grounds Control, and I felt just so happy to see him, I almost couldn't explain it."

"You never dated in college?" I ask.

"Never hooked up, never dated, never thought about him romantically at all. And then he was there, and I felt whatever I was feeling, so I got up the nerve to ask him to dinner, and—well, from there it was just easy. For a guy who runs late, he showed up at that coffee shop at the exact right time."

"That *is* a good story," Penny says. "I didn't realize you'd gone to college, Grace."

Grace grins at this. "Because I've only worked in coffee shops?"

"Well, I guess *yes*," Penny says.

"College isn't just about the degree, or the job market, or how much you'll make later," Grace says. "I was lucky enough to get accepted and to make it work financially, and those four years were amazing. I learned so much, met some of my best friends, and now I run my own business doing exactly what I want."

Penny nods.

"You both have a lot ahead of you," Grace says. "Back when I was your age—oh *shit*. I'm officially a *back when I was your age* middle-aged person."

"You're younger and cooler than Mom," I point out.

"That's a low bar to clear," Penny says, and Grace and I crack up.

"I just don't want the two of you to worry so much about what comes next," Grace says. "The figuring out parts of life can be stressful and chaotic, but it's also some of the best fun I've ever had."

Chapter Twenty

Late on Friday afternoon, my friends and Fran and I plan to meet in one of our usual spots, near Grounds Control and all of my new favorite local shops. Tonight, York Boulevard is completely blocked off to traffic. The sidewalk's somehow too crowded, so I find Su Jin and Ava waiting on the actual street.

"This is even busier than last year," Su Jin says. "Are you ready, Lyds? Is suburbia ever this crowded?"

"Yeah, you should have seen it when they opened a new Sizzler," I say. "It made our local paper."

"Did someone have those big scissors?" Ava asks. "I've always wanted to cut one of those big ribbons with big scissors."

"Dream big," Su Jin tells her as I feel an arm slide around my waist.

There was probably a tiny part of me that worried Fran wouldn't actually be a good girlfriend, that she'd still be trying to hold space for other girls or at least give herself the appearance of being free and unattached. Even while things have been great—better than great, creative ideas exchanged and steamy make-out sessions in her truck and late-night texts that swung me between laughing and thinking and swooning very, very hard—sometimes in quiet moments I'd think back to how things started and how doubtful Fran had seemed about anything that wasn't just *for fun.* But there still hasn't been any of that. And so hopefully that means that tonight—the first night it's been all of us since KBBQ what feels like a million years ago—won't be weird or awkward. How could my friends not see how good Fran and I have it?

"Hey," I say to her, and she kisses my cheek. I register that Ava and Su Jin register the kiss, a real girlfriend move, but I try to just stay right here in the moment. It doesn't have to be some big anxious thing. Everyone will be fine. I always feel a little—well, *nervous* is too strong a word, but Margaret was the one to aggressively friend me at the beginning. I feel lucky that her friends have welcomed me too, but when she's not around I know that I'm less sure of myself.

"Hey. Some kid just gave me free lollipops, so . . ." Fran fans them out, and we quickly fight over the best colors. By the time Tara walks over, only orange ones are left, which of course works out great. She and Fran nod at each other, so I guess we're all fine there.

"Hey, everyone—"

We drown out Margaret's greeting because she looks *so* cute in a pastel sundress with her hair, for once, fanned out loose over her shoulders in perfect beach waves. I'd helped pick out the outfit from an array of extremely cute ones, but it's still kind of stunning to see her in it, looking like the epitome of summer.

"When did you tell Lucas to meet us?" Su Jin asks her as Margaret's frowning over a remaining orange lollipop.

"Like, *now*, so don't be embarrassing, everyone," she says. We all go on high alert, though we're trying to pretend like we're not. But then Lucas is suddenly there, and we all laugh because it's too crowded to see anyone coming anyway. He looks cute in a short-sleeved button-down and nice jeans, his hair cut like Fran's but kind of haphazard because of a few random cowlicks. He is objectively very cute, and I love that he dressed up nice for Margaret. All of my jangly nerves about my own situation settle. I have a really good feeling about tonight.

There are booths lining both sides, with tacos, popcorn, fresh lemonade, jewelry, candles, crystals, T-shirts, tiny pies, seemingly anything you could think of. A section is roped off while a few artists work on giant chalk drawings right onto the sidewalk. I'm not sure my friends notice the drawings right away, but Lucas stops to watch, and so do Fran and I.

"Man, that's amazing," Lucas says as we watch a man add to a drawing of dozens of pastries: pies, croissants, tarts. I can't believe how real they look, and I try to study his shading techniques to figure out how he does it.

"You look inspired," Fran says to me.

"I guess I am, yeah. I mean, not that I'm an artist like that, but creating something out of nothing that tricks your eye, it's kind of like theater in its own way."

Fran glances over at everyone else in our group. "Lydia's so good at just coming up with ideas on how things should look. I wouldn't be getting ready to shoot a film without her."

"No, you'd be fine," I say with a laugh. "But thank you. Also probably no one believes you because I feel like people good at design and creation usually look cool, and I just look boring."

"No way," Lucas, a boy I barely know, says, and I smile. "You can be like one of those tech geniuses. They all wear the same outfit every day and say their brains have more room to think."

"Lucas, she's not boring!" Margaret shrieks.

"No, I am, and that makes me really excited. I basically already am doing that, and now I can say it's just a creative genius sort of goal. Thank you, Lucas."

"I can't wait to see all of Lydia's creative work on the movie," Ava says, and I smile at her as Fran squeezes my hand.

"It's Fran's movie and all the smart stuff is her," I say.

"Just because I'm writing and directing doesn't make it all mine," Fran says. "Lydia's the one with all the other good ideas."

"Not *all* the other good ideas," I say, though I love that she's saying it.

"Are you guys trying to out-compliment each other?" Su Jin asks. "Honestly, it should be annoying, but it's pretty cute."

I can't believe how officially OK everything is. Maybe I could have told everyone how things were going with Fran sooner. Or maybe this is the way, actually, to just be here with everyone, letting them see how good it is. Especially since it's not like it's just Fran and me, I realize how much I care about how everyone gets along. I hadn't understood that part of friendship before—how it has to be taken care of just like a romance. But a sunny day surrounded by my friends and my girlfriend is a great day to realize it.

"Do you want an agua fresca?" Fran asks me.

"I don't even know what that is," I say. "Fresh water?"

Everyone laughs at me, though nicely, and then Fran and Lucas walk off to a nearby booth together to get drinks for all of us. Agua fresca turns out to just be iced fruit juice, kind of like lemonade but with different flavors. Fran gives me the choice of watermelon and cucumber melon, but I can't decide and so we keep switching them back and forth. It already seems silly that I was originally nervous about today, as I look around and see that this is my group, these are my people. It feels like a million years ago that I thought if I could just fall in love and stay in love that no one else would matter. I can't even imagine having Fran if I didn't have these friends, too.

"Do you two need help with your movie?" Ava asks. "I'm sure you're trying to finish it before you're away at school, Fran."

"Oh, I'm not—I'm sticking around." Fran gives me a little look I don't know how to interpret. "But, maybe. Lyds and I were discussing ideal lighting, and if I'm filming, she'd have to hold a lot of reflectors at once, and I'm not sure if that's possible, considering her arms aren't even that long."

"I can help too, considering you'll be filming in my room," Margaret says, stretching out her arms. "Look! A great length."

Everyone's comparing arm spans as Tara corrals us into line for vegan tacos. For some reason, almost all the taco trucks in Highland Park are vegan, but honestly it's hard to tell. They're just all *delicious*.

Fran hands some cash to Su Jin. "Can you order for Lydia and me?"

"Of course," she says, though Su Jin looks as puzzled as I feel. I let Fran pull me away, just a few feet down the sidewalk. We're still in the crowd but not right up against my friends.

"I know you're going back home before long," Fran says. "But I guess it just really hit me for some reason."

I nod, wondering why we have to have this scary talk right after I decided things were safe and right before I'm about to eat vegan tacos. "I'm kind of in denial right now. That's healthy, right?"

Fran grins right at me. Maybe things aren't about to become scary.

"Sure," she says. "Anyway, I want you to know—and you can take your time thinking about this—that even if forty miles don't count as long-distance, I'm not thinking about this as just for the summer."

"Oh my god," I say, kissing her, "me either. I mean, I have, but also— I mean, it's been nice being in the moment with you. But I *like you so much*, Fran."

"This has been…" Fran holds my face in her hands, even though we're in this giant crowd. "I love working with you. I actually like being your girlfriend."

I laugh. "Oh, thanks!"

"You know what I mean. I didn't think being in a relationship was what I wanted, but… I'm glad I went with my gut. Or maybe I went against my gut? I can't even remember now. I just like whatever this is."

"Me too." I glance over to make sure our friends are still waiting for tacos, and they are, so I turn back to Fran to grab her by the shoulders and pull myself up to her height. I'm not completely pro-PDA, but I'm so overwhelmed by Fran and how this feels, to be talking about *the future* with someone I like, and not in the way I thought of before. The future is a real thing we might be building, something we're figuring out one step at a time, together. And right now, it feels impossible not to kiss her.

Someone bumps into me and I pull back, a little, from Fran. "I'm so sorry, we—"

"Lydia."

I turn and look because it can't be. But it is. It's Penny.

Chapter Twenty-One

I run after Penny like I've never run before. Like my life depends on it.

"Penny," I call through the crowds. "Wait for me, OK?"

She doesn't, though, and the truth is I don't blame her. Maybe if I had more righteous indignation at her reaction it would fuel me, but Penny's taller and faster and almost nearly always right.

"Hey."

Speaking of taller and faster, Fran's caught up with me.

"Is everything OK?" she asks. Fran's eyes are so kind, and all I want to do is throw myself into her arms and let her tell me things will be OK in general and specifically. I want to say *no* and have her disagree and not feel like a huge fuckup right now.

"No," I say, but I take a step back from her. "I have to sort this shit out with my sister, OK? It's a long story and I'll tell you the whole thing later, I promise."

"Go handle your sister shit," she says with a grin, and even though I'm losing time I still let myself bury myself in her arms for a few moments. When I extract myself I see that Penny's actually only a few yards ahead of me, and she sees this whole scene unfolding, too.

"Pen—"

She turns and walks off again. I follow after her, more slowly, and eventually we make it all the way back home, in front of Grace and Oscar's.

"You lied to me," she says. Her voice is calmer than I expect, completely steady. TED Talk Penny. "All summer. About—well, quite a lot. Maybe everything."

"No, not all summer," I say. "And it's not really—I wasn't lying. We just said no boys, right? There were no boys at all."

"Oh, sure," she says with a roll of her eyes. "That's what I meant. I certainly didn't mean that you and I had let relationships become destructive forces in our lives and we needed to reexamine our priorities if we were serious about our other goals."

I stare at her. "*Destructive forces?* You make my drama sound like an earthquake."

"Well, what would you call it then, Lydia? We kept falling apart. Like boys were the only thing that—like *romance* was the only thing that truly mattered. When obviously we both know better. We talked about this, remember? And I worked so hard for us to have this summer so that—" Penny shakes her head and I see tears streak down her face. Penny's not me, the girl who cries easily. It takes so much. And right now, I'm the *so much*.

"OK," I say. "You're right. I'm sorry. But—"

"No," she says. "You don't get to be *all casual* right now. You lied to me all summer. And—look, I understand that you don't owe me your identity or however it is to you. But I can't believe you didn't tell me. That you've *never* told me."

I shrug because right now I can't believe I haven't, either. "It's just that before—I don't know, Pen. It was a lot to say, I guess, and there hadn't been anyone who wasn't a boy yet, and I—I don't know."

"I understand that it was up to you," she says. "What you told me about who you are. But once it was—once there was someone you were—"

"Yeah, I know, it was just a lot, Penny, to go from it being this theo-retical that I didn't completely know how to think about to there being this actual girl. I just wanted to really sort it out. I figured because we only agreed to boys, it was fine."

Obviously, saying it aloud, I know lots of my words aren't exactly true. But I've repeated them to myself so many times. I had them ready. I wanted all of it not to be a lie.

"No," she says, "and it's insulting that you think I'd treat gender like that. Boys off-limits, everyone else fine. Plus, if you really thought this was all fine, you *would* have told me. You only didn't because deep down you knew it wasn't actually about boys at all."

"You're right," I say as my stomach clenches in recognition. "I guess I did know that. But also, to be fair, it wasn't just about romance. It was about, like, the balance of romance, right? That was the thing we couldn't get right, how it was all lopsided and obsessive. No friends, forgotten responsibilities, all that? But look at me! I learned how to balance. I fell for someone and you didn't even know!"

Penny watches me for a moment. "Well, congratulations, Lydia. I'm so happy for you."

"No, Pen, I didn't—"

She turns and starts to walk into the house. When I step behind her, she holds up her hand. "I need some time alone."

"Yeah, of course," I say. "But we're OK, right?"

"No," she says, walking into the doorway. "We are definitively not *OK*, and I have no idea how we could be again."

The door shuts right in my face.

∽

I don't really know what to do with myself or how to give someone space when you share a bedroom, so I walk back to the street fair. Fran's already texted that she's gone home for the night, but I assume my friends are still there, and I'm right. I find them eating ice cream at the little park a couple blocks down from Grounds Control.

"Where've you been?" Su Jin asks.

Ava raises her eyebrows a bunch in what I assume is supposed to be a sexy manner. "Makin' out?"

Everyone laughs, but I can't join in considering just how far it is from the truth. And also because that isn't who I am anymore. Sure, the Lydia Jones pre–this summer probably would have sneaked out of a group event as soon as possible to make out somewhere, but I wasn't her anymore. I wanted today with my friends *and* with my girlfriend.

"Just—drama with my sister," I say, finally. "It's a long story."

"Tell us," Tara says.

"It's stupid," I say. "I won't bother you guys with it. Probably I should..."

"Geez, Lyds, we didn't suddenly stop being interested in stupid things," Margaret says. "Ava just spent like an hour telling us about why banana flavoring tastes weird."

"I read an interesting article about extinct banana varieties!" she says, and the rest of them laugh. I missed whatever this is, and I guess that's OK. They're all going on to their own things, and I'm just, again, the girl diverted by relationship drama. But I try to let my stuff get forgotten, and conversation keeps rolling, and suddenly vendors start packing up and the night is over.

Back at Grace and Oscar's, Penny's in bed with her giant head-phones over her ears and a sleep mask on over her eyes. It's a whole lot, but I decide not to get her attention. I'm not really sure how I would anyway.

I get out my phone in bed and ignore the group chat for a text from Fran. *How's the sister drama?*

It'll blow over, I type, despite all evidence literally facing me at this moment. *I'll explain later. I'm so sorry I ruined hanging out tonight.*

It's no problem. I have a family thing tomorrow morning—hang out after?

I agree to that and put my phone on my nightstand. It's not that late but maybe if I can fall asleep now, by the time I wake up, Penny will have forgiven me and then Fran and I can have a big laugh over the whole thing and my friends don't have to know just how much drama my relationships are capable of.

Penny's gone when I get up the next morning. I try not to take it as a sign that my whole plan is doomed. Still, I make an excuse to get out of the group text's plans for breakfast tacos at HomeState. It might not make sense, but I just want everything sorted out. I hate that I finally managed to get this group of friends and then I somehow turned into someone whose drama outweighs everything else going on. What if I am just the girl who has cycles of relationship drama off and on her whole life until she dies?

No, I remember, it's not like last time. My friends are still my friends. And Fran's still my girlfriend. Only Penny's upset, and Penny and I have never stayed mad at each other for long. I'm not in some doomed cycle. Things are going to be fine, and they're probably even going to be fine very soon.

Grace treats me normally when I stop by Grounds Control for coffee and a pastry, which I take as a good sign, and I eat at a corner table while scrolling through Instagram to catch up on everything I missed yesterday. I'm so mad at myself that I lost the time with my friends—yesterday and right now—but maybe time by myself is what I need. Maybe Penny's right and that's all I was supposed to have this summer anyway.

Back at Grace and Oscar's, I curl up with my notepad and try to work on more thoughts for the film. At this point I think I'm set for lighting, and Margaret's room shouldn't need too many embellishments or additional set decoration, but I want to feel fully confident in all of these decisions. Emilia, the classmate of Fran and Margaret's who's going to star in the film, has sent us some outfit ideas, and those colors and fabrics also have to be considered with everything else.

I feel a little guilty about focusing on something that isn't Penny or my own fuckups, but the truth is that Penny's not going to get home sooner just because I'm sitting here doing nothing except waiting for her. Plus there's a timeline for the film, our shoot scheduled. I love the feel of the rush of things, working to outrun the clock. It reminds me of some of my favorite parts of theater.

Fran texts to see if I want to hang out, and even though I was hoping to have already mended things with Penny, I say yes anyway. Plus now at least we're not sneaking around. Not that Fran ever knew we were sneaking around, but it still makes it easier for me.

I hop into her truck when she pulls up and get lost in kissing her for a few moments, maybe more. What's time when you're lost?

"So is everything OK?" Fran asks, her hands off of me and back on the wheel. "Last night and whatever?"

"Oh, sure," I say. I can hear how much more cheerful I sound than I am. "Just this dumb pledge and—it'll be fine."

"A pledge?"

"It was just this whole thing," I say, "with my sister. Since we had all this relationship drama last year—honestly we've been having relationship drama for what feels like our whole lives. I'm a disaster anyway, no one would argue it, but Penny's so together otherwise, but then bring cute boys into the picture and suddenly she's almost as hopeless as I am."

I can hear in my voice that I'm trying to tell this in a charming way, but Fran's expression hasn't changed. This is probably because of the situation and yet all I can think right now is *be more charming!*

"So we did this whole little pledge for the summer," I say. "Not, like, a *pledge* pledge, we didn't hold up our hands with another one on a Bible or do a blood oath. We just promised each other."

Fran's brow is furrowed. We haven't moved from this spot on Grace and Oscar's block. "Promised each other *what?*"

"No boys for the summer," I say. "Just to make sure we got past the drama or whatever. Penny has way bigger goals than getting weighed down by dumb boy stuff. And maybe I don't, but I was still screwing up way too much. There was a whole thing with a performance of *Mary Poppins* and—anyway, we promised no boys the whole summer for, like, a reset."

"So..." She scratches her head, shoves back her hair. "What about me? Us, I should say."

"You're not a boy," I say with a shrug. "Obviously. So I wasn't breaking the pledge at all. Girls were the loophole. You're a technicality."

I think this is cute, but she reels back like I've said something awful.

"I mean, it all seemed fine at first," I continue. I'm sure the more I explain, she'll get it. "You were doing your whole *Fran's a player* thing and I was pretending to let you chase me, but then—"

"*Pretending?*" she asks.

"No, I guess it's more like the whole game of it. You're all tough and mysterious, and I'm all *ooh I couldn't want anything more than tough and mysterious!*"

"The *game* of it?"

"I mean, not that the whole thing was a game, just that at first—"

Fran sighs. "You know, I was stupid enough to feel lucky you were so honest with me when you were ready to actually be in a relationship. It's the kind of thing that never really felt right before but you . . . you felt right. You felt *real*, Lydia."

I want to say that I *am* real, but I can tell it's not the right moment.

"But instead you were playing some shitty game with me?"

"No, it's just how at first you reel girls in with your whole detached, hard-to-get player vibe, and I—"

"I don't *reel girls in*," she says. "I was really up-front with you. Not being in automatic default relationship mode isn't a bad thing or a game, and I'd think you of all people would understand having a long history or whatever doesn't make you some label. Not a slut and not a player, either. Just a fucking *person*, Lydia."

"I'm saying this all really badly. Fran—"

"First I'm a technicality, also I'm a player, also you weren't being honest with me *even when I was thanking you for being so honest*." She shakes her head. "I feel so stupid that I somehow fell for any of this bullshit."

"Fran," I say again. "It wasn't bullshit. I swear."

"You're not even owning it now! Which...well, it's not helping. I feel so fucking stupid."

"You're not stupid—"

"Yeah," she says, "maybe I am. Getting tricked by you makes me feel like I really might be. Have fun back in the suburbs, Lydia."

She sits back in her seat, and I let myself out of the truck and walk back down the block before I can even process it. It's over, and it's like another door, the very last door closing, before I even saw it swinging shut.

I can't believe how fast it all happened, how one moment we were kissing and now we're—I don't want to say *over* but we might be over. Fran seemed so definite and sure of herself, and I have nothing to offer up. Even if what she's saying isn't exactly true, I don't have the words or the proof or whatever Fran needs to see the difference. Suddenly it's like I don't have the right *anything* for Fran at all.

Penny's in our room when I walk back inside, no headphones and no sleep mask. It's unbelievable I could feel hopeful right now, of all times, as my heart might be breaking, but I know it's a good sign.

"Hey," I say.

"*Hey*," she says, but with a roll of her eyes. "We're on *hey* terms now?"

"Pen, please. I promise I—"

"Don't. There's nothing I want to hear from you right now."

"I get that I screwed up," I say. "But you won't even let me explain, and—"

"I planned this whole summer for *us*," she says. "And then you got here and you got this...girl gang I was clearly unwelcome around. You became obsessed with a person named Fran who it turns out *you were dating*. And even though it wasn't how I saw the summer going,

I kept thinking that it was fine because we were being honest with each other and helping each other with our future goals. But what does any of that matter if you were lying the entire time?"

"This was *your* whole idea!" I say. "No boys, more other stuff, right? I did all the other stuff."

"You did so much of *the other stuff* without me," she says. "But when I thought it was because you were learning how to have this healthier, more-balanced life, how could I fault you for that? But of course nothing had changed at all. You left me out *and* you lied, and you didn't grow at all."

"Penny." I don't know what else to say because she's right. She's right about enough, at least. I think my life *is* healthier and better-balanced now, in fact, I'm sure of it. I grew! But I *did* leave her out, and of course that was because, for many reasons, it was all easier without her. And while I'd explained some of that to her already, that friendship was new and scary for me and I was just fumbling through learning how to fit in, I know that none of that sounds the same now. Not with the full story about Fran out there.

Boys are what Penny and I had before. Deciphering texts' meanings and running post-kiss analyses. I trusted Penny's plan, because Penny's basically always right. This summer, though, I saw how much more I thought the two of us could have. College plans and career goals and talking about friendship like two girls who hadn't always figured that out very well. But here we are before the summer's even over, and if Penny can forget about all of that, maybe it turns out that boys are all we had after all.

Chapter Twenty-Two

Grace eyes me warily on our walk to Grounds Control on Monday morning but doesn't say anything. I've been crying a lot and there's nothing I can do to disguise it. Even if I were better at makeup, there's really nothing to do about the fact that my face is all puffy and damp.

The weekend felt longer than maybe the whole summer before it. Penny's still completely freezing me out, and even though I tried to distract myself with rereading my notes on lighting and design for film, it kept making me cry more. What if I can't fix things with Fran? What happens to all our work? Of course it was never just for her. It was for me, too. It was because this is what I do, and what I want to do for the rest of my life, when I allow myself to think that far into the future. If she asked me, even if she's completely done with me otherwise, I'd still help. I'd still set up lighting and pick the right costume and hold the reflectors and make sure every frame looked beautiful.

But I'm not completely stupid. I know that right now, Fran doesn't want to see me. It seems impossible it was only Friday, mere days ago, when Fran confessed that she wanted to make things work even when I was back home. Everything felt possible at that moment, and I saw how it could all be different: a balanced life and a relationship with a person that felt based on something we figured out together.

And now I'm still in LA, but it doesn't matter.

Waze Jeff is in a bad mood when I unlock the door at 5:59, one minute early just to get him over with, and from the way he slams down his reusable mug, he doesn't appreciate it at all.

"Starbucks opens at five," I tell him. "Just so you know. Their lattes are fine."

He gapes at me, and without turning around I can tell that Grace is doing the same. I wait for her to say something, but she's silent.

"Well, I—" Waze Jeff sputters a bit before handing over his credit card. "The coffee here is a lot better. I just really hate my commute. And my boss. It's not great having to deal with someone terrible five days a week."

I swipe his credit card and hand it back. "Yeah, I wouldn't know what that's like."

He makes a face, but I can tell that he's, for once, adding a tip to the payment screen. "Have a good day, ladies."

"You too, Jeff," Grace says, handing him his drink. He dashes out, and I wait for things to get even worse.

But Grace just laughs.

"We should probably have a discussion about customer service," she says. "But that was too enjoyable to worry about, to be honest. And he tipped you twenty dollars!"

"He tipped *us* twenty dollars," I say with a smile. I didn't think anything could make me smile today.

Margaret's there before long, looking the opposite of how I feel. Her braid crown is magnificent, her face is glowing, and she's smiling like she hasn't stopped since Friday night. Maybe she hasn't.

"Lyds! Where were you this weekend?" she asks.

I shrug because I don't know what to say other than that everything is screwed up and I'm not sure I know how to talk to people right now and I just need a lot of space and time to figure it all out or maybe just disappear back into the suburbs altogether.

Grace takes the next customer, and Margaret bumps up against me.

"Friday was so fun."

I sort of nod.

"What's up with you?" She points to me to start pulling espresso shots. "You ignored us all weekend, now you seem all...weird."

"Nothing good," I say. "Can I not talk, please?"

"Lyds." She grabs my arm. "What's going on?"

"Like I said, nothing good. Everything bad. If I talk I'll start crying into these shots, which is disgusting."

"OK," she says, rubbing my shoulder a little. "Come over after work today?"

"I don't know. I might need to just go home."

She shoots me another worried look but doesn't fight me. I keep my head down and stay with the espresso machine until my shift's over. At three, I take off my apron and start back to Grace and Oscar's, hoping my attitude was enough to keep Margaret away.

"Lyds, are you sure you don't want company?"

I was clearly wrong.

"I'm sure," I say, even though of course I do. This is the most alone I can remember feeling. At least when Tate broke up with me, Penny was there. Mom baked me a breakup cake (she didn't call it that, but with its timing, the chocolate-frosted cake couldn't have been anything else). Dad said *that Taylor kid doesn't know what he's missing* while Mom and Penny chorused *His name is Tate!!*

But it doesn't feel right to talk to Margaret. What kind of friendship do we have anyway? I wish I didn't automatically think *built on lies,* but if I was hiding the group from Penny, and Penny from the group, and the full truth from Fran, and—to some degree—Fran from everyone, what else could it be? So I just walk away from Margaret, no matter how much I wish I wasn't.

I don't know what to do with myself once I'm at Grace and Oscar's. All my spare time's been going to the film, my friends, Fran, and Penny. And I don't have any of this anymore, and I'm not sure I want to spend any more time checking my research and my plans, even if it fills the time. Working on it feels so stupid now. Because will Fran even care? Will Fran ever look at me again? Even though I've had a bunch of relationships, I never had a fight like Saturday. Does it even count as a fight when it's just one person justifiably yelling?

I hate how justifiable it was.

We hadn't technically been together that long, but I can't believe how much I miss her, how much I feel her absence. Even just a couple weeks of having Fran as my girlfriend made me count on her, but now there aren't any texts, and there's no pickup truck idling outside for me, and there's no giddy feeling that she could show up at any moment and change everything.

I've always known I was no one special—not someone destined for greatness like Penny, obviously—but this summer it had gotten easy to believe that maybe that wasn't true. The whole reason we were here in the first place was the hard reset Penny and I both needed, and all I can think now is that I'm so screwed up that even a hard reset couldn't fix anything.

The very bad thing about sharing a bedroom with your sister who isn't speaking to you is if you are also dealing with a very broken heart, you end up with both zero privacy and zero sympathy.

When Penny's there, her stupid noise-canceling headphones are ever-present. The sleep mask is also a lot more present than you'd think for hours that are not sleep-related. It's not that this is completely new behavior for her; I know she likes to really focus on audiobooks and podcasts, but it was never constant like this before.

"Hey," I try, and when she doesn't look up, I sit down next to her on the bed and touch her arm. She jerks away and flips up her sleep mask.

"I'm listening to something," she says.

"Can you listen to *me?*" I ask. "For just a minute? Thirty seconds?"

"I can't hear you," she says, sliding the mask back on.

I make a face at her and go back to my side of the room. The group text is busy as always but I still feel like I don't deserve it.

I scroll through Instagram but it feels like torture. Do I want to check in on my friends who don't know how messed-up I am? Or the girl I was falling in love with who wants nothing to do with me? I can't believe I have no one left. No matter how bleak anything else looked before, I'd always had Pen.

I glance over at the stack of books that has now completely taken over the nightstand and grab the top one. It's some self-help-type book about not getting in your own way, whatever that means, and I'm so bored and depressed by social media and the rest of my entire life that I turn to the first page and start reading.

It's hard to know what Penny got out of this, because all the first chapters are about failing at things, and Penny's truly failed at nothing. Even her boy disasters were nothing compared to mine. I can't believe that I let her treat her situation like mine, when her biggest problem was that *boys were fighting over her* while I'd been dumped by the love of my then-life with not a word of explanation.

Me, though, I'm all over these pages. And I guess I'm therefore the exact person who should be reading this book, the person who screws up plans and fails at goals and can't "build relationships" to save my life, if that's how lives could be saved. I guess in some ways, maybe it is. But all I see is a big list detailing exactly how screwed up I am, and it makes me wonder if a book can fix you or if it's just a distraction from the knowledge that you're broken somewhere deep down.

I fold a page over to mark my place and turn off the light. One of the only good things about an early morning job is that the night ends up coming so fast. And tomorrow'll be here before I know it, where nothing will be better but at least I'll have somewhere to go and a job to keep me busy.

∿

Margaret walks in straight over to me the next morning. "I cannot believe you didn't respond to me last night."

"I had to mute the group chat," I say.

"Well, *duh*, we all mute it, it drains your battery otherwise. I meant the texts I sent just to you."

I shrug. "Sorry."

"What's up with you?" Margaret makes a face as she ties on her apron. "Are we in a fight? Are you mad? Did I screw up again? Please tell me if I screwed up."

"You didn't screw up, and I'm not mad." I shrug because what do I even say? I'm a fuckup who doesn't deserve my friends? I'm stupid for thinking I was building something new when really I was rebuilding over the exact same garbage foundation as always? I, per that depressing book, am the girl in my own way. Give me too much time with someone and maybe I'll get in her way, too.

"Just tell me what's going on," Margaret says, but a bunch of people come in and I end up barely looking up from the espresso machine for at least an hour. I like feeling the time slip away like this, drink by drink, time when I don't have to explain or say anything that doesn't have to do with coffee.

I take myself on a long walk after work, no headphones, just me and the city. I can't believe how loud and scary it was to me, how little sense I could make of how it fit together. I love the older parts of this neighborhood, the original storefronts from decades ago, lined right up against new hipster shops and restaurants. And I guess I love whatever it is within me that learned to love something that scared me. It's a part of me that, no matter how I turn it in my head, doesn't seem broken at all.

"Hey."

I literally jump, and then I laugh, because it's just Margaret. "Were you following me?"

"I wish I'd thought of doing something that dramatic. My mom and I ran to Mr. Holmes to get some pastries, and I saw you across the street. This is literally a small town. Also I made my mom buy you a fancy croissant." She holds out a bag and smiles at me. "Seriously, what's going on, Lyds?"

I rub the back of my hand over my eyes, like this is subtle and I'm not crying. But Margaret just slips her arm around my shoulders and squeezes.

"Is it Fran?" she asks, and I actually *laugh* because it's like maybe my friends were just waiting for it to go sideways and—I don't know. Why is that comforting instead of embarrassing?

"It's a lot of things," I say.

"Hang on, let me text my mom to tell her to go home without me," Margaret says, her eyes on her screen. "Unless you want to come over? There's more pastries where this one came from."

"You don't have to bribe me with pastries," I say, and it's in that moment that I realize how far we've come, how at one time pastries were a scary thing Margaret made careless fat jokes about and now, here we are, girls who trust each other. So I say yes and ride back to Margaret's house with her and her mother.

Chapter Twenty-Three

At Margaret's we settle into her room, and something about this setting—the place I was supposed to make a movie with Fran—propels me past the small talk I wish we were having instead. This room seems like the wrong place for it.

"I did this dumb pledge with my sister, because we're disasters," I say, once we're sitting on Margaret's floor on the fluffy pale lavender rug with pastries between us on a beautiful light green plate. Everything in Margaret's home is more beautiful than it needs to be, and I love that. I make a note in that vague list of hypotheticals that my perfect life will be as beautiful and thoughtfully chosen as possible.

"Well," I continue, clarifying, "I'm a disaster and Penny's—"

"A beautiful future president, got it," Margaret says, popping a piece of croissant into her mouth.

"No, just—she had this thing where her boyfriend, who'd seemed fine before, got super jealous of a guy she was volunteering with, and she got a B-minus on a test or something and she flipped out." Penny had told me it was a C, but in retrospect I was pretty sure that was an exaggeration. "My thing was way worse. I'd gotten distracted in the middle of a performance of *Mary Poppins* and I was one of the people in charge of the ropes that kept Elise Winfreid—she was playing Mary Poppins—up in the air, and I missed my cue and—I don't even fully know how it happened, but I wasn't holding the rope at the right time and she went careening."

Margaret gasps, holding her hands to her heart. "Was she OK?"

"Yeah, terrified, obviously, but luckily everyone else could make up the difference once they knew what was happening. But I couldn't hide that it was me who dropped the rope, and considering I was checking my stupid texts because I was convinced Tate had—anyway. A girl almost died. I would have been a murderer."

Margaret laughs. "Um, Lyds, my dad's a lawyer and so I can tell you that it would be involuntary manslaughter at most."

"Do you hate me now that you've heard this story?"

"No, I hate Tate that he made you feel like that! I mean, it's not *good*, but why would I hate you? You're my *friend* and I'm on your side. Plus Elise whatsherface was fine so you're fine. I know you won't make that mistake again."

"Definitely not. Anyway, because of all of that, and being afraid we'd just fall into new disastrous scenarios, Penny arranged this whole thing where we'd stay with Grace and Oscar for the summer and work these jobs and not date any boys at all."

"Wow," Margaret says, her eyes wide. "Were you OK with Penny planning all of that?"

I shrug and tear off a piece of fancy-looking pastry. "Penny's smarter and more mature than me, so, sure. And I did know that something felt off, you know? My last breakup was so hard, and—my life isn't the same up there, you know?"

I take a bite of the pastry and cough until I cry. "Oh my god, why is this *spicy?*"

Margaret cracks up. "That's a jalapeño strawberry bear claw! I should have warned you. Anyway, what do you mean about your life up there?" Her tone softens. "You don't date girls up there?"

I shake my head. "And I'm not friends with any, either. Like, I have my theater tech people, but I've never been good at any of this, Margaret. I'm just this loser who's luckily good with boys. Good enough not to worry too much about friends."

Margaret watches me silently, and I wonder if she's regretting every fun thing I've been included in this summer. Except, no, why would she? It hasn't been like that, some kind of trap to capture potentially less-cool girls. It's been great.

"That doesn't make any sense to me," she says. "You're not a loser, and you're so easy to hang out with. I actually think it's really funny how hung up you got so fast on Fran. I wish it was that easy for me. If not for you I wouldn't have ever asked Lucas to hang out with me."

"I don't think I always knew how to try with friends before," I admit. "And not everyone makes it so easy. You make it *so easy*."

"Only because I wanted us to be friends," she says with a smile. "So ... not to sound like a complete dummy, but ... what's going on, then? Why are you hiding out from the group text and from me?"

"Do I look like I'm hiding out from you now?" I ask, and sneak another bite of the pastry. Now that I'm expecting it, I like the combo, the assault of sweet and spicy at the same time. "It just feels like I've been lying a lot—no, it doesn't *feel like*, I have been lying. And it didn't seem fair for me to lean on you guys or whatever when it was all my fault."

"How have you been lying?" Margaret asks, her eyebrows scrunched up in confusion.

"Well, to Penny, obviously I wasn't stupid enough to think it was actually OK during the summer of no boys to be with Fran. And I didn't tell Fran I was sneaking around with her, and I didn't tell you guys that Fran and I were, like, serious or whatever because I figured you'd just say *Fran's a player* and that you all knew her better than I did and I'd get my heart broken, and also that I acted like I was a normal person when really I'm a friendless loser."

"Oh my *god*, Lyds." Margaret sort of crawls over to me, past the pastries, and throws her arms around me. "You can't lie your way out of being someone who clearly has girl drama—*relationship* drama. We all know. And you're not a friendless loser, you've got all of us, and your theater tech people all *count*. And, yeah, you obviously lied to your sister, but it seems like your sister's someone you need to lie to sometimes."

I shrug. "I probably made her seem worse than she is. She's also really fun and encouraging and it sucks that I did this to her."

"Maybe," Margaret says with a shrug. "But I'm still your friend if you screw up. We're all still your friends. We can even help, you know. We're not monsters."

"I definitely never thought you were monsters. I'm just not very good at any of this. Obviously."

Margaret hops up. "I'm rallying the troops. Ugh, that's a thing my mom says. Aren't I too young to turn into my mom? I thought that was a thing that happened to sad middle-aged people."

"Maybe you're gifted," I say, and she shrieks in laughter as she grabs her phone and sits back down next to me. "What are you doing?"

"We're all going out tonight," she says. "This is what we *do*, Lyds, when someone's having a shitty time. How does Joy sound?"

"I mean, I *wish* I felt joy. I—oh, you mean the restaurant? That sounds great, actually. But you don't have to—"

"Too late, group chat already activated."

I scoop my phone out of my pocket and scroll back through the chat, my four friends, this new thing I should have maybe held on to more tightly the past few days. But now doesn't feel so terrible or like too much time got away from me, really. We grab dinner early as to escape that epic line, and packed around a table overflowing with food, I tell them everything I told Margaret this afternoon. And more—I say more about Fran, even when a few looks flash between my friends, and then because I'm on such a roll with honesty or openness or whatever this is, I even call out those looks, and everyone apologizes, even Margaret who's been really supportive of what she has known about Fran and me.

"I mean, don't apologize," I say. "You all *have* known Fran for a lot longer, and whatever happened with Tara—"

"It's fine," Tara says. "Seriously. Yeah, I cried a lot over Fran Ford, a million years ago, but not because she did something wrong. She just wasn't who I wanted her to be back then. And I was younger and didn't really think about the fact that I could say something about it. I just got my heart broken."

"Yeah, I was always the same," I admit. "I don't know why it changed for me and I spoke up."

"It's our stunningly good influence," Ava says, and everyone laughs.

"Look, I like protecting people," Su Jin says. "So obviously I hated when Tara got hurt, and if I could warn you about the same thing, I was going to. But people change, even Fran Ford, so I *am* sorry if I made you feel weird, Lyds."

I can't believe how safe it feels again, or maybe that it has been this entire summer. I hate that they're all leaving—well, Tara will be close, but I know college will make things different and I'm not sure we'll hang out one-on-one anyway—but I do at least have faith the group chat will live on, and I've somehow earned a permanent spot on it. It almost doesn't seem possible, but I know that it is: Nobody as broken as I thought I was would have this group of friends. I'm so—well, I'm a lot of things because of this. Relieved and grateful and hopeful and also bursting with a huge amount of laughter and food. When I get home and see Penny, headphoneless, I pounce.

"I started reading this the other day," I say, tapping the book on the nightstand.

Her eyes flick over to it. "Good for you."

"Pen, can we talk? I know I screwed up, but—"

"I don't owe you anything," she says, reaching for her headphones.

"Obviously," I say. "But will you listen anyway?"

"Lydia, there's nothing you could say to undo what happened. So I don't see the point in you trying. Let's save both of us the effort."

I pick up the book again because I don't know what else to do. I keep reading through the sad anecdotes, the failures that echo mine. Breakups and professional humiliations, if a high school production of *Mary Poppins* counts as *professional*. I stop for dinner, because Grace is home and makes one of my favorite meals, my great-grandmother's famous summer squash casserole, and even though I just ate with my friends I have a little so that I can share the table with my family and this casserole. It's a little different than when Mom makes it, but it still tastes like home and family. Too bad Penny won't make eye contact with me during dinner. Sometimes something like a casserole seems like it could bridge a divide.

I go back to my room to keep reading. Past the depressing stories, people get better. They get out of their own ways and I wonder if that's all I need. So I walk back to the kitchen and stick a Post-it to the leftovers for Penny (*Better than Mom's, maybe??? Don't tell her I said this!*). I'm not sure if I'm getting out of my own way, but I'm doing *something*. Maybe jokes are better than serious talks right now. Maybe even if you're a little broken, you can work on fixing yourself.

But the next morning my note's in the trash and Penny's still not talking to me. So maybe not.

$\sim\!\sim$

"Has everything been OK lately?" Grace asks me while we're walking to Grounds Control later that week. "I'm never sure if I should mind my own business or—"

"Everything's fine," I say.

"It's OK if it isn't," she says. "You having a job and a place to stay isn't dependent on everything being fine."

"No, I know," I say, but there's something about it that's nice to hear anyway. Grace has always been my coolest relative, the adult I've looked up to most, but before this summer I'm not sure if I was really comfortable with her. She was too cool, too unlike my parents, too different from me somehow. I've always been on my best behavior, and I definitely felt that way when I arrived, especially within the walls of her cool coffee shop. But now the shop is just my job and she's just Grace.

Still, though, none of the details seem right to share right now. I screwed up and managed to lose both my sister and my girlfriend—oh by the way I had a secret girlfriend and yes she's one of your regular customers, Grace—and it's a hundred percent my fault that Penny's schemes backfired and that I'm completely heartbroken. So what's there to discuss now?

Fran's been off beverage duty since our breakup, actually. I knew the film was close to wrapping, so I hope that's the main reason someone else is swinging by with complicated lists of beverages. If Fran's duties have shifted, I don't have to feel guilty that in the environment where she was supposed to agree to perform any task given to her, she might have to speak up just to avoid me, the person who made her feel stupid. Just another person who made her—one of the most brilliant people I've ever known—feel stupid.

Even with that guilt weighing on me, though, it's a relief not to see her every day. Seeing her now that she's not mine would feel terrible, worse than going to school with Tate or anyone before him. I'd never had something like this, something real and built together, and if I couldn't hold it together—well, I hate to think what that means for my future. But the truth is I'm not fixated on my future. How can I be, when my *now* is so screwed up?

Well, it's mostly screwed up. Whenever Margaret gets to work and flashes her smile at me, something settles, and whether or not I deserve my friends, I try to convince myself they're going nowhere. I mean, literally they are, and soon, and so am I—but the group chat rarely rests and I'm starting to trust that it never really will. These girls are here for me, even if I've been stupid. Maybe *especially* when I've been stupid. It won't be the same when we're all in different places, but I know it'll be better than before I knew them.

Right now everyone is organizing a mini road trip this weekend, and this includes me, but I'm not sure about it. It started off as a joke about Ava's retro fast-food obsessions and now Tara's offered to drive us to the oldest Del Taco—about two hours away—on Saturday. I've never truly had this, being packed into a car with friends, driving somewhere that doesn't really matter, something of an adventure. But weekends used to be—mostly—set aside for Penny. And it feels weird taking off for most of the day when things aren't OK with her. Shouldn't I be using my time to fix us? We're *sisters;* we can't stay like this forever.

So I spend less time in the group chat and text Penny instead. More apologies. Ideas for weekend adventures of our own. One more joke about the casserole, just in case. But after days of this, Penny doesn't respond, and so on Saturday morning I crowd into the back seat of Tara's dad's Subaru and head up to Barstow for classic fast-food offerings and some literal distance to match the emotional distance from Penny.

It's easy to forget about that, though, out in the desert—and I let myself. Lucas has asked Margaret to *hang out,* and we all agree it's a date, even without the word being used. Ava's future roommate apparently has no strong opinions about decorating their dorm room and so Ava sounds almost dizzy with retro ideas. Su Jin, on the other hand, isn't sure about her future roommate and asks us to dissect her texts, which we agree are a little stilted and formal, but I point out that's how Penny sounds and Penny's great. And then the literal distance doesn't feel like it's doing its job, and while we're discussing Tara's and Margaret's roommates, I'm really just thinking about what a shitty sister I am, yet again. There's no actual way to put distance between me and that fact.

Penny and Oscar are, not shockingly, watching a Dodgers game when I get back, still somehow stuffed from tacos and real ice cream milkshakes after a two-and-a-half-hour car ride home. I feel better that Penny had something to do and someone to spend time with other than me. But she still doesn't acknowledge me at all, and so even though Oscar invites me to join them, I decide to take a walk alone instead.

My phone buzzes dramatically almost immediately, and I check it with hope. What are the chances Penny and Fran have forgiven me at the exact same moment? But Mom and Dad must have docked again, because a pile of texts and photos appears. I think of the first time this happened, sitting next to Penny in Downtown LA, waiting for a play to start and feeling like everything was still possible.

And I'm not stupid. Yes, I think Penny is being exceptionally hard to talk to right now, and, yes, I thought Fran and I were—well, whatever we were, serious or trusting or open. I thought what we'd built together was strong enough to get through a misunderstanding. But I deserve to be cut out. I lied to two of the people I cared about most—and, honestly, in some ways I lied to my friends too, I was just lucky enough that they had either forgiven me or didn't really see it that way. A few weeks ago I felt like I was finally grasping the stuff that seemed to come naturally to everyone else: sisterhood, friendship, a relationship rooted in reality and not happily-ever-after fantasies. And now I feel like all of it is way more complicated and maybe I understood nothing at all.

While I'm scrolling Mom and Dad's endless messages and badly framed photos, I see that the group chat is already making plans for tonight. Being available for Penny—or an out-of-the-blue but not unwelcome *wyd*—is clearly not working, so after my walk I change into slightly cuter clothes and wait outside for Tara to swing by again. This time I'm the first one she picks up, and I wonder if she also thinks it's awkward, the coolest and least cool people in the group, also the two exes of Fran Ford.

"What are you doing?" Tara yells out the window as I reach for the handle of the back passenger-side door. "I'm not your chauffeur."

I laugh to cover the fact that I'm super embarrassed and get into the front seat next to her. "Sorry. I just never ride in the front seat."

"*Ever?*"

"No, like, with any of you. I'm the extra friend, the newest one. I feel like I haven't earned it yet."

Tara laughs. "You don't have to *earn it*. You just have to get to the car first. Call shotgun. Whatever."

"I'm awkward at everything," I say. "At a lot of things, at least."

"I think that's just being a person," she says. "Also I know we seem like this group that's been tight forever, but it's not exactly like that. Senior year just kept throwing us together and this formation sorta gelled."

"Does it suck that it happened right before you're all going away?"

Tara shrugs. "I can't speak for everyone, but I'm looking forward to meeting people at school, seeing what's next. These girls aren't going anywhere."

"Except literally," I say, and she laughs again.

"Yeah, except that." She pulls up to Margaret's house but doesn't take out her phone yet. "I'm aware everyone somehow thinks I'm still hung up on Fran, even though it was years ago and I've dated people since. So you're hearing it directly from me that I'm not. I have nothing

at stake to tell you that—if you want, it's really none of my business—
you shouldn't give up on her yet."

"What do you mean? I haven't given up on her, she's the one—"

"No, I know, but try texting her, or however you normally get in
touch. She's not going to reach out to you, I'm sure of that, but you're
right that things were different with the two of you. I'd give it a shot."

"I really messed up," I say.

"Yeah, again, I can tell you think that's really unique, but a lot of it
is just being a person. People mess up. And you know Fran. She's got
all that swagger but she's so soft. She needs extra care."

Tara takes out her phone and texts Margaret that we're outside.

"Thank you," I say. "Do you want me to—"

"Lyds, if you're about to ask me if you should sit in the back seat,
I'm gonna scream."

"I wasn't—"

Tara cracks up. "You completely were."

Margaret gets into the back seat. "What'd I miss?"

"I'm extra awkward," I say.

"Oh, so nothing new at all, got it."

Once we've picked up Su Jin and Ava, Tara drives down the freeway
to a nearby neighborhood, parking next to a strip of little shops and
restaurants. We're still all kind of full from our taco road trip, so we snack
on ice cream and donuts and Frappuccinos, even though Margaret
and I feel a little bad supporting Starbucks, though at least it's not the
one close to Grounds Control. Ava hits up every single vintage store,
though sometimes the rest of us wait outside, and Margaret makes
me coach her through "casually" texting Lucas, which I'm able to
transition into an official hangout invite.

"You're a genius," Margaret tells me as our group gets back into Tara's car to head back to their part of town. I love that everyone's so ready to change plans for Margaret. "If left to my own devices I'd still be figuring out the right emoji to respond with."

"I'm definitely not a genius," I say. "You just don't have to worry so much when someone obviously likes you. He *likes* you. All emojis are the right emoji."

"Well, maybe not *all*," Su Jin says, and begins texting us a string of questionable choices while we're riding back to Highland Park. By the time Tara finds a parking spot near the tiny park not too far from Grounds Control, most of us are literally crying from laughing so hard. Margaret, only *gently* shoved by us, joins Lucas on the swings, while we kind of mill about and make conversation with Lucas's friends. Every single one of them is, honestly, pretty cute, and when a boy offers to get us agua frescas from a nearby taco truck, I see in his eyes that I could end tonight with kissing him, if I really want that.

I don't, though, and not just because of Tara's words from earlier. Maybe she's right, and maybe there's still a chance with Fran, but even if she's not right—I'm not ready yet. I don't care that right now there's no future happily ever after I can see for myself. I'm heartbroken, my sister's shut me out of her life, and my friends are all leaving. And the last thing that's going to solve any of this right now is kissing a random stranger in a park.

I mean, obviously, we still let Lucas's friends treat us to agua frescas. Later we return the favor and get bagfuls of tacos for the whole group. I notice a vibe between Tara and a hot skater type in Lucas's group, so I make sure to nudge them together whenever it's possible. Tara, who's obviously a wiser person than I am, knows what I'm up to, but I notice she doesn't resist, either.

And maybe that's why I feel like it's not the worst idea to listen to Tara's earlier advice, or maybe I just feel lonely watching my friends flirt with their cute former classmates, but I sit down on a bench a little bit away from everyone and get out my phone.

I messed up SO BADLY, and I don't deserve another chance. But I miss you, and I would love a chance to talk and maybe explain.

I'm about to hit send, but I look up and see these amazing girls who are now part of my life. When later we're all piled in the car again, I won't have to worry about them judging me or rolling their eyes about Fran. It's safe to get their advice. It's safe to tell them everything, again.

Chapter Twenty-Four

Penny manages to continue ignoring me in a way that's honestly impressive. No matter how mad I was, there's no way I could have held out this long. But Penny, of course, masters everything she takes on, and so now her skills involve lightning-fast placement of headphones over ears, agile slips past me out the doorway, and a newfound ability to look only at Oscar and Grace during dinner, no matter where I scheme to sit.

Fran, though, isn't like Penny. After my friend-sourced text to her on Saturday night (ultimately we landed on *I'm sorry, and I miss you, and I'd love to talk, but only if you want to. xo),* my phone buzzed on Sunday morning with a *Maybe.* I suddenly felt powerless without my friends, but I reminded myself that while I loved their advice, I'd managed plenty of this on my own already. So I let some time pass, because not looking too eager wasn't playing a dishonest game, it was just a smart move right now.

No pressure, just let me know. You know where to find me.

Since I sent it and got no response, I do worry I should have brought in my friends again. I wanted it to be cute and a little flirty and familiar, but maybe it was just weird. But if I'd screwed up in the whole realm of honesty, being completely myself—including the weird parts—probably *is* what I should do. If I can't fix me and Fran, it shouldn't be because I don't try, and it shouldn't be because I don't offer up the real me.

I try not to dwell too much on the possibility that the real me won't be enough. Living in the now is really annoying sometimes.

By midweek, Fran and I are still exchanging only the bare minimum of texts, usually with only one-word replies from her, often just *maybe,* and I'm not sure how we're going to come back together. Not that I'm going to give up. My sister might still be ignoring me, but that doesn't mean I can't be inspired by her and her practiced skills and her stacks of *you can do it if you overcome your own flaws* books piled between us still. I'm not sure how much better they're really making me. Yeah, I have a lot of flaws, but those aren't the only things that hold girls back. I know that people at school wouldn't whisper *slut* if I were a boy, and I know that if Fran had been a boy with romantic comedy tastes that other boys would have leaned in and listened instead of making her feel shitty about her taste and her future.

But, still, flaws are flaws, and even if I won't fix them all with a stack of books by smiling blonde women, I hope Penny notices that I'm trying. I hope she knows that with every page I read, I feel a little more like I understand her and her seemingly endless journey to do every single thing as well as possible with as little risk as necessary.

But right now I'd risk a lot of things to get back to the people I miss the most.

"Lydia," Grace calls, late in my shift on Thursday, stepping out from the back office. Margaret and I were using the downtime, of course, to experiment with rocket-themed latte art. The good news is that we're getting slowly better over time. The bad news is it's very easy to make rockets that look like dicks, and we might have to rethink our entire strategy.

"Sorry," I say, tossing out our latest experiment before Grace can see how truly perverted it looks. Margaret snickers. "We promise we're not wasting too much milk or espresso."

"I'm not worried about this whole thing you two have going," Grace says with a smile. "Since it's pretty slow today, I thought I'd take off when the next shift shows up. Want to grab a late lunch with me?"

Grace *never* leaves work early, but I decide not to dwell on this because I'm thrilled for any and all extra time with her. Even if a lecture on sisterhood or getting along in her household is forthcoming. I mean, that doesn't really sound like Grace, but we haven't really tested her so far this summer until now.

"I have to run a few errands," Grace tells me when we're walking back to her house so she can get the car. "But they can all be accomplished in Old Town Pasadena, so we can grab lunch and then walk around for a while. Sound good?"

"I have no idea what Old Town Pasadena is, but it sounds fancy. Do I need to change?"

Grace laughs. "I thought you stopped being so nervous about how you looked and dressed. No, it's mainly just a bunch of chain stores in historic buildings and should depress me more than it does, especially as a small business owner. But I do like having a Sephora so close."

"I wasn't *nervous* about how I look or dress," I say. "I mean, I guess I *was*, technically, just as it related to the whole aesthetic at Grounds Control. Not in general."

"I love that you think that, when I wear, like, one of the same seven faded T-shirts and one of the same two pairs of jeans basically every day," Grace says with a laugh.

"Yeah, but you have this whole retro badass thing going on."

"I'll pretend you don't mean *old* when you say *retro*. You realize these are all my T-shirts, right, that I was the one who bought them new, once upon a time?"

I laugh instead of admitting I'm not sure that I thought that. Shops in Grace's part of town are so good at selling those perfectly faded-by-time T-shirts and jeans. I didn't think about the fact that the time could be your own.

"You never see fat girls in Instagram posts about coffee shops like yours," I say. "People like you and Margaret will say I look fine or that I don't stick out, but it's not like I'm just making that up. The whole Insta aesthetic is thin, so when you and her don't get why I say things like that, it's like, look at reality."

I all but smack my own hand over my own mouth because I can't believe I just said all of that to one of my favorite people, someone who's been so generous with her time and home and business this summer. I wouldn't even *have* this summer without Grace. And I'm not sure I even knew I was thinking all of that! It must have been building up, and maybe all the words from all of Penny's self-help heroines pushed it over the top. And now here it all was, out in the open.

"You're completely right," Grace says. "I think I forget about that aspect because—well, Lydia, look at how well you fit in! You've made friends so easily, Margaret clearly adores you and I'm sure the rest of her gang does, too. And Fran—"

"What about Fran?" I ask in a tone I hope is casual, even though obviously I just interrupted her *aggressively*.

Grace laughs softly. "It's just the two of us. Do I have to pretend there's nothing going on between you and Fran?"

"Right now, trust me, there's nothing going on between me and Fran at all, because I screwed up so much," I say. "But, yeah. I didn't know you knew. I wasn't trying to sneak around or lie or anything—"

"Oh god, Lyds, no explanation needed," Grace says. "I dated my first girlfriend for about a year and a half without telling almost anyone."

"Wait, what?" I stammer, and then feel like an absolute jerk. "Sorry, not to sound so weird. I just had no idea."

"I forget that people don't know," Grace says, as we reach her block and walk around the back to the alley that leads to her garage. "My last long-term relationship before Oscar was also with a man, and so there are so many people in my life who just assume I'm straight because of that. And it often doesn't come up, so I don't have a chance to correct them and..." She shrugs. "I don't want to speak for you or your identity, so speaking for only myself, I'll just say that it can be a complicated part of being bi."

"I feel like I haven't even figured out the complicated parts yet," I say as she lets me into the Prius. "Liking Fran was just... well, it was so easy."

"Well, *yeah*," Grace says, chuckling. "Fran's some kind of teen dreamboat. It's ridiculous."

"I really thought you had no idea," I say.

"You two weren't exactly subtle," Grace says, still laughing. "Your eyes practically turned into hearts whenever she walked in, and she did plenty of maneuvering to somehow always be waited on by you."

I smile, despite the fact that Fran's responses to me are still only one or two words each. If I dwell just in this moment like I'm trying to do these days, maybe we're not over. Suddenly I'm thrilled that other people noticed, because, just maybe, what other people saw between us is still there.

"Can I ask?" We're stopped at a stoplight, and Grace outlines a circle around us with her hands. "This car is a safe space, I'm a pretty nonjudgmental bisexual. Was the thing with Fran to avoid the no-boy convent thing?"

"*No,*" I say. "I really was going to take the summer off from romance, just like I said. Just flirt with Ben and his pastries and leave it all at that. I just…I felt like I fell for Fran the second I said that stupid Phil thing. She's so funny and she just has this…I don't know. Her whole vibe. It was like I was drawn to her. But, yes, it was convenient she didn't technically break any of my rules, though obviously Penny doesn't see it that way. And I made Fran feel like what you just asked is true, that I was with her because of the stupid pledge, and not just that the stupid pledge made me lie to Penny when what I should have done was—honestly, I don't know what I should have done. But not *lie.*"

"Sisters are hard sometimes," Grace says. "I lied to your mom plenty."

"About dating girls?"

"Well, sure. If she knew I liked girls, I thought she would tell our parents and then they'd stop letting me have girls sleep over."

"*Grace,*" I say, a little scandalized, and she cracks up.

"Look, were there perks to being a closeted queer nineties teen? Absolutely. But I lied plenty about other unrelated things, too. Sometimes it's easier. Sometimes you feel like you're sparing someone's feelings. Sometimes, fair or not, they're just the least of your concerns and you're simply trying to get by."

"Yeah," I say. "All of that."

"And Penny's . . . very different from you," Grace says. "I know. But I also know that she's reasonable and seems willing to hear all perspectives in a way that I'm definitely not as good about. She's open to new things, and so sharp and perceptive."

"Yeah, OK," I say. "All of that, too."

"So give Penny a chance, is what I'm saying," Grace says. "Also time. She'll get there. She just runs on a different schedule than you."

"I'm worried no one's getting there," I say. "I'm trying to live in the moment and not skip to the end in my head, but right now it's hard not to think we'll be like this for the next year, and then—hopefully—I'll get into college, but then I'll leave and that's it. And Fran will never forgive me and I'll stay brokenhearted and—"

"That won't be it," Grace says, as she pulls the car into a parking garage. "I promise. And remember that you've got me, too. I know you'll be home before long, but you can call me—sorry, I forget people your age never call anyone, you can DM me on TikTok or whatever is cool. And if the drive won't kill you, you can also pick up some weekend shifts if you'd like."

"I probably have to check with Mom and Dad before I officially agree, but I'd love that."

Grace and I get burgers and fries before starting on her errands, and I hear more about her secret high school girlfriend and all of the fun sneaking around they did, back before social media and iPhones even existed. I fill her in more on Fran, and she agrees with my friends that it doesn't seem over yet and that I shouldn't give up. I'm still not sure about that, but it's nice to hear from anyone who says it. It's really nice how many people, it turns out, believe in me.

Penny still ignores me that night, but I try to believe Grace about the longer schedule. Hopefully it's not *too* long. I'd hate to go back home with this silence still between us, and right now it's hard to see a way out of it.

It feels like magic, but the next day, while I'm back on espresso machine duty, Fran walks in. Margaret nudges me as if I don't know exactly how it sounds when Fran Ford walks into Grounds Control, but Grace, a pro, doesn't look back at me at all. With everything out in the open, I'm glad she can still be cool about things. I shouldn't be surprised, though; Grace is the coolest person I've ever known.

"She's only getting one drink," Margaret whispers. "She's here for you, not because her movie bosses are making her. It's *a sign.*"

"Maybe it's one drink for the director or something," I whisper back. "We have no proof who that drink is for."

"I wish you could write a cute message," Margaret says. "Too bad we're not better at latte art that's not hearts or ferns."

"Or dicks."

She practically cackles. "Go with a heart, I think. Not a dick or a fern."

"The fern latte was the drink I was calling when I accidentally called her Phil," I say, and splash the fern design into the foam like it's my very first day again. Everything—truly almost everything—has changed since then, but I carry it over to the counter as if it hasn't, as if it's Day One.

Fran's waiting nearby, her expression as blank as I've ever seen it. Her gaze drifts over to me.

"Double fern latte for Phil," I say, and I see the corners of her mouth pull up.

"Thanks," she says.

"Fran—"

"I have to go," she said. "Big day on set."

"OK," I say, watching her go. And then there's three more drinks up, and I can't dwell on Fran anyway. The rhythm of work keeps me going, and all of a sudden it's hours later and the image of her stepping out the door is slightly less vibrant in my head. I can at least function like Fran's not the only thing I'm thinking about.

"She only got her own drink," Grace says, proving my theory about how I'm functioning very, very wrong. "Margaret's right. That was a really optional latte. You can definitely take it as a good sign."

I shrug as I wipe down the countertop around the espresso machine. "I'm not sure about that. I know what you're saying makes sense, but she was really eager to go."

"Maybe it actually is a big day on set," Margaret says, and I realize the two of them heard our entire non-exchange. "Ooh, doesn't Fran love all those swoony old movies? You should do some big romantic gesture."

"What old movies?" Grace asks.

"Like *Sleepless in Seattle* and *You've Got Mail*," Margaret says, and Grace cracks up.

"You two have a real knack for making me feel ancient as hell."

"Grace, those movies are *older than we are*," I point out.

"I'm not sure how you think that's helping. Though Margaret has a point. I love big gestures. Though I guess you can't meet on top of the Empire State Building like in *Sleepless in Seattle*. Wait, though, doesn't the other one end with a giant corporation putting an indie bookstore out of business?"

I shrug. "It seems romantic when it happens, though. You get all caught up."

"Sure." Grace frowns. "I'll just say if Oscar had secretly been the owner of Starbucks, I don't think we would have had the same ending."

"Ugh, no, that's not the end," Margaret says. "The end is them meeting in a beautiful park and kissing. And there's a beautiful park just across the street, Lyds."

Grace's eyebrows shoot up. "That park that used to be a gas station?"

"Grace, can you tamp down your Gen X snarkiness for, like, two seconds? We're trying to plan a grand romantic gesture. I thought you said you liked those."

Grace holds up her hands. "You're right, but, please, if you plan a romantic gesture in a park, I'm just saying it should be one that didn't used to be a gas station. That's all. Garvanza Park is gorgeous. Ask her to meet you there."

Yes, of course I like the sound of all of this, but it's Grace and Margaret's plan. I'm not sure how it'll actually go over, so I keep my phone in my pocket and stay as busy as possible for the rest of my shift. I ask Margaret if she wants to get pizza after, but she points to Grace instead of answering.

"What, are you going to tell us the pizza place also used to be a gas station and we shouldn't go there, either?"

"We haven't taken many photos for our shop Instagram or site lately," Grace says. "I've just been recycling the same set of professional photos of our drinks and pastries. So I thought I'd mix it up a little, post more candids. I was thinking about what you said yesterday, and I think you should be part of Grounds Control's aesthetic."

"No, I didn't mean—oh my god, look at me, I'm—"

"Yeah, *obviously*," Margaret says. "Grace told me in advance so I brought my hair stuff to make it all sleek and Insta-ready. You already have the cute lip gloss on, and if you're behind the counter, no one'll know you're wearing some shirt promoting a school musical that happened a hundred years ago."

"You don't have to do this just to make a point," I say to Grace.

"It's not just a point about you. It's also a point about our customers, that I might be part of gentrification in this part of town, but I opened this shop for everyone, I tried to keep my prices down so that it wasn't out of touch with the budgets of families who've always lived in this neighborhood. I work with local vendors. And I still went for this whole social media aesthetic that made people feel left out. I'm working on that. So let me."

Margaret redoes my hair, and we both touch up our lip gloss while Grace rolls her eyes. She really is extra snarky today, but I've also never felt so close to her.

"You know what this would be a great time for?" Margaret asks, shooting me a sly look.

"Yes!" I gesture to the espresso machine. "Do you want to do the honors?"

"What are you two up to?" Grace asked, sounding a little exhausted with us if you ask me.

"Just you wait, Grace," Margaret says, and I stand basically over her shoulder while she gives the rocket latte art her very best effort.

We shriek with laughter because it's still really, really bad. Grace walks over to take a look, and I feel like her eyebrows nearly shoot off her face.

"That's more than mildly pornographic," she says, though she starts laughing, too.

It seems like our big plan might be dead, and we won't be leaving anything behind after this summer at Grounds Control. But then Grace takes photos of Margaret and me behind the counter, and photos of the tables, too—with customers' permission, of course. I know Grace is only doing this because of what I said yesterday, but when I check the new posts later, I see how Grounds Control *does* look different, does look like a place that wouldn't have scared me on my first day. I'm leaving something behind, after all.

Even so, I'm still a little worried people will be rude in the comments. But when I check later that night, there's only four, and they're all variations on *my favorite baristas*. One's from Fran.

So I text her an invite to the park.

CHAPTER TWENTY-FIVE

I buy a little bouquet of flowers at the nearest supermarket on my way to the park the next day. Once I'm there, though, it all feels stupid, the bright flowers for a girl who might never take me back, the park that doesn't look anything like a Manhattan movie, and me, who screwed up and then maybe hasn't changed at all and doesn't deserve this chance.

But then Fran walks up, wearing a faded blue T-shirt and jeans, her hair freshly trimmed since the last time I've seen her, and maybe none of the dumb stuff matters.

"Hi," I say.

"Hey."

"Fran, I'm so sorry."

She nods at the flowers. "Those for me?"

"Uh, obviously. Who else would I have flowers for?"

She grins and takes them from me, her hands brushing mine. "Maybe you were on your way to someone's grave."

I laugh and pretend to take them back. "Don't joke about my flowers."

"They're my flowers now, I can joke all I want." She nods to a bench. "Want to sit?"

I agree, and we head over, sitting close but not girlfriends close.

"Some of the stuff you said was pretty bad," Fran says, and my heart hammers in my chest. "I know that people think I'm—I don't know.

People will say shitty stuff to my face because they think I'm tough, or because I'm butch, and it's *fucked up.* And I try to live my life in this really straightforward way and then you—Lydia, you blew it all up."

"Fran, I'm *so sorry,*" I repeat, "I—"

"No," she says, "let me finish. I'm saying you blew it up in a good way. Senior year was rough, and then the PA gig wasn't what I thought it would be, and I was thinking maybe my future wasn't going to include any of the things I thought I wanted. And then this girl comes along who believes in me and challenges me and doesn't think my ideas aren't worthy. So even though there's a lot about relationships I wasn't sure about, I took this chance."

"And I screwed it all up."

Fran turns to look at me. "Yeah, a little. But I don't think I handled it very well, either. I know shit's probably complicated with your sister, and—well, I kept replaying it in my head, it being some game, me being some technicality to you, but also it's unfair of me to act as if what we had wasn't real. You might have started off building your side on lies, but everything we built after was pretty great, Lydia."

I don't know where any of this is going, but I'm grateful anyway. I've never talked something out like this before. Normally it's over, and when it's terrible and messy and I'm heartbroken, I'm left just to wonder. For Fran to lay it all out like this isn't something I'm sure I deserve, but it's genuinely great. No matter what it means for us.

"I should have told you right away," I say. "The stupid pledge, the fact that I was sneaking around, my whole disastrous tendencies."

Fran smirks. "You're just fulfilling the disaster bisexual stereotype. I should have considered myself warned."

"What? That's a stereotype?" I smile, even though I'm not sure this moment should make me happy. "I always thought I didn't fit in with like all of the LGBTQ+ kids at my school, like they all had these clear identities, and I was worried they'd just see me as a slut. I mean, they *already* saw me as a slut, add bi to that—"

"That's the other thing," Fran says.

"Me being a slut?"

"*No.* I know you're still working out your identity, that I'm the first girl you've been with, and maybe I owed you a little more patience there, if you couldn't talk to your family or figure out the right way to explain things to me. Remember, you're my first girlfriend, too, technically, and I'm not having a bunch of these talks, either."

"I don't think you owed me anything, considering I lied to you."

Fran smiles, leans in a little. "I think that's for me to decide. I'm also not really sure you lied. You were just—"

"A disaster?"

"Something like that." She's closer still. "Lydia?"

"Yeah?"

"Are you not interested in giving this another shot, or am I not being clear enough I'm trying to kiss you?"

"The second!" I wrap my arms around her shoulders, even as I'm laughing, and find her lips with mine. Her fingertips graze the sides of my face as we kiss, and it's all old and new at the same time. We've always been great at this part, anything physical, but something feels stripped bare and clean between us, like Fran's fresh haircut. I rub my fingertips at the nape of her neck where the short hairs feel prickly and soft at once.

"Get a room," someone mutters, and we look up to see a bunch of tween skate kids sneering at us. We crack up and head away from them, slipping behind a leafy tree to wrap up in each other's arms again.

"I need you to know," I say. "I swear that I never thought of you as a technicality or a loophole, Fran. I just said that so—"

She kisses my neck, uses just enough pressure that my knees feel a little weak. "Yeah, Lyds, I know."

"It's not because you're a girl, either. It's just that you're so funny and interesting and talented, and when I'm with you—well, I just don't want to risk it again."

"What, getting yelled at by those kids?" she asks with a grin.

"*No.* You wondering for even like one second that I don't value you the way I do. Also I thought you weren't into PDA."

"We're behind a tree and hardly anyone's around. I think we can get away with a little, don't you?"

I do, and soon her lips are on mine again and she feels so safe and sure and *real.* However it started, whatever either of us once thought, we're through all of that now. I know I can't expect things to be absolutely perfect, but right now it's all out there in the open. I wonder how much different everything would have been, all the pining and the disastrous breakups and everything in between, if I'd been so open with everyone. And does this mean that I never was, that I was so worried about getting my happy future, and so worried I didn't deserve one in the first place, that I forgot to even be myself?

I feel this fear zipping through me, and then I remind myself that I'm only seventeen, hopefully I haven't wasted too many years being not great in relationships, and also, my very hot girlfriend is kissing me under a beautiful tree in a beautiful park in the middle of a city, just like in a movie. There'll be plenty of time to stress about stuff later. This moment was built to live inside of for as long as it lasts.

We're still wrapped up in each other when we hear nearby footsteps.

"Ugh, we told you guys to get a room!"

Fran and I crack up, and she grabs my hand and leads me away from the giggling skate tweens and out of the park. Her pickup truck is parked nearby, and I make the familiar climb inside, so grateful to be here again.

She drives us to a diner, and we split a meal like we did on our first official date. Fran tells me about all the classes she's registered for at the community college, where she'll get to learn about film and writing and gender, all the stuff she cares about.

"I really thought I'd fucked up my whole future by not applying to film school," she says, dipping a french fry into a tiny side of ranch dressing. "But now it doesn't feel that way anymore. It's a really cool school. I should have looked at the course catalog sooner."

"Sometimes we do things only when we're ready for them," I say. "Sorry, I've been reading a lot of self-help books lately. Hoping Penny will be impressed with my commitment to one of her favorite pastimes."

"How are things with her?" Fran asks.

"Not great. She's still completely ignoring me, and my parents will be back in less than two weeks. I feel like if I can't fix things while we're sharing a room and having really great summers, there's no way I'll be able to up at home when there's so much space between us."

"Maybe she needs space," Fran says. "I mean, I needed space from you to think."

"Right, but you're my girlfriend, and she's my sister."

Fran laughs. "Yeah, sure, but that doesn't mean she doesn't need space, and sharing a room with the person you need space from is probably not helping. And I can tell you're not someone who needs space when things get weird, but you were smart enough to get it was what *I* needed. So what does Penny need?"

I finish the rest of my grilled cheese instead of admitting that I don't know. Unbelievably, a few of the skater kids sit down at the booth with adults I assume are parents of one of them, and the kids screech in recognition when they spot us.

"We said to get a room!" one of them yells.

"A room for what?" I yell back. "We're just eating a sandwich!"

Fran hides her face behind her hands. "Oh my god."

"You said you wanted the real me."

"I don't think I actually said that, and—the real you yells at children?"

"At child *bullies*!"

She laughs and lowers her hands to look at me. "I missed you. Do you know we were supposed to start filming my short this week?"

"Of course I know that, I put it in my calendar app like Penny taught me," I say. "My friends are still all free to help, I'm sure. Margaret's semi-dating that cute boy from the street festival, but that just means we probably have an extra person to help us, if we need it. Want me to get the group chat on it?"

Fran shrugs, but I see that she's thinking. After her haircut, the tousle part of her hair doesn't hang into her eyes anymore, so she's got nowhere to hide her intense gaze as I practically feel her work through this.

"OK," she says, a slow smile appearing on her face. "If and *only if* everyone really still wants to help. Someday I won't be a person who asks others to work for me for free, but while I am, I can at least not be an asshole about it."

I'm already halfway through writing the text to my friends. "I missed you too, Fran. But I'm also glad that . . . I don't know. I feel kind of weird explaining it, but the whole deal with my sister this summer is because I *was* a disaster. My relationships were like the center of my whole universe and so when things were good I didn't have room for anyone else, and when they were bad it was like one of those black holes that sucks a bunch of garbage into it."

"I haven't taken a science class in a while, but I don't think that's what black holes do," Fran says.

"Oh, come on, you get my point! Anyway, I did miss you, so much, but it also was good because—"

"The black hole didn't suck up any garbage this time?" Fran grins at me.

"Hardly any. I like that my life is you and my friends and this movie and thinking about the fall musical and whatever else. I hope that doesn't sound weird, like I don't like you enough or something."

"Oh, god *no*," Fran says. "Of course it's good you don't just have me. No offense, but that sounds terrible."

"Like black hole garbage?"

"Something like that." She reaches out and threads her fingers through mine. Considering we've been eating fries and a grilled cheese sandwich, we're both pretty greasy, but I'm still glad we're holding hands. "Seriously, Lydia, thanks for believing in me when it felt like no one else did."

"You're really easy to believe in," I say. "I can't wait to see what you do next."

"Let's see if I even do this."

I hold up my phone with my other hand. "Everyone's in. We're totally making your movie, Fran."

Chapter Twenty-Six

By the time all of us—Fran, Margaret, Ava, Su Jin, Tara, Emilia, who's playing the only human role, and me—are crammed into Margaret's room to film, I realize that it's really happening. With Fran's phone set up on a tripod, I see that the image framed is exactly as I'd planned it, with the tulle and fairy lights balanced perfectly with the worn stuffed animals who were the other stars of the show. Emilia, who was in the same class as my friends, is shorter than all of us, with glossy black hair that keeps sliding into her face. Dressed in jeans and a plaid button-down, she's perfect casting for a younger version of Fran, a girl who was still figuring some things out.

I guess, to be fair, we're all girls who are still figuring some things out. But I'm proud of everyone in this room for all the things we seemed to have accomplished already. Everyone else has college plans, and I got an email from Mr. Landiss just last night that I'd be in charge of set design for REACT this coming school year, which I'd hardly expected after *Mary Poppins*. Darren Nygard, who's going to head up lighting, immediately started a group chat for all the tech leads, and I pushed myself to stay involved and even to agree to an in-person meetup in a couple weeks at the Panera across the street from school. No, REACT will never be a substitute for what I'd found with my new friends this summer, but maybe I'm not as bad with groups as I thought. It's at least worth trying.

Fran films the short script multiple times. It seems perfect to me from the beginning; Emilia captures how unsure and awkward it can be to figure out life, and even though Ava and Su Jin were initially only reading the imaginary friends' dialogue as a placeholder, their stuffed animal voices are so good that Fran asks if they can record the dialogue with her later to edit in for the final cut. But because the stuffed animals can't—obviously—actually move, Fran is filming from multiple angles so she can use some cuts and zooming-in effects to create a feeling of movement anyway. Every time she moves her phone, there's a little work for me in keeping the background consistent, and I like how it's different from theater this way. Onstage, once the production starts, and a scene plays out, we can only move forward. But here on film we get to adjust, figure out new perspectives, find all the ways we can tell this one story.

I wonder what the film club is like at my school and decide as long as it doesn't conflict with REACT, I might want to check it out, too.

We all go out afterward, even though it's weirdly exhausting to spend just a few hours filming the same minutes over and over. It reminds me of late nights at Denny's after opening nights, except then REACT would be frantically figuring out how not to make any of the same mistakes the next night. Tonight we're just celebrating that the film was shot, on Fran's phone and backed up to several clouds, and ready for her to edit. Obviously, we all feel victorious in this, but I see from how everyone watches Fran that we also know that it's her thing and she's achieved something big.

"Do you want to see if the boys want to hang out?" Margaret asks as our check arrives and we're figuring out how to split the bill seven very uneven ways. "I mean, no pressure, obviously, just an option."

"If by *the boys* you mean Lucas's whole group, yeah," Tara says, and even though she always sounds casual, Ava and Su Jin and I hear it in her voice and shriek at the same time.

"You want to see that hot skater girl again," I say.

"They're actually nonbinary and also going to USC this fall," Tara says, instead of *no,* and we try not to tease her too much. Margaret, who's sitting next to me, nudges me slightly.

"Do you want to invite your sister?" she asks. "If it's a whole group of us, maybe it'd be fun for her?"

"That's really sweet of you to offer, but she's still not talking to me. I'm trying to respect her and give her space, but—I don't know. I feel like nothing's going to break through, and when my parents show up next week it'll still be like this, and then it'll be like this my whole senior year, and then if I'm lucky enough to get into one of my dream colleges, I'll move away and we'll just never speak again."

"That escalated quickly," Su Jin says.

"Oh my *god,*" Margaret says. "I can't believe we didn't think of this the other week when we were talking about big gestures. Like we only talk about big gestures for romance and stuff, but maybe your sister needs a big gesture, too."

There's something about her words that feels so right to me. If the whole summer was supposed to be about exploring life outside of romance, wasn't taking something normally only for romance into another place fulfilling exactly what Penny wanted?

"OK," I say. "What do you think is a good big gesture for a sister?"

"It's not *a* sister," Fran says. "It's *your* sister."

"Yeah, doesn't she like TED Talks and leaning in?" Margaret asks.

"Ladies who give life advice on Insta Live," Su Jin adds.

"Books about listening to your heart," Ava says. "Chasing that dream! Following your own road!"

"Just empowering white lady shit," Tara says.

"Oh my god, yes," Margaret says. "Fran, can you film Lyds like a TED Talk, like she's wearing a pantsuit and talking to a big crowd about how important her sister is to her and how much she screwed up?"

"I don't own a pantsuit," I point out.

"Yeah, and I'm not sure where I'm getting a big crowd in a TED Talk auditorium," Fran says. "But what about like one of those YouTube videos you sent me that she sent you, Lydia? We can definitely make one of those look just as professional, and you can upload it privately and only send the link to your sister."

"I'd feel weird being on camera," I admit. "I'm more of a behind-the-scenes person. Like you! You got someone else to play you in your movie. Wait, Emilia, can you play me in—"

"*No*," Margaret, Su Jin, and Fran say at the same time.

"No one has to see it but your sister," Fran says gently.

"And us, obviously," Su Jin says.

"It'll mean way more to her this way," Margaret says. "Come on, I haven't texted Lucas yet. Let's get this thing written tonight. My room's still half set up."

"You should go have fun with Lucas and his friends," I say. "I'll solve Penny myself. Or I won't. But—"

"Everyone cute will still be there tomorrow night," Margaret says. "Let's first make sure you don't permanently estrange your only sister."

So we pile back into Tara's car and Fran's truck and reassemble in Margaret's room. While my friends, Fran, and Emilia watch other videos for inspiration, I sit with my notepad, scribbling out everything I want to say to Penny. After about my tenth start, Fran walks over and sits down next to me on the floor.

"The thing about these videos is they look a little slick, but in the better ones, clearly people are just speaking from the heart. If you do that, it'll be fine."

"Well, I don't want it to be *fine,* I want it to be perfect. Penny doesn't do anything halfway, and I owe her to try as hard as possible."

"You don't do anything halfway, either," Fran says. "You figured out the entire production design of my film, you got me this whole crew of girls I never would have had the nerve to ask, and this is on top of the fact that you just got awarded a huge position with your school's theater department. I know that your sister's this intense overachiever, but have you looked in a mirror lately?"

"I'm nothing like Penny," I say, but I feel what she's saying. It isn't just how Fran sees me, it's all those objective truths stacked up, amounting to something. I'm definitely not broken or unlovable or worthless. It turns out I've maybe been a lot of good things all along, and I just needed to let people in to see that—including myself.

"Maybe you have more in common with your sister than you think," Fran says, and kisses my cheek before rejoining my friends in their YouTube spiral. I start again and decide to keep going, even when I know it's not perfect, because I don't want to keep my friends all night and also because *I'm* not perfect and that won't be news to Penny.

Perfection isn't the point, after all. Being myself and giving Penny what she actually needs is all that matters right now.

Margaret does my makeup while my notepad gets passed around and my friends and Emilia offer a few suggestions. I can't believe I'm lucky enough to have these girls in my life, but I also know I'd do the same for any of them, and I hope in the future there are a million chances I'll get to pay them back.

Fran sets up her phone to record me, but I screw up so much right away that Ava and Emilia, the two actors in the room, swoop in and talk about eye contact and tone and enunciating, and I'm worried I'll screw up again when Su Jin shouts, "Just be a person, Lyds." Everyone laughs, and Fran immediately starts filming again.

"Hey, Penny, I used to think it was so weird you loved all these videos, but after watching some of your favorites, it made more sense. I know you love guides and rules for life, and I think one reason I never looked for stuff like that is I've practically always had you. Even though you're technically my little sister, I never think of you that way. You always seem to know more than me about everything, and it's why I never argued against your plans for this summer. I knew that you were right about us and boys. There was way too much drama and we couldn't keep going like that."

I take a deep breath—why do I feel like I've forgotten how to breathe when I feel like I talk nonstop all of the time?—and try to keep my eye contact with Fran's phone. Everyone in the room must be staring at me—I can practically feel it—but I try to keep my focus right there. Breathing and the phone.

"The thing I really learned, though, had nothing to do with boys. And that's not because of Fran, that's because of *me*. I spent so long thinking if I could just fall in love, I'd be fine and I wouldn't have to worry about the rest of life, because the rest of life seemed way scarier to me. I couldn't figure out friends or school or my future, and so every time it fell apart with someone it wasn't just like I was losing *them*, it was like I was losing everything.

"This summer changed all of that. I love working at the coffee shop, and I may even get good at it someday, especially if Grace lets me keep working weekends. I made real, true friends for the first time in my life, and I realized maybe the problem wasn't that other people made it too hard, it was that I hadn't invested any of my own energy into making it easier. And I'm taking theater more seriously now, too. You might think that I always did, because REACT takes up so much of my time, but it's cool to research colleges and think about what kind of life I could have after. Plus it was amazing working on Fran's film, and maybe that's something I could think about, too. My future feels really open, now, not hinging on getting someone to fall in love with me forever but like it's up to me most of all.

"And, honestly, I wouldn't have figured any of that out without you. It's not just the summer, and it's not just the pledge. It's spending time together, feeling encouraged by you, seeing you not as this all-knowing perfect sister but just another girl who's also figuring out what she wants from life.

"And I get that I really, really screwed up, and I hurt you, and I lied. I have so much more I want to talk about with you, but none of, like, the nuances matter if you don't believe me that I'm sorry, and if you're not ready to actually talk to me. But we'll be back home by the end of next week, and before long school will start and you'll be all stacked high with extracurriculars and I'll have some stuff going on too and—Pen, I just don't want to lose what we found this summer."

I realize I'm about to cry, but I decide to push through, since I'm almost at the end.

"I'm here and I'm ready to talk to you whenever you're ready for me. And I promise you I will work so hard to make sure I never make you feel like this again."

Fran uploads it almost immediately, and sends the private link to me. I text it to Penny, and then it's just all of us in this room where I've just aired way more about myself than I'd expected. But my friends just pull me into hugs and don't tease me at all for how much I end up crying.

Fran drives me back to Grace and Oscar's, and even though I feel like we could spend at least a full twenty-four hours talking about today, I kiss her good night and hop out of the truck, scared and eager at the same time to see my sister.

Penny's sitting up on her bed when I walk into the bedroom, and we make eye contact for what feels like the first time in ages.

"Did you get my video?" I ask, and she nods.

"That was . . . very nice of you," she says. "And you looked really nice on camera."

I wave my hand. "Margaret did my makeup. And Fran knows how to film to make things look better or whatever."

"You could just take a compliment," Penny says. "Also, thank you for everything you said. And, obviously, I know you didn't mean to hurt my feelings. But sometimes that feels terrible as well, as if my feelings didn't even come to mind for you."

"Only because you always seem so great." I sit down across from her on my bed, gently, casually, hoping this moment isn't about to end. "You know that I always felt like you were perfect and judging me for not being like you and—I mean, obviously I've gotten to know you a lot better, but I think sometimes it's still hard to understand you're not just like a thousand percent confident about everything and living your life exactly as you want it to be."

"I feel the same way about you," she says.

"God, that's weird," I say, and she laughs. I'm not sure I've seen anything as good as my sister laughing right now. "I seriously feel terrible I lied to you this summer. But also I didn't always feel like I was lying, and some stuff is just kind of weird to talk about."

"I've done a lot of reading," Penny says, and I'm afraid she's about to rattle off a bunch of statistics about LGBTQ+ youths or whatever, "and the last thing you owed me was your identity. Especially if it was something you're still in the middle of exploring."

"It's weird to talk about," I admit. "Not that there's something weird about being bi, just—I don't know. I didn't completely know how to talk about it, and then things with Fran happened kind of fast, and—well, that's when I should have told you. Not because I owed you my identity but because we made a pledge this summer."

Penny grins. "I hope you never thought I actually meant that gender is such a binary thing that I only defined it as a *no boy* summer. I would have called it a *no romance* summer had I known. But I suppose I do admire you working loopholes like that."

"Pen, *working loopholes* sounds so dirty," I say, and we both crack up. "I'm really sorry about that part, OK? Even if it was technically allowed. Obviously I knew that it wasn't. I just didn't want to let you down and I also didn't want to stop seeing Fran."

She nods. "I just kept thinking that you've always had it so much easier than me. Even though this summer's made me realize we both have various things we're dealing with. And for you to end up with someone, after all of this, you dating someone and with a million friends, it wasn't only that you'd lied. It was more proof that everything always worked out for you."

"Nothing has ever worked out for me like this before," I say. "And I do need things that are just mine. If I only replace romance with promises to you, things aren't going to go well."

"I *never* said to replace romance with anything to do with *me*," Penny says, but she's still smiling. "You do seem different, Lydia. My plan may not have worked out as I thought it would, but I think we still achieved some of our original goals anyway."

"Pen, I learned that counting on happy endings later instead of living in the moment is a recipe for disaster," I say.

"So, can I meet Fran?" Penny asks.

"Yeah, obviously, of course. I think you'll like her a lot. Actually, I think tomorrow night we're going out with a bunch of people to the park, long story, but you should come."

"What's *a bunch of people?*" she asks.

"Margaret and Su Jin and Tara and Ava and Lucas, this guy Margaret's kind of dating, some cute skater Tara thinks is hot, some seemingly unattached boys, all of which are cute."

"Hmm, maybe," Penny says, but she smiles, and I think it's a *yes* and move over to sit next to her.

"Can I hug you?"

She frowns. "That doesn't sound like us."

"Oh, shut up," I say, and tackle her into a hug.

Penny starts laughing, practically in hysterics. "Lydia, remember when you thought you invented *live, laugh, love*?"

"I did *not*, that was Grace's joke!"

"I choose to remember it this way," Penny says, and now I'm laughing, too. Grace leans into the doorway, her eyebrows way high on her face.

"I thought someone was crying," she says.

Penny wipes her eyes. "I just remembered the time Lydia thought she invented *live, laugh, love*."

Grace all but doubles over laughing, while I try to yell the truth over their laughter. Soon all three of us are crying on the bed, and Oscar leans in and then quickly backs out, which only makes us laugh harder. I'm afraid Grace will say something embarrassing about being happy the two of us are talking again, but of course Grace is too cool for that and only offers to bring in some ice cream, which we quickly agree to. And then we have so much to catch up on. Not just these nearly two weeks of not talking, but everything I normally would have told her but didn't about Fran, and the film, and my friends, and of course everything from her life, too.

The summer hadn't turned out anything like we'd expected, but it turns out that was exactly what I needed. And I'm pretty sure, for once, that Penny feels the same way.

EPILOGUE

Penny's waiting for me when I get out of my seventh-period Western Civilization class, as promised. She skirts rules because she's an office aide during final period, a strategy to cut back on her non-AP classes to pass/fail electives only, therefore upping her GPA <u>and</u> giving her extra time for homework. Even Penny's class scheduling is smarter than anyone else I know.

"I promised you I'd walk you over," she says. "So I'm here."

I roll my eyes but it's just for show. "I'll really be fine. It's not a big deal."

"It's a big deal in a good way," Penny says, falling into step beside me, as I make my way down the hallway in the direction of Ms. Howe's classroom. "You can walk me to my first practice because that'll be a big deal, too."

Penny had initially thought about volunteering her statistics brain to help out the boy's baseball team, but their season was so far away, and she hadn't felt super welcomed when she'd brought up the idea to Coach Yates. But the girls' soccer coach, Ms. Alvarez, overheard the conversation and offered Penny a role as a student manager if she was willing to learn about a different sport instead. Now my sister eats and breathes soccer statistics and has already hung out a few times with girls on the team and bought a professional whistle.

"OK, I can take it from here," I say as we reach Ms. Howe's classroom as well as all the posters that announce LGBTQ+ Club First Meeting Today After School Yes We Have Snacks.

I'd assumed I'd have to make some big coming out announcement to even get into the first meeting, but I'd decided to risk awkwardness and do it anyway. I hadn't thought about the fact that—now that she wasn't a secret in any way—I posted tons of photos of Fran on my Instagram, and once *Imaginary Friends* was up on her new YouTube channel, I shared a screencap of it with the caption *I'm so proud of my girlfriend for her beautiful short film!* and then, of course, everyone knew.

Darren asked on the REACT leaders group chat why I wasn't already part of the LGBTQ+ Club, and instead of making up an answer about too many extracurriculars or whatever, I told the truth, that I'd never felt like one of those solid-identity enamel-pin kids and wasn't sure it was for me. And then at our first in-person REACT meeting of the year, the other leaders swiped my backpack from me, and when it came back to me a few minutes later, a shiny *disaster bisexual* pin glittered at me and I screamed in excitement. I immediately felt like part of the club, and so today I'll officially become part of the club for real.

"I'll hang around the library until you're done so you have a ride home," Penny tells me, starting to head down the hallway.

"You can go, I'll get a ride home from someone, I'm sure," I say. It was nice to feel confident about that fact. "But want to do something then? Even if it's just like our homework in a less boring place than home?"

"Perfect. See you then, Lydia."

Penny waves and walks off. My phone buzzes in my pocket, and I check it to see that Penny's texted *I'm proud of you, all right?* I text back the rolling eyes emoji, but then a heart and prayer hands. *Thanks, Pen.* I turn around and wait only a moment before I walk through the open door.

ACKNOWLEDGMENTS

Thank so much to my editor, Maggie Lehrman, for your thoughtfulness and warm support of this book. Working with you on it was truly a wonderful experience.

Thank you to my agent, Kate Testerman, for all your work and enthusiasm.

Thank you to the entire team that worked on this book, including Deena Fleming, Jeff Östberg, Kristin Dwyer, the Abrams publicity team, everyone on the Abrams school and library teams, and anyone I forgot to call out here—I truly appreciate every single minute of work that goes into this book.

Before I began work on this book, I feared that due to a bunch of stuff that felt completely out of my control that I would never write again. Thank you, thank you, thank you to my friends Kayla Cagan and Jasmine Guillory, who made sure that I did not stop, and who told me very specifically to keep going when I mentioned I had the idea for this very book. For anyone who's struggling to create art during bleak times, I hope you have those friends who can guide you through, and if you don't, take this as a gentle shove from me to keep going.

Thank you to everyone who chatted with me about Nora Ephron, especially Melissa Baumgart and Elise Laplante. Thank you to all members of Ladies Meat Night for all the KBBQ (and other assorted meats

ACKNOWLEDDGMENTS

and friendship). Thank you to Drama Club for all the conversations about water-related sets at the Taper; you're all my Jellicle Choices worthy of Jimmy Awards.

Thank you to my entire writing community, in Los Angeles and beyond, and to all my friends, though those Venn diagrams overlap quite a bit! Thank you to my mother, Pat Spalding.

Finally, writing queer YA books during a time in history where so many books like mine—and including mine!—are being banned only makes me more determined to write books where queer people get happy endings. There is enormous pushback against the rights of the LGBTQ+ community, and I'm constantly angry, especially at the harm directed at young queer people. That said, I'm so grateful to everyone doing work to fight this hate: activists, teachers, librarians, parents, and so many more.

Read more from Amy Spalding

"Amy Spalding knows that best friendships are love stories, and this one is complex, earnest, and unflinching. A must-read for anyone who's ever had or lost a friend."

—Becky Albertalli, *New York Times* bestselling author of *Simon vs. the Homo Sapiens Agenda*

Told in dual timelines—half of the chapters moving forward in time and half moving backward—*We Used to Be Friends* explores the most traumatic breakup of all: that of childhood besties.

ABOUT THE AUTHOR

AMY SPALDING is the author of several novels for teens, including *Kissing Ted Callahan (and Other Guys)*, *The Summer of Jordi Perez (and the Best Burger in Los Angeles)*, and *We Used to Be Friends*, which Becky Albertalli called "complex, earnest, and unflinching." She lives in Los Angeles.